BOTTOMS UP TO MARS

"I can tell you for sure we will not turn Mars into a prison colony."

"I wish I could promise we won't let tourists carve their initials into those arches."

"Still you will try."

"Yes."

"We have a treaty, then."

"Agreed. No tourists, no prisons."

Lev hugged his coat tighter over his pressure suit. The crawler's speed brought biting cold. "Very solemn treaty."

"Deserves a beer."

"Indeed. I suggest we drink our reserve well before the lander crew comes."

"Very wise."

"Another historic agreement?"

"Yeah, the First Martian Beer Protocols."

"We are being diplomatically silly."

"Of course. All diplomats are."

**—from "All the Beer on Mars"
by Gregory Benford**

ISAAC ASIMOV'S

MARS

Edited by Gardner Dozois

ACE BOOKS, NEW YORK

ISAAC ASIMOV'S MARS

An Ace Book / published by arrangement with
Davis Publications, Inc.

PRINTING HISTORY
Ace edition / September 1991

ISBN: 0-441-37375-5

Ace Books are published by the Berkley Publishing Group,
200 Madison Avenue, New York, New York 10016.
The name "ACE" and the "A" logo
are trademarks belonging to Charter Communications, Inc.

PRINTED IN THE UNITED STATES OF AMERICA

10 9 8 7 6 5 4 3 2 1

Grateful acknowledgment is made to the following for permission to reprint their copyrighted material:

Mars Needs Beatniks by George Alec Effinger, copyright © 1983 by Davis Publications, Inc., reprinted by permission of the author; *The Catharine Wheel* by Ian McDonald, copyright © 1983 by Davis Publications, Inc., reprinted by permission of the author; *Green Mars* by Kim Stanley Robinson, copyright © 1985 by Davis Publications, Inc., reprinted by permission of the author; *The Difficulties Involved in Photographing Nix Olympica* by Brian W. Aldiss, copyright © 1986 by Davis Publications, Inc., reprinted by permission of the author; *All the Beer on Mars* by Gregory Benford, copyright © 1988 by Davis Publications, Inc., reprinted by permission of the author; *Retrovision* by Robert Frazier, copyright © 1988 by Davis Publications, Inc., reprinted by permission of the author; *Live from the Mars Hotel* by Allen M. Steele, copyright © 1988 by Davis Publications, Inc., reprinted by permission of the author; *The Great Martian Railroad Race* by Eric Vinicoff, copyright © 1988 by Davis Publications, Inc., reprinted by permission of the author; *Windwagon Smith and the Martians* by Lawrence Watt-Evans, copyright © 1989 by Davis Publications, Inc., reprinted by permission of Scott Meredith Literary Agency, Inc.

ACKNOWLEDGMENTS

The editor would like to thank the following people for their help and support: Susan Casper, who helped with the scut work involved in preparing the manuscript; Shawna McCarthy, for having the good taste to buy some of this material in the first place; Sheila Williams, who has labored behind the scenes on *IAsfm* for many years and played a part in the decision-making process involved in the buying of some of these stories; Ian Randal Strock, Charles Ardai, and Scott L. Towner, who did much of the basic research needed; Florence B. Eichin, who cleared the permissions; Cynthia Manson, who set up this deal; and thanks especially to my own editor on this project, Susan Allison.

CONTENTS

ISAAC ASIMOV'S

LIVE FROM
THE MARS HOTEL

Allen M. Steele

*"Live from the Mars Hotel" was purchased by Gard-
ner Dozois and appeared in the mid-December, 1988,
issue of* IAsfm, *with an illustration by George
Thompson. This was Steele's first sale, but it didn't
take him long to follow it up with a string of sales to*
IAsfm *that quickly established him as one of our most
popular new writers. (Steele is pleasingly prolific, and
we have several more stories by him in inventory.)
In 1989, he published his critically acclaimed first
novel,* Orbital Decay, *one of the most talked-about
debut novels in some time; it subsequently won the
Locus Poll as Best First Novel of the year. His most
recent book,* Clarke County, Space, *has been nomi-
nated for the Philip K. Dick Award.*

*One of the most interesting of the new hard-science
writers, Steele has been compared to Golden Age
Heinlein by no less an authority than Gregory Benford
. . . and you may see why in the hard-edged, yet gently
ironic, story that follows, which takes us traveling
very far indeed to hear the music of home . . .*

1

Rachel Keaton; program director, WBXL-FM, Boston

I first heard the Mars Hotel while I was working as a jock at KMCY in St. Louis. At that time 'MCY—"Mighty Mickey, the rock sound of St. Louis"—had a progressive contemporary format, and the playlist represented much of the progressive music that was coming out then. The experimental groups from the Far East, the latest British invasion, and of course the acoustic revival. This was the early '20s, y'know, and there was some interesting stuff coming out even before the Mars Hotel appeared, so the timing was right for their first single.

Looking back on it, I think I was one of the first jocks in the country to play it, and that was a matter of being in the right place at the right time. About six months earlier the D.J. who handled the Sunday afternoon acoustic show, Ben Grady, had left 'MCY to become music director at a Los Angeles AOR station. The acoustic revival was just getting started and I had developed a taste for it, the work that was coming out of Nashville and Austin and Muscle Shoals, so I managed to bug Heidi Schlosberg, who was the program director at the time, into letting me take over Ben's show.

It was a lot of fun, because many of these artists were recording on obscure labels, so finding stuff to play was a little like, y'know, exploring new territory. But I kept discovering guys who had skipped back forty, fifty years and were reviving David Bromberg or Johnny Cash or the Earl Scruggs Revue. It was a neat time to be in the music business, since it was finally dredging itself out of the glitzy Hollywood-punk scene where it had been stuck for . . .

I'm sorry. (Laughs.) I'm getting off the subject. Where was I?

Right. Well, I got Ben's old show and renamed it "The Wireless Hour," and one Sunday afternoon in—I guess it was '22, maybe '23—Heidi walked into the air studio with a single in her hand. She had been in that day doing some extra work left over from last week, which included opening all those boxes of records that radio stations get swamped with all week. Well, she had this one single she had just taken out of a box, and the moment I spotted it in her hand, I knew it had to be two things. One, because it wasn't a ceedee and was pressed on old-fashioned vinyl instead, it had to be from some small, destitute label. Second, it had to be good, because she had obviously listened to it in Studio B and thought it was so hot that she had not bothered to master it onto a cart yet.

"Put this on," she says, handing me the disc. "You'll love it!"

I took it out of her hand, saw that it was on a label I had seen a couple of times before, Centennial Park Records, which was a little Nashville company which had started up a couple of years earlier and hadn't put out anything special. The "A" side was an old Bob Dylan, "Knockin' on Heaven's Door." The "B" side was "Sea Cruise," the old classic. The band was something called the Mars Hotel.

I gave Heidi this look, because she was into heavy metal and thought, y'know, that Hiroshima was God's gift to pop music. "Trust me," she says. "You'll eat it up." So I cued up the Dylan song and segued it in after the next couple of ad spots. I didn't expect anything special, right?

I dunno. What can I say that hasn't been said before? It was fantastic. I could tell that the band, whoever they were, were only three guys: a vocalist on guitar, a bass player, and somebody on synth doing piano, percussion, and pedal steel. There's been a million bands like that and a million people have done Dylan, most of the time badly. But these guys made "Knockin' on Heaven's Door" sound like they had just written it. Very fresh, stripped-down. Unpretentious. They played like they meant it, you know what I mean?

So I look up and say, "Who are these guys?" Heidi grins at me and asks, "Where do you think they're from?" I glance at the label again and say, "Well, they're obviously from Nashville."

She just shook her head. "No, they're from Mars."

Alan Gass; former station supervisor, Skycorp/Uchu-Hiko Arsia Base, Mars

Well, it's no secret that life at Arsia Base was rough. Always will be rough, or at least until someone gets around to terraforming Mars, which is a wild-eyed fantasy if you ask me. But even if you disregard the sandstorms and the scarcity of water, the extremes of heat and cold and . . . well, just the utter barrenness of that world, it's still a hell of a place to live for any extended period of time.

I guess the worst part was the isolation. When I was station manager we had about fifty men and women living in close quarters in a cluster of fifteen habitat modules, buried just underneath the ground. Most of these folks worked either for Skycorp or the Japanese firm Uchu-Hiko, manufacturing propellant from Martian hydrocarbons in the soil which was later boosted up to the Phobos fuel depot, or were conducting basic research for NASA or NASDA. The minority of us were support personnel, like myself, keeping the place operational.

A lot of us had signed on for Mars work for the chance to explore another planet, but once you got there you found yourself spending most of your time doing stuff that was not much different than if you had volunteered to live underground in Death Valley for two years. For the men working the electrolysis plant, it was a particularly hard, dirty job—working ten or twelve hour shifts, coming back to the base to eat and collapse, then getting up to do it all over again. The researchers didn't have it much easier because their sponsoring companies or governments had gone to considerable expense to send them to Mars and they had to produce a lifetime's worth of work during their two years or risk losing their jobs and reputations.

The base was located in a visually stunning area, the Tharsis region, just south of the equator near the western flank of Arsia Mons. When you went outside there was this giant, dead volcano looming over you, and on a clear day you could just make out the summit of Olympus Mons way off to the northeast. But after a few weeks the novelty would wear off. You'd become used to red rocks and pink skies, and after that what would you have? There was never any time for sightseeing. After awhile you started looking forward to the next big sandstorm, just to watch this giant swirling red curtain coming toward you like the wrath of God. (Laughs.) You wouldn't spend much time watching because the wind could shred your suit in a minute, but at least it was exciting.

Anyway, one night I had just come off my shift in the command module and I was walking back to my bunkhouse through the connecting tunnel, which was called Broadway. I was beat, and I didn't feel like going to the wardroom because I wasn't hungry—not that the food was particularly appetizing anyway—but the way to Module Five took me past the wardroom, Module Three, which we called the Mars Hotel. I had just walked past Three when I heard a guitar being played and someone singing.

I really didn't notice it at first, because I figured it was coming from a tape, but then I heard another guitar joining in and someone else beginning to sing, and then there was an electronic piano chiming in. But the second guy couldn't sing and the piano was a little off-key, and suddenly I realized that I wasn't hearing a tape.

That stopped me in my tracks. I don't know if I can describe that feeling of puzzlement and wonder. It was like a rare bird had just flown down Broadway. I mean, which was stranger? Seeing a rare species, or just seeing a bird in the first place? I backed up a couple of steps, wondering if I was hallucinating, and looked through the open hatch.

Partial transcript of an interview with the Mars Hotel, originally broadcast on NBC's "The Today Show," July 27, 2022 (Note: this interview was taped and edited in advance in order to contract the time differential during Earth-Mars transmissions)

Judith King, host: "So how did you come up with the name for your group?"

Tiny Prozini, lead guitarist: "Um . . . which of us are you asking?"

King: "Any one of you."

Joe Mama, synthesizer player: "During that last nineteen minute delay we thought it over and decided that we wouldn't tell you that we used to be called the Mars House of Ill Repute, but the record company made us change it because it was too long to fit on the label."

Gary Smith, bass guitarist: "You shouldn't ask Joe straight questions like that, I'll warn you right now."

Mama (to Prozini): "I told you we should have used a different name. Now we're going to have to answer that question for the rest of our lives."

Prozini: "Look who's talking. No, it's . . . (Laughter.) See, there's two reasons. One, the ward room here is called the Mars Hotel. It was once called the Mars Hilton, but it somehow got shortened. Second, there's an old album by the Grateful Dead, whom we all admire, called *From the Mars Hotel*. The ward room is the place where we've always rehearsed, and we've all been influenced one way or another by the Dead, so it sort of came natural.''

Smith: ''After we started jamming together and people here at the base started coming to listen to us during their off-shifts, they tried to stick us with names.''

Mama: ''Things like, y'know, the Tharks, the Mike Mars Blues Trio, John Carter and His Bare-Ass Barsoomians . . .''

Smith: ''Worse things, when we sounded bad, like Dry-Heaving Sandworms . . .''

Prozini: ''Eventually the name that stuck was the Mars Hotel Band, which sort of made us sound like a Ramada Inn lounge act that plays bar mitzvahs. (Laughter.) Before long the last part of the name was dropped and we became just, y'know, the Mars Hotel.''

King: ''I see. And when did you start playing together?''

Mama: ''When we got sick of Monopoly.''

Prozini: ''Please forgive him. The steel plate in his head . . .''

Smith: ''Tiny got us started, though he won't admit it.''

Prozini: ''Oh, I will admit it! I just didn't want to take all the credit.''

Mama: ''Don't worry. You won't.''

Smith: ''Oh, hell. If nobody will give you a straight answer, I will! (Laughter). Tiny and I were shooting the breeze one night in Module Six, our bunkhouse, about the things we missed out here, and one of the things was live music. We're both from New England—he's from Massachusetts, I'm from New Hampshire—and as we talked it turned out that we had both gone to the same places where you could hear live, acoustical music. Bluegrass, blues, folk, rockabilly . . .''

Prozini: ''I'm telling the story, so get lost. (Laughter.) And it further turned out that both of us knew how to play guitar. Well, I knew Joe here had a portable Yamaha synthesizer that he had smuggled out here and was hiding in his geology lab . . .''

Mama: ''Hey! I told you not to say anything about that!''

Prozini: ''Don't worry about it. You're famous now. Anyway, I managed to pull some contacts on the Cape and get a couple of guitars shipped to us on the next Mars-bound ship, and once we roped Joe into the combo, we started playing together in the Mars Hotel. And it was just like that.''

King: ''I see. From what your audience here on Earth has

heard so far, you principally cover songs other people have written. Some of them quite old, in fact. Why aren't you writing songs of your own, about Mars?''

Prozini: ''Well, uh . . .''

Smith: ''We're lazy.'' (Laughter.)

Mama: ''Actually, I'm working on composing an epic twenty-hour opera inspired by old 'Lost In Space' episodes. It's tentatively entitled 'Dr. Smith Unbound.' ''

Prozini: ''You're a sick man, Joe.''

Gary Smith; former bass guitarist, Mars Hotel

That was a pretty ridiculous interview, as I recall it. We had just heard that ''Knockin' On Heaven's Door'' had cracked the Top Forty in the U.S. and Canada, which we had never dreamed would happen, when we got a request from Skycorp's P.R. office that we do an interview for ''The Today Show.'' We didn't take it seriously because, really, we didn't take *any* of it seriously. ''We're music stars? They've got to be kidding!'' That sort of thing.

But, deep down inside, when we actually got around to doing the interview, the question that we dreaded the most—although none of us really discussed it—was the one we got about why we weren't writing our own songs. When you watch the tape you can see how we avoided answering that completely, with Joe's remark about ''Lost In Space'' being the closest we came to giving a reply. But we had answers for that.

One, of course, was that we *liked* playing the old stuff. It was what made us feel good, what took our minds off the hellhole conditions out there and so forth. That's really how the Mars Hotel got started in the first place. None of us aspired to be professional musicians. We didn't even care if we had an audience or not, although we didn't mind when base personnel started gathering in the ward room during our sessions. An audience was something that was thrust upon us, just as fame on Earth was thrust upon us by circumstances beyond our control. It just started with the three of us sitting in the Mars Hotel, trying out things like ''Kansas City'' or ''Police Dog Blues'' or ''Willie and the Hand Jive''—we were out to entertain ourselves, period.

But secondly—and this was what we didn't want to admit— none of us could write songs worth a damn. Not that we didn't try. At one time or another each of us said, "Hey, I'm going to write a song about Mars," and that person would disappear for a while, think think think, y'know, and come back to the other guys with something. "Here's a song, let's try it." And it would always turn out as some hackneyed, pretentious bullshit. Metaphorical nonsense about raging sandstorms and watching Phobos and Deimos rising and how I miss you, my love, now that we're worlds apart. Boring shit, not at all the kind of thing any of us wanted to play.

After a while we just gave up, saying to ourselves and each other, "Screw it, I'd rather do 'Johnny B. Goode' any old day." But our failure to produce anything original that said something about the human condition out there really gnawed on us, though I kept thinking that there had to be a good song somewhere about watching the sun rise over Arsia Mons. But it really bugged Tiny, who was probably the most creative of the three of us, who worshipped Woody Guthrie and Bob Dylan and Robert Hunter. I know for a fact, because one of the guys who shared his bunkhouse told me, that he secretly kept attempting to write songs, late at night when he thought no one was watching. I kinda felt sorry for him. It was like masturbation—an ultimately futile attempt to scratch an unscratchable itch.

Alan Gass

After Tiny and Gary got those guitars—I think they bribed Billy DeWolfe, who was one of the regular pilots for the Earth-Mars supply runs, into smuggling them aboard the *Shinseiki*—and they put together the band with Joe, I had to keep after the three of them constantly to do their jobs. Tiny and Gary were both miners—"the Slaves of Mars," we called them—and Joe was a soil analyst in the geology lab, so they all had important industrial functions to fulfill, and it was my job to make sure that Skycorp got its money's worth from them.

As a band, they were pretty funny to watch. Gary looked normal enough, since he would just stand there wearing his bass. But you've seen the pictures of Tiny. He was literally a giant. Six-foot-four, three hundred pounds, almost all of it muscle. Sometimes he wouldn't even bother to sit in a chair, but would lie on the floor with his guitar resting on his huge chest, playing along with his eyes closed.

Joe was the strangest of the bunch. He looked a lot better in the pictures you've seen, if you can believe that. (Laughs.) His Japanese and American bloodlines had crossed to produce one freakish-looking individual: narrow, squinty eyes, jug ears, too tall and skinny, with his hair cropped so short that he was almost bald. "Joe Mama" wasn't his real name, but I don't think anyone knew his real name. He would put his mini-synth in his lap and as he'd play—looking like he was typing, the way he held his hands—his eyes would narrow even more and his mouth would hang open and his head bob back and forth as if his neck was made of rubber. If you didn't know better, know that he was an M.I.T. graduate with a near-genius level I.Q., you would have sworn he was an idiot.

The funniest thing, though, was how they sounded when they were rehearsing in the Mars Hotel. It was a big, steel cylinder, you've got to remember—very bare, hardly any furniture except for some tables and chairs and a couple of data screens suspended from the ceiling. As far as acoustics go, it sounded like they were playing in a tin can. The sound would reverberate off the walls and make them sound louder than they really were, and you could hear them all over the base. At first a few people minded, but once they got good—believe me, they were just awful at first—people stopped complaining and started coming by to listen. After a while, I stopped being strict with them about keeping their hours on the clock. Their music was like a little piece of Earth. God knows they were good for morale.

Salvador "Sal" Minella; chief dietician, Arsia Station

I think their best moment was on Christmas night in '21, when they played for the beer bust we held in the Mars Hotel. Everyone knows what they sounded like that night, because that was the performance that Billy DeWolfe taped and brought back to Earth.

You know that DeWolfe was the one who smuggled Gary's and Tiny's guitars out there, right? Well, DeWolfe was a pipeline for all sorts of things. You sent him a message asking for something and arranged a cash transfer from your bank account back home to his, and unless NASA or Skycorp caught him he would make sure that it was loaded into the cargo lander of either the *Enterprise* or the *Shinseiki* when it left Earth the next time. You might have to wait nine months or more, but if Billy could get it for you, he'd do so, with only a slight markup.

We had long since arranged for eight cases of Budweiser to make it aboard the *Enterprise* in '21, because the timing was that the ship would arrive just in time for Christmas. Al Gass had already arranged with Skycorp for some freeze-dried turkey to be sent out, but Billy and I figured that the crew would appreciate some suds more than the turkey. Christmas dinner and the party afterwards would be held in the ward room, and I managed to twist Tiny's arm into getting his band to play after dinner.

To make a long story short . . . well, you've heard it already. It was a damn good show. We drank beer, we danced, we had a good time. We forgot about Mars for a while. You can hear a little bit of that in the background on the tape, but a lot of the stuff was edited out, like Joe playing a weird version of "White Christmas" and that sort of thing.

About halfway through the evening, I spotted Billy DeWolfe standing near the stage, which we had made out of a collapsed cargo pallet, with a cassette recorder in his hand. I don't think the band noticed what he was doing—and if they did, they wouldn't have cared—but I wandered over to him and said, "Hey, you trying to steal the show or something?"

Billy just grinned and said, "I'm only getting something to show the folks back home what they're missing." I remember getting a kick out of that. Never stopped to consider if the son of a bitch was serious.

Billy DeWolfe; former Skycorp/NASA deep-space pilot

It wasn't my idea at first to record the Mars Hotel so I could take the tape to a record company. It's just that the trip back to Earth is as long as the trip out, and since the command crew doesn't get to ride in the zombie tanks like the passengers, you have to find things to entertain you during that long haul. I made the tape so I would have something to listen to while I was standing watch, that's all, so it pisses me off when people say that I was trying to rip off the band.

I didn't consider taking the tape to a record producer until much later. I had been listening to it over and over, and at some point it occurred to me that it was too bad that people on Earth couldn't hear the Mars Hotel. Then, the more I listened to it, I realized that it was a really good tape. There was hardly any background noise, and what there was sounded just like the audience sounds you hear from any recorded live performance. I thought it was as good as any ceedee or tape I had ever heard. By the time the *Enterprise* rendezvoused in LEO with Columbus Station, I had decided to contact a cousin who lived in Nashville to see if he could provide me with any leads to the record companies there.

Why didn't I ask permission from the band? (Shrugs.) I was embarrassed. I knew none of those guys were into this for the money, or even to be heard beyond Arsia Base. They wouldn't have given themselves the chance to make it big. But I wanted to do them a favor by trying to give them that chance. Hey, if doing somebody a favor is criminal, I plead guilty.

Gary Smith

Did we mind what Billy did? Of course we minded! (Laughs.) We bitched about it all the way to the bank!

Excerpt from "Martians Invade Earth!" by Barry O'Conner; from Rolling Stone, *June 21, 2023*

DeWolfe was turned down by every major record company on Nashville's "Music Row" before he approached Centennial Park Records with his tape of the Mars Hotel. Indeed, company president and producer Saundra Lewis nearly ejected the space pilot from her office as well when she heard that DeWolfe had not been authorized by the group to represent them. She also did not believe that the tape had been recorded on Mars. "My first thought was that it had been recorded in a basement in Birmingham, not in the ward room of the Mars base," Lewis recalls.

However, she was impressed by the tape, and after extensive double-checking with Skycorp, she established that Tiny Prozini, Gary Smith, and Joe Mama were, in fact, active personnel at Arsia Base. Even though the Mars Hotel had no previous track record, Lewis decided to take a gamble. Centennial Park Records, while it had gained some respect among connoisseurs of acoustical bluegrass, blues, and rockabilly, was close to bankruptcy. "Since a virtually finished product was already in our hands, I felt like we had little to lose by cleaning it up and releasing it,'' she says. With DeWolfe acting as the group's agent, the company got permission from the Mars Hotel to release an edited version of the tape as an album, entitled *Red Planet Days*.

"We were surprised that a tape of one of our sessions had made its way to Nashville,'' says Tiny Prozini, "and for a little while we wanted to strangle Billy. But we figured, 'What the hell, maybe it will even sell a few copies,' so we gave in and signed a contract.'' Prozini leaned back in his chair and shrugged. "But we had zero expectations about it. I even said that we'd find copies in the cut-out bins by the time we got home.''

Yet when *Red Planet Days* was released and the single was sent to rock and country stations in the U.S. and Canada, there occurred one of those unanticipated surprises which happen in the music industry once every few years. In hindsight, it can be explained why the album took off like a bullet; it was released at a time when the public was beginning to rediscover the acoustic, grass-roots sound. This was particularly the case on college campuses where students, sick of several generations of formula hard-rock, were once again listening to dusty LPs recorded in their grandparents' time by Jerry Jeff Walker, Howlin' Wolf, and the Nitty Gritty Dirt Band. A new band which had that old sound filled the gap. Yet there was also the fact that this was an album which had been recorded on Mars, by a group that was *still* on Mars.

"It added a certain mystique, no doubt about it,'' says Lewis, "and I'll admit that we marketed that aspect for all it was worth.''

Within two weeks of its release, "Knockin' On Heaven's Door'' was added to the heavy-rotation playlists of every major-market radio station in the country, and *Red Planet Days* was flying off the shelves in the record stores. By the end of the month, Centennial Park Records went back to press for a second printing on the disc, the first time the company had ever done so with one of its releases.

"It's the damnedest thing I ever saw,'' says WNHT Program Director Ben Weiss, who is credited with being the first New York City radio manager to add the Mars Hotel to his station's playlist. "No one even knew what these guys looked like. Not one concert appearance.''

Which was precisely the problem for Centennial Park Records. The company, which only months before had been on the verge of filing under Chapter Eleven, now had a runaway hit. Unfortunately, neither a follow-up album nor a concert tour was possible, for the band was thirty-five million miles away. It was a record producer's nightmare.

"Naturally, we had to bring the mountain to Mohammed," says Lewis . . .

Gary Smith

I can't say that we were overwhelmed by the news that the disc had become a hit. In fact, we were sort of *under*whelmed. For one thing, it seemed like a distant event, and not just because of the miles involved. None of us even had a copy of the ceedee, because it hadn't been pressed by the time the last supply ship had left Earth. During a transmission from Skycorp SOC someone had held a copy up to the camera for us to see, but that was about it. We had never heard it played on the radio, of course. In fact, we barely remembered what we had played that night. So it was no big deal. It was almost as if *we* hadn't made the tape.

We were going back to being space jocks by then. The novelty of playing together was beginning to wear thin, and there was a lot of work that had to be done at the base before summer, which is sandstorm season there. But I also think we were unconsciously defending ourselves against this celebrity status which had been thrust upon us. Not that it wasn't fun to play music, but somehow people had started pointing fingers at us, saying, "Ooooh, *superstars*!" We hated that shit, and we wanted to get away from it.

But, y'know . . . (Shrugs.) That wasn't the way it worked out. About a month before the next supply ship, the *Shinseiki*, arrived in Mars orbit, we received a priority message from Skycorp, signed by the CEO himself. It told us that our contracts had been terminated and that we were to return to Earth aboard the ship. We later found out that Skycorp had struck a deal with Saundra Lewis and a Los Angeles concert promoter. Skycorp was scratching our contracts so we could come to L.A. to cut another album and then do a concert tour.

• • •

Alan Gass

I'm not sure that they wanted to stay, but I don't think they wanted to go either. Mars gets under your skin like that. It seems like a terrible place while you're there, when you're working in spacesuits that smell like week-old socks and living in tin cans, but secretly you come to love Mars. I've been back for several years now, and there isn't a day when I don't think about the planet and wish I was back there.

I think Tiny especially realized that he was leaving something special behind. But no one gave them a choice. Skycorp, which had taken a beating from the press because of the cost overruns and fatalities incurred by the powersat project, had seen a chance at good publicity in the Mars Hotel. There's a clause in the fine print of everyone's contract that says the company reserves the right to terminate an employee's duty whenever it pleases, and Skycorp called in that clause when it made the deal with the record company. Joe, Tiny, and Gary weren't fired so much as they were, to use the old Army phrase, honorably discharged, but the deal still stank anyway.

The night before they left on the *Shinseiki*, they played one last gig in the Mars Hotel. Everyone showed up, and everyone tried to put a good face on it, but it was different than before. It was definitely a goodbye show, and no one wanted to see them go. But more than that, there was this sense that the Mars Hotel, the band, didn't belong to Mars anymore. It was another resource which had been dug out of the rocky red soil and flung out into space for someone else to use.

The band was also very somber. They played as well as they always did, but they didn't seem to have their hearts in it and they didn't play for very long. After they did "Sea Cruise" they just put down their instruments and smiled uncomfortably at everyone—the place was very quiet then—and mumbled something about needing some sleep before the launch next morning, and then they sorta shuffled out of the ward room. Just like that, it was over.

Saundra Lewis; producer, Red Planet Days *and* Kings of the High Frontier

I don't know why it didn't work out . . .

(Long pause.) No, no. Scratch that. I know, or at least I think I know, why the Mars Hotel bombed after we got them back here. It's just hard for me to admit it, since I was part of it.

In the music business we tend to put talents into convenient little niches, thinking that if we can put a label on that which we can barely comprehend, we somehow control the magic. So the little niche that was carved for the Mars Hotel was "oldies band from Mars." Once we had made that label, we went about forcing them into the niche.

Once we got them back to Earth and into a studio in L.A., we got carried away with the realization that, unlike with *Red Planet Days*, here was a chance to tinker with the band's style. The euphemism is "fine-tuning," but in this case it was meddling. The unexpected success of the first album had made us overconfident; at least I, as the producer, should have reined myself in.

But we hired backup singers and session musicians by the busload, and added strings and horns and electric guitars and drums and choruses, thinking that we were improving the quality while, in fact, we were getting away from that elegant, stripped-down sound that was on *Red Planet Days*. Joe's mini-synth was replaced by a monstrous, wrap-around console he could barely operate, for example. Nor did we listen to their ideas. Tiny wanted to do "John Wesley Harding," for instance, but we decided that we wanted to have a more country-oriented approach, so we forced them into doing Willie Nelson's "Whisky River" instead, saying that it was bad luck to do two Dylan songs in a row. (Laughs.)

The only bad luck was that there were too many cooks in the kitchen. *Kings of the High Frontier* was an overproduced catastrophe. In hindsight, I can see where the errors of judgment were made, where we had diluted the very qualities that made the band strong. But worse than that, we failed to recognize a major reason why people liked the Mars Hotel. But we were too busy fooling with the magic, and it wasn't until they went out on the road that the lesson was learned.

Gary Smith

The promoter had booked us into medium-sized concert halls all over the country. The tour started in California and worked west through the Southwest into the South and up the east coast. It should have been just the three of us, and maybe doing small clubs instead, but the record company and the promoter, who were pulling all the strings, decided to send along the whole mob that had been in the studio doing the album.

We had no creative control. There was virtually nothing that we could veto. Each night, we were trying to do soulful, sincere versions of ''Knockin' On Heaven's Door'' on these huge amphitheatre stages with three backup singers, a couple of guitarists, a drummer, two horn players, and a piano, so there was this wall of sound that just hammered people back in their seats. And in the middle of this orchestra there were me and Tiny and Joe, wearing these silk silver jumpsuits that were some costume designer's idea of what we wore on Mars, while overhead spun a giant holographic image of Mars.

So it was all slick Hollywood-Nashville bullshit, the exact opposite of everything we wanted our music to be, manufactured by twits and nerds with a cynical outlook on what people wanted. (Shakes his head.) Well, you can't sell people what they don't want. Even though the concerts were almost all sell-outs, from up on the stage we could see people wincing, frowning, leaving their seats and not coming back. I stopped reading the reviews after a while, they were so grim. And *Kings of the High Frontier* was D.O.A. in the record stores, of course.

It ended in Baton Rouge at the tail-end of the tour. It had been another hideous show, and afterwards, while all the session players were drinking and screwing around in the hotel, the three of us slipped out and caught a cab to an all-night diner somewhere on the edge of town. At first all we wanted was to get an early-morning breakfast and to escape from the Nashville bozos for a little while, but we ended up staying there until dawn, talking about everything that had happened over the past few months, talking about what had happened to *us*.

We knew that we were sick of it all—the stardom, making crap records, touring—so there was practically no argument over whether we should break up the band. We didn't even try to think of ways to salvage something from the wreckage; all we wanted to do was to give the Mars Hotel a mercy killing before it became more embarrassing.

No, what we discussed was *why* things had turned so sour so quickly, and somehow in the wee hours of the morning, drinking coffee in the Louisiana countryside near the interstate, we came to the conclusion that we had been doomed from the moment we had left Mars.

It wasn't just the way *Kings of the High Frontier* had been made, or that we were doing George Jones instead of David Bromberg or Willie Nelson instead of Bob Dylan because someone decided that we should have the Nashville sound, whatever that is. No, it was the fact that we had been playing music that had been born on Earth, but we were doing it *on Earth*. What had made the Mars Hotel different many months before had been the fact that we were playing Earth music . . . on Mars.

It was a strange notion, but it made more sense the longer we considered it. We had taken a bit of human culture to Mars, and then exported it back. It was the same culture, we hadn't changed the songs, but what was different was that it had been performed by people living on another world. Back here, we were just another band doing a cover of "Sea Cruise." People take culture with them wherever they go, but what makes a frontier a home is when they start generating a culture of their own. We had been proving, without really realizing what we were doing, that it was possible to do something else on Mars than make rocket fuel and take pictures of dead volcanos.

It was then that Tiny surprised Joe and me. He pulled out of his jacket pocket a small notebook and opened it. I had seen him, now and then during the tour, sitting by himself and writing in it, but I had never really paid attention. Now he showed us what he had been doing—writing songs.

They weren't bad. In fact, they were pretty good. There was one called "Olympus Mons Blues," and another piece that hadn't yet been titled, about running from a sandstorm. Not sappy or stilted, but gritty, raw stuff. Great Mars Hotel material.

"But this isn't for us," he said when I commented that we should try playing them before we ended the tour. "At least this isn't anything that can be played here. I've got to go back *there* for this stuff to make sense, or if I'm going to write anything else about it."

It was ironic. While we had been on Mars, Tiny hadn't been able to write anything about the place. It took coming back to Earth for the words to finally come out. But his memories were beginning to dry up, the images were beginning to fade. Tiny knew that he had to go back if he was going to produce any more Mars songs. Nor would anyone appreciate them if they were sung from any place else but Mars.

He had the notion to apply for another duty-tour with Uchu-Hiko, since Skycorp obviously would be displeased if he tried to get his old job back from them. Joe was also up for it, but I wasn't. I liked breathing fresh air again, seeing plants that weren't growing out of a hydroponics tank. They didn't hold that against me, so we decided that, once we had fulfilled our contract obligations by finishing this tour, we would formally dissolve the band.

Afterwards, I moved back up to New Hampshire and started a small restaurant in North Conway with the money I had made. On weekends I played bass with a small bluegrass jug-band, but otherwise I lay low. I got postcards for a while from Tiny and Joe, telling me that they were now working for the Japanese and were being trained at the Cape for another job at Arsia Station.

A month before they left for Mars on the *Enterprise*—by coincidence, the pilot was to be Billy DeWolfe, who had gotten us into this mess in the first place—I got a final card from Tiny: *"We still need a bass player. Please reconsider. C'mon down and we'll make room for you."*

I didn't write back, figuring that he was just being cute. The shuttle went up to Columbus Station and the *Enterprise* launched from the Cape a few days later, and Joe and Tiny were on their way back . . .

(Long pause.) Funny. I almost said, "On their way back home." I guess it was. I guess it always will be now.

Billy DeWolfe
When Tiny and Joe climbed through the hatch into the manned lander, I never thought for an instant that I would be the last person to see them alive. I would have been piloting the lander down myself, if it weren't that I had to close down the *Enterprise* and bring the cargo lander down. I suppose I should consider myself lucky.

There weren't any great last words from either of them that I can recall, only Joe grinning and saying, "See you later," just before I shut and dogged the airlock hatch. I remember both of them being happy as hell to be back, though. During the two days since they had come out of the zombie tanks, while we were on our final approach and Mars was getting bigger and bigger, they had been talking about music, working on a song together—and they had been talking about *making* music, not just playing the oldies. (Laughs.) They said that when they were ready, they would give me a new tape to take back to Earth with me, as long as I didn't take it to Nashville.

And y'know . . . suddenly, they were gone. I was on the command deck safeing everything for the return flight when Arsia Control came over the comlink, saying that they had lost telemetry with the lander.

Alan Gass

We buried them where we found them at the crash site, northeast of the Tharsis Montes range just above the equator. We wrapped Joe and Tiny, along with the three other people who had been in the lander, in the parachutes that had tangled after aerobraking, and buried their bodies under piles of rocks. I went back a few weeks later to place markers we had made from pieces of the wreckage. The floor of the desert shifts around a lot, so I don't know if the graves are even visible anymore.

Billy found their instruments in the cargo lander, and they're now in the Mars Hotel, hanging on the walls. Some country music museum wanted us to ship them back, so they could put Tiny's guitar and Joe's mini-synth on display, but we refused. It's more appropriate that they stay on Mars . . .

It's funny that you ask. A few days ago I got a letter from a friend who's still stationed there, telling me that somebody's been playing Tiny's guitar. Guy from Florida, who wanted to try it out and thought it was okay to take it down from the hooks. I don't think anyone minded very much. Besides, my friend says he's pretty good . . .

THE DIFFICULTIES INVOLVED IN PHOTOGRAPHING NIX OLYMPICA

Brian W. Aldiss

"The Difficulties Involved in Photographing Nix Olympica" was purchased by Gardner Dozois and appeared in the May, 1986, issue of IAsfm, with an illustration by George Thompson. Aldiss doesn't appear in the magazine nearly as often as we'd like, but each appearance has been memorable. In the subtle and quietly profound story that follows, he takes us along to a military base on a future Mars, and shows us that what's most important is not so much what you see, but how you see it.

One of the true giants of the field, Brian W. Aldiss has been publishing science fiction for more than a quarter of a century and has more than two dozen books to his credit. His classic novel The Long Afternoon of Earth *won a Hugo Award in 1962. "The Saliva Tree" won a Nebula Award in 1965, and his novel* Starship *won the Prix Jules Verne in 1977. He*

*took another Hugo Award in 1987 for his critical
study,* Trillion Year Spree: The History of Science
Fiction, *written with David Wingrove. His other
books include the acclaimed Helliconia trilogy—*Helliconia Spring, Helliconia Summer, Helliconia Winter—, The Malacia Tapestry, An Island Called
Moreau, Frankenstein Unbound, *and* Cryptozoic! *His
latest books include the collection* Seasons in Flight
and the novel Dracula Unbound. *He lives in Oxford,
England.*

It was unprecedented for anyone stationed on Mars to refuse
home leave. Ozzy Brooks refused. He secretly wanted to photograph Olympus Mons.

For his whole two-year tour of duty, Sgt. Brooks had saved
money and hoarded material. Had made friends with the transport section. Had ingratiated himself with the officer in charge
of rations. Had gone out of his way to be nice to practically
everyone in Atmosphere Control. Had wooed the guys in the
geological section. Had made himself indispensable in Engineering.

Almost everyone in Fort Arcadia knew and, within their
lights, liked little Sgt. Brooks.

Brooks was small, dark-skinned, lightly built, neat-boned—
ideal fodder for Mars. He had nondescript sandy hair which
grew like lichen over his skull, with eyes to match. He had
what are often referred to as ageless looks, and the rather blank
stare that goes with those looks.

Behind that blank and inoffensive gaze lay ambition. Brooks
was an intellectual. Brooks never got drunk. He rarely watched
TV screenings from Earth. Instead, he could be seen reading
old books. He went to bed early. He never complained or
scratched his armpits. And he seemed to know everything. It
was amazing that the other troops stationed in Fort Arcadia
liked him nevertheless: but Brooks had another qualification.

Ozzy Brooks was Fort Arcadia's Martian *t'ai chi* master.
He taught two classes of *mar t'ai chi*, as he himself called it:

an elementary class from eight to ten in the morning and an advanced class from eight to eleven in the evening. Even men for whom *mar t'ai chi* was not compulsory joined Brooks's classes, for they agreed that Brooks was a brilliant teacher; all "felt better" when each session was finished. Brooks's teaching was an antidote to the monotony of Mars.

After dismissing one of his morning classes, Brooks slipped out of his costume, put on denims, and strolled across the dome to Engineering, to work on the larger format camera he was building.

"What do you need a camera for on Mars?" Sgt. Al Shapiro asked.

"I want to photograph Olympus Mons from the ground," Brooks said.

Shapiro laughed, with contempt in the sound.

Brooks's secret in life was that he did not hate anything. He hated no man. He did not hate the Army, he did not hate Mars. All the rest of the men, his friends, spent long hours trying to decide whether they hated the Army or Mars most. Sometimes Mars won, sometimes the Army.

"It's the boredom. The monotony," they said. Referring to both or either.

Brooks was never bored. In consequence, he did not find life monotonous. He did not dislike Army discipline, since he had always strictly disciplined himself. Certainly he missed women; but he consoled himself by saying that instead he had this unique opportunity to know the Red Planet.

He loved Mars. Mars was the ideal place on which to do *t'ai chi*. Despite his ordinary name, Brooks was an exotic. While his grandmother, a refugee from Vietnam, had had the fortune to marry a seventh-generation American, his great-grandparents were Chinese from Szechwan Province. A *t'ai chi* tradition had been passed down in the family from generation to generation. Ozzy Brooks hugged this knowledge to himself: Mars, with its lighter gravity, was the perfect planet on which to develop his art. Some wise Chinese ancestor, many generations ago, had invented the postures of the White Crane *with Mars in mind*.

Under Brooks's American-ness ran a strong delight in his oriental heritage. He believed that it was a Chinese who had discovered the perfect way to live on another planet, in harmony with its elements, using those elements to become more perfect in oneself. Mars—he had realized this almost as soon as he had disembarked from the military spaceship—was the most Chinese of planets, even down to the *sang-de-boeuf* tint of its soil, the color of ancient Chinese gateways and porcelains.

In Brooks's mind, Mars became an extension of China, the China of long ago, crammed with warriors, maidens as fair as white willows, and tombs loaded high with carvings and treasure. Beyond the dome of Arcadia, he thought he saw Cathay.

It was some while before he realized he had a friend in Sgt. Al Shapiro.

He was working in the engineering laboratories, inserting the shutter mechanism in the 8×10 camera now rapidly nearing completion, when Shapiro strolled up. Shapiro was small, light on his feet, and darker in complexion than Brooks. He smiled at Brooks through a hank of black hair which hung across his face.

"What are you really going to use that camera for, Ozzy?"

"Pictures—like I told you. What else?"

"You're not going to be able to take it back to Earth in your kit. It's too heavy."

"What a nuisance," said Brooks, blandly.

Shapiro hesitated, then said, "You should photograph Mars with it, same as you said. Maybe I could help."

The remark took Brooks aback. He regarded Al Shapiro as a wooden man, cut off from his fellows, often to be seen reading the Army manuals other guys shunned. Al didn't even do *t'ai chi*. Could there be a vein of imagination under that stolid surface?

Mistaking his surprise, Shapiro lowered his voice and said, "Most guys see nothing in Mars, nothing at all. Except the officers. Do you notice when we're out doing maneuvers, Colonel Wolfe always says, 'Mars is fine fighting country'? That's how a professional soldier sees it, I guess. What do the men say about it? 'The dustbowl'—that's what they call Mars, the squaddies. They can't see it except as a torn-off chunk of America's Badlands. They've got no imagination. Me—I've had a think about it . . ."

"How do you see Mars, Al?" Brooks asked, very calm and in control again.

Shapiro gave his flitting smile.

"How do I see it? Why, when I take a look out there, I see it as a fantastic piece of natural engineering. Uncluttered by trees and all the vegetation that hides Earth. Mars is honest, a great series of cantilevers and buttresses and platforms. God's naked handiwork. I'm the only guy I know who'd like to get out there among it all."

"Some of the men like to go out for the pigeon shoots," Brooks said.

There were Mars jeeps which toured nearby gulleys firing off clay pigeons in all directions. These shoots formed one of the few outdoor recreations available. But no one ever ventured more than a mile from the fort.

Shapiro shrugged. "Kid stuff . . . I'd just like to figure on doing something memorable with my time on Mars. I've only got a month before they ship me back to Chicago."

Brooks put out his hand.

"That's the way I think too. I wish to do something memorable."

And so they came to draw up plans to photograph Olympus Mons from the ground.

Al Shapiro was as resourceful as Ozzy Brooks in getting what he wanted. He actually enjoyed the Army, and knew how to exploit all the weaknesses of that organization. They indented for a week's base leave, they set about bribing Captain Jeschke in Transport to secure the unauthorized loan of a Mars jeep, they bartered services in return for supplies.

"I should be a general—I could run Mars single-handed!" Shapiro said, laughing.

And all the while, he went ahead with his work in Engineering, and Brooks taught *mar t'ai chi*, instructing his squads how to love Mars as the ally of all their muscular exertions— thus, in his quiet way, subverting the army's purpose, which was to make the men hate the planet and anything on it which moved and was not capitalist.

Occasionally, maneuvers were undertaken in conjunction with the EEC dome in Eridania. The men had to fire missiles on the arctic ranges, or crawl around, cursing, in the red dust. Brooks saw then that his subversion had not had much effect.

Everyone wanted to go back to Earth. They had no vision. He longed to give them one.

"Before we leave here, we must make a model of Nix Olympica, and study it from all angles, so that we decide the ideal position to which to drive." Brooks nodded sagely as he spoke and looked sideways at Shapiro.

"Cartography," said Shapiro. "Lou Wright owes me a favor. Let's try Cartography."

They obtained more than maps and photographs. As the most prominent physical feature on Mars, the extinct volcano had warranted a plastic model, constructed by a bygone officer in the Army Geological survey. Brooks inspected it with interest before rejecting it.

"It's too small. We can make a much better one between us," he said.

What he felt was that this army model of Olympus was contaminated by its source; it had no poetry. Whoever had ordered it had probably been concerned with how the sides of the crater could be scaled, or how the cordera itself might provide a base for ground-to-space missiles.

Brooks molded his model of the gigantic volcano in plastic, coloring it with acrylics. Shapiro occasionally came over to admire his work.

"You see, the formation is about the size of the state of Missouri. It rises to all of fifteen miles high," Brooks said. "The best idea is to approach it from the east. The lighting will be best from the east."

"What's your lens?"

"I'm taking a selection. The point about an 8 × 10 camera is that it will give terrific definition—though it feeds on sheet film, and I'll need a tripod to keep it steady."

"I can make you a tripod."

They surveyed the model of Olympus critically when it was finished. Brooks shook his head.

"It's a good model," Shapiro said. "Photograph it here against a black background and we can save ourselves a trip."

Although Brooks rarely laughed, he laughed now. Laughed and said nothing.

He was serenely happy drawing up his own map, entering the sparse names of features in fine calligraphic style, precision-drawing contour lines. The most dangerous aspect of the trip was its distance. They were contemplating a drive of almost seven hundred and ninety miles, with no filling stations on the way, and then the journey back. They would be unlikely to see anyone the whole trip, except possibly a patrol moving between the Arcadia base and the hemisphere of the planet held by the enemy.

No possible danger could deter Brooks. His mind was filled with his delight in having found a friend and in the prospects ahead. Ever since Mariner 9 had executed its fly-over back in 1971, Olympus Mons, the largest volcano in the solar system, had frequently been photographed, by both satellites and rockets. But never as *he* would photograph it, with all the skill of an Ansel Adams.

He could visualize the prints now. They would be majestic, expressing both the violence and the deadness of the Martian landscape; he would create a serenity out of the conflicting tensions. He would create such an image that it would remain definitive: through the elusive art of photography, he would create a monument not only to the sublimity of the universe, but also to the greatness and the insignificance of mankind in the scheme of things.

With such exalted thoughts in his mind, Brooks had no room for fear.

The two men left Arcadia early one morning. Clad in suits, they slipped through one of the personnel locks in the main dome and made their way over to the transport hangar. There a stretched Mars jeep was waiting, loaded with fuel and supplies. As it rolled into the dim dawn light, the half-tracked vehicle resembled a cumbrous beetle.

There was little room to move in the cab. When they slept, their hammocks would be strung overhead. The ironically named Fort Arcadia was situated close to fifty degrees North, in the veined recesses of the Arcadia Planita. It was summer in the northern hemisphere of Mars, and they had a straight-forward drive southwards to the giant volcano, according to the maps.

They reckoned on traveling for fourteen hours a day, and averaging something close to twenty-seven miles per hour, the best they could hope for over trackless terrain. They nodded with pleasure as the shabby collection of prefabricated buildings disappeared behind them, and they were alone with Mars. Shapiro was driving.

A chill, shrunken sun had pierced through the mists of the eastern horizon, where layers of salmon pink dissolved into the sky. The shadow of their vehicle spread across a terrain which resembled Earth's Gobi Desert. Dust lay in sculptured terraces, punctuated here and there by rocks of pumice. In the far distance to their right, a series of flat-topped escarpments suggested a kind of order completely lacking nearer at hand; they made their way through a geological rubbish dump.

This formless landscape was familiar to them from their military exercises. They had crawled through it, dressed in camouflaging sand-robes. Nothing moved but dusts and rusts; the rest—unlike Earth's restless territories—had endured without change for billions of years. It had no more life to offer than the Geological Survey map of the route pinned to the dash.

There was no cratering here, as in the southern hemisphere, to lend interest. Their one concern was to steer south, avoiding rocks and dust drifts. After the first hour of travel, with Al Shapiro at the wheel, Brooks began to want to talk.

Shapiro, however, had gone silent. As the sun climbed in the pinkish sky, he became more silent. He offered the information that his family came from the Cicero area of Chicago, and then gave up entirely. Brooks, tired of trying to make conversation, resorted to whistling.

The sun arched overhead. The two sergeants took the wheel by turns, driving till the sun sloped to the west, to sink behind a low dust cloud. They had covered three hundred and seventy miles, and were pleased with their good progress. With nightfall, Shapiro found his voice again and was more cheerful; they ate a companionable supper from their rations before climbing into their hammocks and sleeping.

Once in the night, Brooks woke and peered out of the window. The stars and the Milky Way were there in glory, remote yet curiously intimate, as if they shone only for him, like a hope at the back of his mind. He was caught between the tensions of awe and enjoyment, like a troglodyte before its god, unable to tear his gaze away from the glitter until an hour had passed. He climbed back into his hammock, smiling into the fuggy darkness, and slept.

· · ·

Next dawn revealed no sign of the dust storm glimpsed at sunset—to Brooks's secret relief. Joy came to him. He sang. Shapiro looked doleful.

"Are you okay?" Brooks asked.

"I'm fine, sure."

"Anything worrying you? You wanted to get out among it all, and here we are."

"I'm fine."

"The Tharsis Bulge should be in view in an hour or two. Tomorrow we'll be within sight of Nix Olympica."

"Its name's Olympus," Shapiro said, sourly.

"I like to call it by the old name, Al. Nix Olympica... That was the name bestowed on it before anyone had ever set foot on the planet, or even left Earth. Nix Olympica is the old name, the name of mystery, of remoteness. I like it best. I'm going to photograph Nix Olympica and give a new image to Earth, before they come and build a missile site in the crater. Let's hope the atmosphere stays clear of dust."

Shapiro shrugged and brushed his hair from his eyes. He said nothing.

They were rolling by six-thirty. By eight, the terrain was changing. Petrified lavas created a series of steps over the ancient sand-rocks. Their gravimeter began to show fluctuations in the gravity field.

Brooks pointed ahead.

"There's the Tharsis Bulge," he said. "From here it stretches to south of the equator."

"I can see it," Shapiro said, without answering Brooks's excitement.

They began to steer south-east until the low wizened lips of Alba Patera lay distantly to their left. The view ahead became increasingly formidable.

The Tharsis Bulge distorted half a hemisphere. Earth held no feature as majestic. At its northwestern bastion stood the grim sentinel shape of Olympus, its cone rising a sheer fifteen and a half miles above the surrounding plain. As yet, they were too distant to see more than a pimpled shoulder of the Bulge looming above the ancient lands like a great bruise. Black clouds of dust rolled above the bruise. From the clouds, lightning showered, flickered like burning magnesium wire, died, flickered elsewhere. High above both Bulge and dust clouds, wispy white clouds formed a halo in the dark sky.

They climbed. The engine throbbed. The hours passed, the landscape took on power. It was as though the ancient rock breathed upwards. Despite the jeep, Brooks could feel the strength of the great igneous upthrust through the soles of his feet—the "Bubbling Well," as *t'ai chi* had it.

He breathed air deep into his *hora* center. But Shapiro sank back in his seat.

"You are suffering agoraphobia, Al," Brooks said. "Don't worry. Now we have something marvelous to distract your mind."

Brooks's intention was to drive some way up into the Bulge until Nix Olympica lay to the west; from there, he estimated he could photograph the formation at its most dramatic, with falling ground behind it.

The terrain which had been merely rutted now became much more difficult to drive. Long parallel fractures, remarkably uniform in spacing and orientation, ran downhill in their path. There was no way of avoiding the fracturing; as the map indicated, the faults extended for at least a hundred miles on either side of their course. Each fracture had straight, almost vertical, cliffs and reasonably flat bottoms. They found a point where a landslide had destroyed a cliff. By working their tracks on alternate sides, they contrived to slip down a small landslide to the bottom of the fracture, after which it was simple to drive along it. It was the width of an eight-lane highway.

Cliffs boxed them in on either side. The sky above was leaden, relieved by a strip of white cloud low ahead. It was just a matter of proceeding straight. No canyon on Earth was ever like this one.

Brooks pointed into the shadowed side of the fracture at the foot of the cliff. A trace of white lay across small boulders.

"It's a mixture of frost and snow, by the look of it," he said.

The sight delighted him. At least there was one natural process still functioning on the dead surface of the planet.

"How're we going to get out of this fault?" Shapiro asked.

"We're in a crack at least two and a half billion years old," Brooks said, more or less to himself. Even Cathay was not that ancient.

"And the satellites can't pick us up while we're down here," Shapiro said.

But Brooks would have nothing of misgivings. They would emerge somehow. He had never enjoyed himself so much.

"Just imagine it—once a great torrent rushed along here, Al. We're on an old riverbed."

"No, this wasn't formed by water," Shapiro said expertly. "It's the result of stresses in the Martian lithosphere. You'll be looking out for fish-bones next."

Although Brooks was silenced by this rejoinder, he spent the next hour alert for signs of departed life. What a triumph to see a fossil in the fracture walls! Once he cried out and stopped the jeep, to peer more closely at the cliff; there was nothing to be seen but a pattern of splintering in the rock.

"Nothing living has ever lived here—not ever," Shapiro said, and began to shiver.

It was impossible to say anything sympathetic, but Brooks understood how Shapiro felt. These unknown spaces chilled Shapiro as much as they excited Brooks; it was what came of being born in a crowded Chicago slum. Besides, he understood intellectually how absurd it was to be experiencing such intense pleasure in such a forbidding place. The mountains of Western Szechwan Province, from which his Chinese ancestors had come, might be almost as unwelcoming as this.

It turned out that Brooks's light-heartedness was not misplaced. The fracture cut into another at an oblique angle. Vast ramps, as smooth as if designed by a mortal architect, led up to the general level of the Bulge. The jeep climbed with ease, and they emerged onto the rainless elevations of the Tharsis Bulge. They were 1.3 miles above the datum, Mars's equivalent of sea level. The read-out also showed a free-air gravity anomaly of 229 mgals. The wall of yellowish black dust had disappeared. Visibility was good in the thin atmosphere. The sun shone as if encased in lucite. There was a glazed aspect, too, to the great smooth features of the inclined plain about them, where strange bumps and undulations suggested bones under the basaltic skin.

"Wonderful!" Brooks said. He began to tease himself. "All we need now is for a devil to emerge and dance before us. A devil with a red and white face."

"For god's sake . . ." Shapiro protested. "Take your photographs and let's get home."

But Brooks wanted to climb out and dance. He was sick of being cooped up in the cab of the vehicle, sick of the perpetual noise of the engine and air-purifier. It would be a time for the *t'ai chi* solo dance, even with the space suit on. He would celebrate Mars as no one else had done.

He controlled himself. A few more hours driving and they would see Nix Olympica itself. The sun was already descending. They had to make as much distance as they could before dark.

With nightfall, an electrical storm swept down from the heights. They stopped the jeep beside a corroded boulder. Flickering light surrounded them. Shapiro spent an hour checking through all the equipment, climbing restlessly about, and muttering to himself.

"One failure and we're dead," he said, catching Brooks's eye. "No one could get to us in time if anything went wrong. We embarked on this caper far too thoughtlessly. We should have planned it like a military operation."

"We shall see Nix Olympica tomorrow. Don't worry. Besides, imagine—wouldn't this spot really make a dramatic tomb?"

Shapiro was apologetic next morning. He did not realize that the desolate spaces of Mars would have such a bad effect on him. He knew he was acting foolishly. It was his determination to take a grip on himself. He was looking forward to seeing Olympus, and would be fine, he felt sure, on the way home. There was just—well, the realization that their lives balanced on a knife-edge.

Clapping him affectionately on the shoulder, Brooks said, "Life is always lived on a knife-edge. Don't worry."

By ten that morning, when the sun was shining through its blue glaze, they caught sight of a dark crust beyond the curve of the horizon. It was the volcano.

Both men cheered.

The volcano grew throughout the day, arising from behind the humps of the Bulge. Hour by hour, they gained a clearer impression of its size. It was a vast tomb of igneous rock which would have dominated any continent on Earth. It would have stretched from Shapiro's Chicago to Buffalo, obliterating Lake

Erie. It would have stretched from Switzerland to London, obliterating Paris and most of Belgium. It would have stretched from Lhasa in Tibet to Calcutta, obliterating Mount Everest like a molehill on its way.

Above its shoulders, where the sky was indigo, little demons of lightning danced, corkscrewing their way down into its scarred crust.

It could not be imagined or described. Only photographed.

Brooks brought his films from the refrigerator. He had three SLR cameras besides his homemade "tank." He went to work with cameras, lenses, and filters when they were still over four hundred miles from the giant caldera of Olympus. In the thin air, it appeared deceptively close.

Talking excitedly as he worked, Brooks tried to explain what he felt to Shapiro, who drove with his gaze on the ridged ground ahead.

"Back in the eighteenth century, painters discriminated between the beautiful, the picturesque, and the sublime. You'd need to dream up another category for most of Mars, particularly the dull bits round Arcadia. You wouldn't find much that would square with definitions of 'beautiful' or 'picturesque,' but here we have the sublime and then some . . . This monster has all the elements of awfulness and grandeur which the sublime requires. I wonder what the great painters would have made of Nix Olympica. . . ."

The sun climbed to zenith, and then began to slope away down the western sky.

"Turn direct south, Al. Speed it up, if you can. I want to catch the sunset behind Nix. It should be wonderful."

Shapiro managed a laugh. "I'm doing my best, Ozzy. Don't want to shake the buggy to pieces."

Brooks began loading low-grain fast film into his cameras.

They were traveling over ground composed of flow after flow of lava, one wave upon another, slags, powders, and ejecta cast upon the previous outpourings in grotesque patterns, as if the almost indestructible material had been bent on destroying itself, to the depth of hundreds of fathoms.

Whatever ferment had taken place over eons of time, those eons were themselves now eons past; since then, only silence covered the forbidding highlands—silence without motion, without so much as a wisp of steam from a solitary fumarole.

"Stop here!" Brooks exclaimed suddenly. "Where's that tripod? Oh, god . . . I must get on top of the jeep and film from there."

Grunting, Shapiro did as he was told. Brooks screwed his helmet on, draped his cameras and telescopic lenses over one shoulder, and climbed to the ground. He stood for a while, staring at the ground sloping towards the distant formation, and the sky, in which thin cloud curled like feather some five miles overhead. He took several shots at various shutter speeds almost without thought.

Looking back on his modest life, without distinction of any kind, he could hardly believe his luck. Night was descending on Mars, and he was here to photograph it. Even if Earth soon blew itself up, still he was here, and could record the moment.

His luck was crowned as he started to photograph from the top of the vehicle, using the 8 × 10 tank, steadying it with the tripod.

Phobos, the innermost moon, appeared to rise from the west—its orbital period being less than Mars's rotation period.

It glittered above the barricades of Nix Olympica. An ice cloud trailed like a pennant above the great volcano. The setting sun emerged from under a band of mist, spilling its light like broken egg along the horizon. The volcano was black in silhouette against the sky. The tank's shutter clicked, as moment by moment the light enriched itself.

Totally engrossed, Brooks slotted a polarizing filter over the lens. Click. Wonderful. Click. Click.

The universe closed down like an oyster on the strip of brightness. The sun seemed to flare and was gone, leaving Nix Olympica to prop up its sky. Brooks opened up his aperture and kept shooting. He knew he would never witness anything like this again. Tomorrow night, they would be on their way home, racing the sinking gauge on the oxygen cylinders. Then it would be up to him to try and recreate this moment in his darkroom, where the hard work would be done.

Next morning, both sergeants were stirring before dawn.

"I've got to capture the first ray of light to touch those crater walls," Brooks said. "Let's try to get fifty miles nearer."

"How about something to eat first, Ozzy?"

"We can eat for the rest of our lives. You drive, okay?"

Shapiro drove while Brooks fussed over his equipment. He

threw the vehicle recklessly forward, caught by Brooks's excitement.

He laughed.

"This'll be something to tell people about."

"No mistake there," Brooks said. "Maybe I'll publish an album of the best shots. Hey, Al, maybe we should climb the crater while we're here!"

"Forget it. Fifteen miles up in a space suit, with no climbing gear! I'm not mad even if you are."

They were racing across the bulbous incline. A worn stump of rock loomed ahead.

"Stop and I'll climb that," Brooks said.

When they got to it, the rock proved to be a small cone, a hundred yards across and several feet high. Unmoved by Shapiro's protests, Brooks unclamped the portable ladder from the jeep and climbed to the top. The crater was plugged with ancient magma and covered with dust. He got the tripod and the cameras in place just as the sun rose from behind a shoulder of Tharsis.

Click. This time, the fortress of Olympus was bright against a dark sky. For a moment, the outline of Tharsis was printed in shadow on its eastern flank. Click. Then like an iceberg of untold mass, it was floating on a sea of shadow. Click. The shadow withdrew across the plain towards the men. Mists rose. Click. For no more than five minutes, the great mesa was softened by evaporating carbon dioxide fumes. Click.

"Wonderful, wonderful!" said Brooks. He found that Shapiro had followed him up the ladder. Rapture was on both their faces. They hugged each other and laughed. They took shots of each other standing by the volcanic cone.

They forgot to eat and, throughout the morning, drove as fast as they could towards the volcano. It was a magnet, bathed in light.

At midday, they stopped to drink ham-and-green-pea soup.

They were still over one hundred and fifty miles from Olympus. It spread grandly before them: its great shield, its summit caldera—not a vent as in Earth's familiar stratovolcanoes but a relapse of the summit region—its flanking escarpments, its pattern of frozen lava runs, which from this distance resembled tresses of hair. From above, as Brooks knew, Nix Olympica resembled the nipple of a Martian Juno.

They gazed out at this brilliant formation as they slurped down their soup. It occupied one hundred and twelve degrees of their vision, although it was still so distant.

Shapiro turned from the sight and checked their instruments.

"We're doing okay, but getting near the safety margin on both fuel and oxygen. Are you almost ready to turn homewards, Ozzy?"

Brooks hesitated, then spoke in a nonchalant manner. "I'm almost ready. There's just one thing left to do. We've got some fine photographs in the bag, and by the time I bring the negatives up, there just could be a masterpiece or two among them. The only problem is the question of scale. Since there's no means of comparison in any of the pictures, you can't get an idea of the magnitude of Nix."

They looked at each other. Shapiro said, "You want me to leave you here and then drive the jeep nearer, so that you can have it in the foreground?"

"I don't want the truck in. Besides, I need to be mobile myself. I want you in it, Al—the human figure. I want to put you forward in the landscape. Then I move around taking shots."

Shapiro became rigid.

"I won't do that, Ozzy."

"Why not?"

"I won't do it."

"Tell me why."

"Because I just won't."

"Look, Al, we'll never be out of sight of each other. We'll be in radio contact. You'll be able to see the jeep all the while. All you have to do is stand where I put you. It'll take an hour, no more."

"No, I said. I'm not standing out in that landscape alone. That's flat, okay?"

They glowered at each other.

"You go out there. I'll take the damned pictures."

"I'm not afraid to go out there. Come on, Al, we've come all this way. There's nothing to be scared of, for Christ's sake. One hour, that's all I ask."

Shapiro dropped his gaze, clenching his fists together.

"You can't make me do it."

"I'm not making you. What's so difficult? You just do it."

"Suppose something happens?"

"Nothing has happened here for century after century. Not a thing."

Shapiro expelled a sigh. His face showed the tension inside him. His skin gleamed in the flat light.

"Okay. I'll do it, I guess."

"Okay." Brooks hesitated then said, "I appreciate it, Al. The medics haven't yet got round to naming a fear of wide open alien spaces, but they will. I know it must take some fighting."

"I'll conquer it. Just don't talk about it," said Al, his teeth chattering, as Brooks helped him secure the helmet of his suit.

"Sometimes there's need for talk. Remember, the same demons and spirits haunt wide open spaces of Mars as those of Earth. No difference really, since all apparitions are in the mind. If we import demons, then we can conquer them, because they must obey our laws."

"I'll try and bear that in mind," said Shapiro, forcing his teeth to stop chattering. "Now let me out before I think better of it."

All the while Brooks drove back and forth about that portion of the Bulge, taking his historic shots of Nix Olympica, he was aware of what the distant white figure was undergoing as it stood alone in the grotesque landscape. He proceeded without haste, but he worked as fast as possible, concentrating now on his wide-angle lenses.

The end result of the men's endeavor was the series of photographs which became historic records of mankind's expansion through the solar system. They rank as works of art. As for Brooks, despite a period of fame, he eventually died in penury. General Shapiro ended up as Officer Commanding Mars Base; his memoirs, in four volumes, contain an account of his first reconnaissance of Olympus—which differs considerably from the facts as set down here.

WINDWAGON SMITH AND THE MARTIANS

Lawrence Watt-Evans

"Windwagon Smith and the Martians" was purchased by Gardner Dozois and appeared in the April, 1989, issue of IAsfm, *with an evocative illustration by David Lee Anderson. Although Watt-Evans was already a well-known novelist, and had sold some short fiction to gaming magazines, he made his first short fiction sale to a mainline science fiction magazine in 1988, with his widely popular story "Why I Left Harry's All-Night Hamburgers," a story that won our 2nd Annual Readers' Award, and later went on to win a Hugo Award as well. Watt-Evans has gone on to publish several more pieces in the magazine—with several more in inventory. Public response to them has remained strong, with a poem of his winning in the poetry category this year, and this, the whimsical story of a journey to a Mars that ought to have been, winning the* IAsfm *Readers' Award as the best Short Story of 1989.*

Lawrence Watt-Evans's many novels include The Wizard and the War Machine, Denner's Wreck, The Cyborg and the Sorcerer, With a Single Spell, Shining

Steel, *and* Nightside City. *Coming up is an anthology he's edited,* Newer York. *He lives in the Maryland suburbs of Washington, D.C., with his wife and two children.*

I reckon most folks have heard of Thomas Smith, the little sailor from Massachusetts who turned up in Westport, Missouri one day in 1853 aboard the contraption he called a windwagon. He'd rigged himself a deck and a sail and a tiller on top of a wagon, and just about tried to make a prairie schooner into a *real* schooner. Figured on building himself a whole fleet and getting rich, shipping folks and freight to Santa Fe or wherever they might have a mind to go.

Well, as you might have heard, he got some of the folks in Westport to buy stock in his firm, and he built himself a bigger, better windwagon from the ground up, with a mainmast and a mizzen both, and he took his investors out for a test run—and they every one of them got seasick, and scared as the devil at how fast the confounded thing ran, and they all jumped ship and wouldn't have more to do with it. Smith allowed as how the steering might not be completely smooth yet, though the idea was sound, but the folks in Westport just weren't interested.

And last anyone heard, old Windwagon Smith was sailing west across the prairie, looking for braver souls.

That's the last anyone's heard till now, anyways. A good many folks have wondered whatever became of Windwagon Smith, myself amongst them, and I'm pleased to be able to tell the story.

And if you ask how I come to know it, well, I heard it from Smith himself, but that's another story entirely.

Here's the way of it. Back in '53, Smith headed west out of Westport feeling pretty ornery and displeased; he reckoned that the fine men of Westport had just missed the chance of a lifetime, and all over a touch of the collywobbles and a bit of wind. Wasn't any doubt in his mind but he could find braver men somewhere, who would back his company and put all those mule-drawn freight-wagons right out of business. It was just a matter of finding the right people.

So he sailed on, and he stopped now and then and told folks his ideas, and he was plump disconcerted to learn that there wasn't a town he tried that wanted any part of his windwagon.

He missed a lot of towns, too, because the fact was that the steering *was* a mite difficult, and he didn't so much stay on the trail as try to keep somewhere in its general vicinity. He stopped a few times to tinker with it, but the plain truth is that he never did get it right, not so as one man could work it and steer small. After all, the clippers he'd learned on didn't steer with just a tiller, but with the sails as well—tacking and so forth. If Smith had had more men on board, to help work the sails, he might have managed some fine navigation, instead of just aim-and-hope.

After a time, though, he had got most of the way to Santa Fe, but had lost the trail again, and he was sailing out across the desert pretty sure that he was a good long way from where he had intended to be, when he noticed that the sand was getting to be awfully red.

The sky was getting darker, too, but there wasn't a cloud anywhere in it, and it wasn't but early afternoon; it just seemed as if the sun had shrunk up some, and the sky had dimmed down from a regular bright blue to a color more like the North Atlantic on a winter morning. The air felt damn near as cold as the North Atlantic, too, and that didn't seem right for daytime in the desert. What's more, Smith suddenly felt sort of light, as if the wind might just blow him right off his own deck, even though it didn't seem to be blowing any harder than before. And he was having a little trouble breathing, like as if he'd got himself up on top of a mountain.

And the sand was *awfully* red, about the color of a boiled lobster.

Well, old Windwagon Smith had read up on the West before he ever left Massachusetts, and he'd never heard of anything like this. He didn't like it a bit, and he took a reef in the sails and slowed down, trying to figure it.

The sand stayed red, and the sky stayed dark, and the air stayed thin and he still felt altogether too damn light on his feet, and he commenced to be seriously worried and furled the sails right up, so that that windwagon of his rolled to a stop in the middle of that red desert.

He threw out the anchor to keep him where he was, and had a time doing it, because although the anchor seemed a fair piece lighter than he remembered, it almost took him with it when he heaved it over. Seemed like he had to be extra careful about everything he did, because even the way his own body moved didn't seem quite right; of course, being a sailor, he could keep his feet just about anywhere, so he got by. He might have thought he was dreaming if he hadn't been the levelheaded sort he was, and proud of his plain sense to know whether he was awake or asleep.

Just to be sure, though, he pinched himself a few times, and the red marks that left pretty much convinced him he was awake.

He stood on the deck and looked about, and all he saw was that red, red sand, stretching clear to the horizon whichever way he cared to look. The horizon looked a shade close in, at that; wasn't anything quite what it ought to be.

He didn't like that a bit. He climbed up aloft, to the crow's nest up above the main topsail, and he looked about again.

This time, when he looked to what he reckoned was west, he saw something move, something that was blue against the blue of the sky, so he couldn't make out just what it was.

It was coming his way, though, so he figured he'd just let it come, and take a closer look when he could.

But he wasn't about to let it come on him unprepared. After all, there were still plenty of wild Indians around, and white men who were just as wild without any of the excuses the Indians had, seeing as how they hadn't had their land stolen, or their women either, nor their hunting ruined. They could be just as wild as Indians, all the same.

He slid down the forestay and went below, and when he mounted back to the maintop he had a sixgun on his belt and a rifle in his hand.

By now the blue thing was closer, and he got a good clear look at it, and he damn near dropped his rifle, because it was a ship, a sand ship, and it was sailing over the desert right toward him.

And what's more, there were three more right behind it, all of them tall and graceful, with blue sails the color of that dark sky. Proud as he was of his work, old Windwagon had to admit

that the ugliest of the four was a damn sight better-looking than
his own windwagon had ever been, even before it got all dusty
and banged up with use.

They were quieter, too. Fact is, they were near as silent as
clouds, where his own windwagon had always rattled and clattered like any other wagon, and creaked and groaned like a
ship, as well. All in all, it made a hell of a racket, but these
four sand ships didn't make a sound—at least, not that Smith
could hear yet, over the wind in the rigging.

He was pretty upset, seeing those four sand ships out there.
Here he'd thought he had the only sailing wagon ever built,
and then these four come over the horizon—not just one, but
four, and any of them enough to burst a clipper captain's heart
with envy.

If they were freighters, Smith knew that he wasn't going to
get anywhere near as rich as he had figured, up against competition like that. He began to wonder if maybe the folks back
in Westport weren't right, but for all the wrong reasons.

The sand ships' hulls were emerald green, and the trim was
polished brass or bone white, and above the blue sails they
flew pennants, gold and blue and red and green pennants, and
they were just about the prettiest thing Smith had ever seen in
his life.

He looked at them, and he didn't know what the hell they
were doing there or where they'd come from, but they didn't
look like anything wild Indians would ride, or anything outlaws
would ride, so he just watched as they came sailing up to his
own ship—or wagon, or whatever you care to name it.

Three of the sand ships slowed up and stopped a good ways
off, but the first one in line came right up next to him.

That one was the biggest and the prettiest, and the only one
flying gold pennants. He figured it must belong to the boss of
the bunch, the commodore or whatsoever he might be called.

"Ahoy!" Smith shouted.

He could see people on the deck of the sand ship, three of
them, but he couldn't make out any faces, and none of them
answered his hail. They were dressed in robes, which made
him wonder if maybe they weren't Indians after all, or Mex-
icans.

"Ahoy!" he called again.

"Mr. Smith," one of them called back, almost like he was

singing, "Come down where we can speak more easily."

Smith thought about that, and noticed that none of them had any guns that he could see, and decided to risk it. He climbed down, with his rifle, and he came over to the rail, where he could have reached out and touched the sand ship if he stretched a little.

He was already there when he realized that the strangers had called him by his right name.

Before he could think that over, the stranger who had called him said, "Mr. Smith, we have brought you here because we admire your machine."

Smith looked at the strangers, and at the great soaring masts and dark blue sails, and at the shiny brass and the sleek green hull, and he didn't believe a word of it. Anyone who had a ship like that one had no reason to admire his windwagon. He'd been mighty proud of it until a few minutes ago, but he could see now that it wasn't much by comparison.

Well, he figured, the strangers were being polite. He appreciated that. "Thanks," he said. "That's a sweet ship you have there, yourself."

While he was saying that, he noticed that the reason he hadn't been able to make out faces was that the strangers were all wearing masks, shiny masks that looked like pure silver, with lips that looked like rubies. The eyes that showed through were yellow, almost like cat's eyes, and Smith wasn't too happy about seeing that. The masks looked like something Indians might wear, but he'd never heard of any Indians like these.

He said, "By the way, I'd be mighty obliged if you could tell me where I am; I lost my bearings some time back, and it seems as if I might be a bit off course."

He couldn't see which of the strangers it was that spoke, what with the masks, but one of them said, "My apologies, Mr. Smith. It was we who brought you here. You are on Mars."

"Mars?" Smith asked. He wasn't sure just how to take this. "You mean Mars, Pennsylvania? Down the road a piece from Zelienople?" He didn't see any way he could have wound up there, and he'd never heard tell that Pennsylvania had any flat red deserts, but that was one of the two places he'd ever heard of called Mars, and he didn't care to think about the other one much.

"No," the stranger said, "the planet Mars. We transported

your excellent craft here by means that I am unable to explain, so that I might offer you a challenge.''

Now, Smith knew something about the planets, because any sailor does if he takes an interest in navigation, and he knew that Mars was sort of reddish, and the red sand would account for that nicely. He looked up at that shrunken sun and that dark blue sky, and then at those sand ships like nothing on Earth, and decided that one of three things had happened.

Either he'd gone completely mad without noticing it, and was imagining all this, which didn't bear thinking about but which surely fit the facts best of all; or somebody was playing one hell of a practical joke on him, which he didn't have any idea how it was being done; or the stranger was telling the truth. For the sake of argument, he decided he'd figure on that last one, because the second seemed plumb unlikely and the first wasn't anything he could figure on, never having been mad before and not knowing just how it might work. Besides, he'd simply never judged himself for the sort of fellow that might go mad, and he wasn't in any hurry to change his mind on that account.

So he figured the stranger was telling the truth. Whether it was magic, or some sort of scientific trick, he didn't know, but he reckoned he really was on Mars.

And he didn't figure he'd ever find his way back to Earth by himself.

"What sort of a challenge?" he asked.

He sort of thought he saw the middle stranger smile behind his silver mask.

"I," the middle stranger said, "am Moohay Nillay, and I am the champion yachtsman of all Teer, as we call our planet." Smith wasn't any too sure of those names, so I may have them wrong. "I have the finest sand ship ever built, and in it I have raced every challenger that my world provided, and I have defeated them all. Yet it was not enough; I grew bored, and desired a new challenge, and sought elsewhere for competitors who could race against me."

Smith began to see where this was leading, but he just smiled and said, "Is that so?"

"Indeed it is, Mr. Smith. Unfortunately, our two worlds are the only two in this system bearing intelligent life, and your world has not produced many craft that will sail on sand. I am not interested in sailing upon water—our planet no longer has any seas, and I find the canals too limiting. I might perhaps find better sport on the seas of your planet, but the means by which I drew you here will not send me to Earth. I have been forced to wait, to search endlessly for someone on your planet who would see the obvious value of sailing the plains. To date, you are only the second I have discovered. The first was a man by the name of Shard, Captain Shard of the *Desperate Lark*, who fitted his sea-going ship with wheels in order to elude pursuit; I drew him here, and easily defeated his clumsy contrivance. I hope that you, Mr. Smith, will provide a greater test.''

"Well, I hope I will, Mr. Nillay. I'd be glad to race you." Smith didn't really think he had much of a chance against those sleek ships, but he figured that it wouldn't hurt to try, and that if he were a good loser, Mr. Nillay might send him back to Earth.

And of course, there was always the chance that his horse sense and Yankee ingenuity might just give him a chance against this smooth-talking Martian braggart.

Well, to make a long story a trifle less tiresome, Smith and the Martian agreed on the ground rules for their little competition. They would race due south, to the edge of a canal—Smith took the Martian's word for just where this canal was, since of course he didn't know a damn thing about Martian geography. Whoever got there first, and dropped a pebble into the canal without setting foot on the ground, would win the race.

The Martian figured it at about a two-day race, if the wind held up, and he gave Smith a pebble to use—except it wasn't so much your everyday pebble as it was a blue jewel of some kind. Smith hadn't ever seen one quite like it.

If Smith won, he was to have a big celebration in the Martian's home town, and would then be sent back to Earth, if he wanted. If he lost, well, he wouldn't get the celebration, but if he had put up enough of a fight, made it a good race and not a rout, the Martian allowed as he might consider maybe sending him back to Earth eventually, just out of the goodness of his heart and as a kind gesture.

Smith didn't like the sound of that, but then he didn't have a whole hell of a lot of choice.

"What about those other folks?" he asked, figuring he needed every advantage he could get. "I'm sailing single-handed, and you've got two crewmen and three other ships."

The Martian allowed as how that might be unfair. Captain Shard had had a full crew for his ship, and Mr. Nillay hadn't been sure whether Smith had anyone else aboard or not, but since he didn't, since he was sailing alone, then Mr. Nillay would sail alone, too. And the other three ships were observers, just there to watch, and to help out if there was trouble.

Smith couldn't much quarrel with that, so after a little more arguing out details, the two ships were lined up at the starting line, Smith's windwagon on the left and the Martian sand ship on the right, both pointed due south.

One of the other Martians fired a starting pistol that didn't bang, it buzzed like a mad hornet, and the race was on.

Old Windwagon yanked the anchor aboard and started hauling his sheets, piling on every stitch of canvas his two little masts could carry, running back and forth like a lunatic trying to do it all by himself as fast as a full crew, all the while still keeping an eye on his course and making sure he was still headed due south.

Those sails caught the wind, and before he knew it he was rolling south at about the best speed he'd ever laid on, with nothing left to do but stand by the tiller and hope a crosswind didn't tip him right over.

When he was rolling smooth, he glanced back at the Martian sand ship, and it wasn't there. He turned to the stern quarter, and then the beam, and he still didn't see it, but when he looked forward again there it was, a point or two off his starboard bow, that tall blue sail drawing well, full and taut, and that damn Martian yachtsman standing calm as a statue at the tiller.

And although it wasn't easy over the rattling and creaking of his own ship, Smith could hear the Martian sand ship make a weird whistling as it cut through that red sand.

Well, seeing and hearing that made Smith mad. He wasn't about to let some bossy little foreigner in a mask and a nightshirt beat him *that* easily, no sir! He tied down the tiller and ducked below, and began heaving overboard anything he thought he could spare, to lighten the load and help his speed.

Extra spars and sails, his second-best anchor, and the trunk with his clothes went over the after rail; he figured that he could come back and pick them up later if he needed them. When the trunk had hit the ground and burst open, he turned and looked for that Martian prig, and was about as pleased as you can imagine to see that he was closing the gap, gaining steadily on the Martian ship.

Then he hit a bump and went veering off to port, and had to take the tiller again.

Well, the race went on, and on, and Smith gained on the Martian little by little, what seemed like just a few inches every hour, until not long after sunset, while the sky was still pink in the west, the two ships were neck and neck, dead even.

It was about at this point that it first sank in that they weren't going to heave to for the night, and Smith began to do some pretty serious worrying about what might happen if he hit a rock in the dark or some-such disaster as that. He hadn't sailed his windwagon by night before.

He wasn't too worried about missing a night's sleep, as he'd had occasion to do that before, when he was crewing a clipper through a storm in the South Pacific, or spending his money ashore in some all-night port, but he *was* worried about cruising ahead under full sail across uncharted desert in the dark.

It helped some when the moons rose, two little ones instead of a big one like ours, but he still spent most of that night in a cold sweat. About his only consolation was that the crazy Martian was near as likely to wreck as he was himself.

It was a mighty cold night, too, and he wrapped himself in all three of the coats he still had and wished he hadn't been so quick to throw his trunk over.

About the time when he was beginning to wonder if maybe the nights on Mars lasted for six months, the way he'd heard tell they did way up north, the sun came up again, and he got a good look at just where he stood.

He'd pulled ahead of the Martian, a good cable's length, maybe more. He smiled through his frozen beard at that; if he just held on, he knew he'd have the race won.

So he *did* hold on, as best he could, but something had changed. The wind had died down some, and maybe the Martian had trimmed his sails a bit better, or the wind had shifted a trifle, but by the middle of the afternoon Windwagon saw that he wasn't gaining any more, and in fact he might just be starting to lose his lead. He wasn't the least bit pleased, let me tell you.

He started thinking about what else he had that he could throw overboard, and he was still puzzling over that when he topped a low rise and got a look at what lay ahead.

He was at the top of the longest damn slope he'd ever seen in his life, a slope that looked pretty near as big as an ocean, and down at the bottom was a big band of green, and in the middle of that green was a strip of blue that Smith knew had to be the canal.

And it was downhill almost the entire way!

The green part wasn't downhill, he could see that, but that long, long red slope was. It wasn't steep, and it wasn't any too smooth, but it was all downhill, and that meant he didn't want to lighten the ship any more at all.

He tied down the tiller again and hung down over the side, pouring on the last of his axle grease so as to make the most out of that hill.

When he got back up on deck and looked back he could see that he was gaining quickly now, pulling farther and farther ahead of the Martian's lighter ship. And that canal was in sight, straight ahead! He figured he just about had it won.

And then the wind, which had been just sort of puffing for a while, up and died completely.

By this time he was rolling hell-for-leather down that hill, at a speed he didn't even care to guess, and he didn't stop when the wind died—but that flat stretch of green ahead suddenly looked a hell of a lot wider than it had before.

He pulled up the tiller entirely, to cut the drag; after all, the canal stretched from one horizon to the other, so what did he need to steer for? He could still maneuver the sails if he had to.

He went bouncing and rattling down that hill, thumping and bumping over the loose rocks and the red sand, praying the whole way that he wouldn't tip over. He didn't dare look back to see where the Martian was.

And then he was off the foot of the slope, crunching his way across that green, which was all some sort of viney plant, and his wagon went slower, and slower, and slower, and finally, with one big bounce and a bang, it came to a dead stop—a hundred feet or so from the canal.

Smith looked down at those vines, and then ahead at that blue water, and then back at the Martian sand ship, which wasn't much more than a dark spot on the red horizon behind him, and he just about felt like crying. There wasn't hardly a breath of wind, just the slightest bit of air, enough to flap the sails but not to fill them.

And what's more, the vines under his wheels weren't anywhere near as smooth as the red sand, or the prairie grass back on Earth, and he knew it would take a good hard tug to get the old windwagon started again.

If he could once get it started, he figured that he could just about reach the canal on momentum, without hardly any wind; the vines sort of petered out in about another twenty feet, and from there to the canal the whole way was stone pavement, smooth white stone that wouldn't give his wheels the slightest bit of trouble.

But he needed a good hard push to get off those vines and get moving, and the wind didn't seem to be picking up, and that Martian was still sailing, smooth and graceful, closer and closer down the slope.

And thinking back, Smith recalled that the sand ship had a blade on the front. He hadn't seen much use for it back on the sand, but he could see how it would just cut right through those vines.

He looked about, and saw that a dozen or so Martians, in their robes and masks, were standing nearby, watching silently. Smith wasn't any too eager to let them see him lose. If there was ever a time when he needed some of that old Yankee ingenuity he prided himself on, Smith figured this was it.

He looked down at the vines again, and thought to himself that they looked a good bit like seaweed, back on Earth. He was stuck in the weeds, just like he might be on a sandbar or in shoal water back on Earth.

Well, he knew ways of getting off sandbars. He couldn't figure on any tide to lift him off here, but there were other ways.

He could kedge off. He hauled up the anchor, and heaved it forward hard as he could—and the way his muscles worked on Mars, that was mighty hard. That anchor landed on the edge of the pavement, and then slid off as he hauled on it, and bit into the soft ground under the vines.

That was about as far as he could haul by hand, though. For one man to move that big a wagon, even on Mars, he needed something more than his own muscle. He took the line around the capstan and began heaving on the pawls.

The line tautened up, and the wagon shifted, and then inched forward—but he couldn't get up any sort of momentum, and he couldn't pull it closer than ten feet from the pavement, where it stopped again, still caught in the vines. When he threw himself on the next pawl the anchor tore free.

He hauled it back on board and reconsidered. Kedging wasn't going to work, that was pretty plain; he couldn't get the anchor to bite on that white stone. So he was still on his sandbar.

He thought back, and back, and tried to remember every trick he'd ever heard for getting a ship off a bar, or freeing a keel caught in the mud.

There was one trick that the men o' war used; they'd fire off a full broadside, and often as not the recoil would pull the ship free.

The problem with that, though, was that he didn't have a broadside to fire. His whole armory was a rifle, two sixguns, and a couple of knives.

He looked back up the slope, and he could see the sand ship's green hull now, and almost thought he could see the sun glinting on Mr. Nillay's silly mask, and he decided that he was damn well going to *make* himself a broadside—or if not a broadside, at least a cannon or two.

The wind picked up a trifle just then, and the sails bellied out a bit, and that gave him hope.

He went below and began rummaging through everything he had, and found himself his heavy iron coffeepot. He took that up on deck, and then broke open every cartridge he had and dumped the charges into the pot; he judged he had better than a pound of powder when he was through. He took his lightest coat, which wasn't really more than a bit of a linsey jacket anyway, and folded that up and stuffed it in on top of the powder for a wad. He put a can of beans on top for shot, and then rolled up a stock certificate from the Westport and Santa Fe Overland Navigation Company and rammed it down the coffeepot's spout for a fuse.

The sails were filling again, but the wagon wasn't moving. Smith figured he still needed that little push. He wedged his contraption under the tiller mounting, and touched a match to the paper.

It seemed to take forever to burn down, but finally it went off with a roar like a bee-stung grizzly bear, and that can of beans shot out spinning and burst on the hillside, spraying burnt beans and tin all over the red sand. The coffeepot itself was blown to black flinders.

And the wagon, with a creak, rolled forward onto the pavement. The sails caught the wind, feeble as it was, and with rattling and banging the windwagon clattered across that white stone pavement, toward the canal.

And then it stopped with a bump, about ten feet from the edge, just as the wind died again.

Smith just about jumped up and down and tore at his hair at that. He leaned over the rail and saw that there was a sort of ridge in the pavement, and that his front wheels were smack up against it. He judged it would take near onto a hurricane to get him past that.

He looked back at the Martian sand ship, with its long, graceful bowsprit that would stick out over the canal if it stopped where he was, and he began swearing a blue streak.

He was at the damn canal, after all, and the Martian was just now into the vines, and he wasn't about to be beat like that. He knew that he had to *drop* the pebble, not throw it, so he couldn't just run to the bow and heave it into the water. He was pretty sure that that old Martian would call it a foul, and rightly, if he threw the confounded thing.

And then that old horse sense came through again, and he ran up the rigging to the mainyard, where he grabbed hold of the starboard topsail sheet and untied it, so that it swung free. Hanging onto the bottom end, he climbed back to the mizzenmast, up to the crosstrees, still holding the maintopsail sheet, and dove off, hollering, with the pebble-jewel in his hand.

He swooped down across the deck, lifting his feet to clear it, and then swung out past the bow, up over the canal, and at the top of his swing he let the pebble drop.

It plopped neatly into the water, a foot or two out from the canal wall, while that Martian yachtsman was still fifty feet back. Windwagon Smith let out a shriek of delight as he swung wildly back and forth from the yardarm, and a half-dozen Martians applauded politely.

By the time Smith got himself back down on the deck, Mr. Nillay had got his own ship stopped on the pavement, and he was standing by the edge of the canal, and even with his mask on Smith thought he looked pretty peeved, but there wasn't much he could do.

And then a few minutes later the whole welcoming committee arrived, and they took Smith back to their city, which looked like it was all made out of cut glass and scrimshaw, and they made a big howdy-do over him, and told him he was the new champion sailor of all Mars, the first new champion in nigh onto a hundred years, and they gave him food and drink and held a proper celebration, and poor old Mr. Nillay had to go along and watch it all.

Smith enjoyed it well enough, and he had a good old time for a while, but when things quieted down somewhat he went over to Mr. Nillay and stuck out his hand and said, "No hard feelings?"

"No, Mr. Smith," the Martian said, "no hard feelings. However, I feel there is something I must tell you."

Smith didn't like the sound of that. "And what might that be, sir?" He asked.

"Mr. Smith, I have lied to you. I cannot send you back to Earth."

"But you said . . ." Smith began, ready to work himself up into a proper conniption.

"I did not believe I would lose," the Martian interrupted, and his voice still sounded like music, but now it was like a funeral march. "Surely, a sportsman like yourself can understand that."

Well, Smith had to allow as how he *could* understand that, though he couldn't rightly approve. It seemed to him that it was mighty callous to go fetching someone off his home planet like that, when a body couldn't even send him back later.

Old Nillay had to admit that he had been callous, all right, and he damn near groveled, he was so apologetic about it.

But Smith had always been philosophical about these things. It wasn't like he'd had a home anywhere on Earth; all he'd had was his windwagon, and he still had that. And there on Mars he was a hero, and a respected man, where on Earth he hadn't been much more than a crackpot inventor or a common seaman. And the food and drink was good, and the Martian girls were right pretty when they took their masks off, even if they weren't exactly what you'd call white, being more of a brown color, and those big yellow eyes could be mighty attractive. What's more, what with Martians being able to read minds, which they could, that being how they could speak English to Smith, the women could always tell just what a man needed to make him happy, and folks were just generally pretty obliging.

So Windwagon Smith stayed on Mars and lived there happily enough, and he raced his windwagon a few more times, and mostly won, and all this is why he never did turn up in Santa Fe and why he never did find any more investors after that bunch in Westport backed out.

And I know you may be thinking, well, if he stayed on Mars, then how in tarnation did I ever hear this story from him so as I could tell it to you the way I just did, and all that I can say is what I said before.

That's another story entirely.

RETROVISION

Robert Frazier

"Retrovision" was purchased by Gardner Dozois and appeared in the August, 1988, issue of IAsfm *with an intriguing illustration by Janet Aulisio. Frazier published dozens of poems in* IAsfm, *and elsewhere, throughout the 1980s—he is, in fact, one of the genre's best known and most respected poets, and he has published more poetry in* IAsfm *over the years, by a considerable margin, than any other contributor. Toward the end of the decade, he began writing prose stories, as well. He made his first prose sale to* IAsfm *in 1988, and has since sold several more to us, as well as to markets like* Amazing, New Pathways, *and* In the Field of Fire. *Several chapbooks of his poetry have been published, and, at last word, he is at work on a novel. He lives in the wilds of Nantucket, within hailing distance of his friend and sometime collaborator, Lucius Shepard.*

In the haunting and disquieting story that follows, he shows us that the old saying about how we live on only in the memories of those who loved us may be a good deal truer than we think . . .

Anxious to reach the hospital at the hub of Rio Base, Joaquim Boaz Cristobel hurried along the corridor of the innermost ring. He stretched his stride to its limit, pushing past the slow-moving crowds that toured the Brazilian colony as part of a cultural exchange program. Unable to navigate around a group of Matis in their Amazonian tribal dress, he pushed through them until he encountered a man who blocked his way completely. The face was familiar, he thought—then realized abruptly that it was his own.

Joaquim was not surprised by the mirrored wall, for the colonists frequently used such partitions to break up the monotony of their Martian life; yet he was surprised—and shocked—by his own appearance. He looked more aboriginal than the Matis: his black hair in dirty twists, salt and pepper stubble on his chin, eyes shot through with a fine capillary pink. He looked like shit. He *felt* like shit. Between extra shifts at the lab and night hours spent with Celina at the hospital, he'd barely slept. Christ, not at all. He brushed flat his rumpled blue lab coat, ran his fingers through his hair. He had to look good for his mother; she'd always demanded that.

In the next section of the ring, a corridor branched in toward the hub complex, and Joaquim hitched a ride on an electric dolly that was delivering chemical tanks to the hydroponic gardens there. The hub corridor and the ground level of the hub itself were abuzz with evening activity; the bigwigs down at the Sao Paulo shuttleport must have reserved a big transport for the tour this time, judging by the number of visitors. The dolly operator said the cryotanks must have cost a fortune. She wished she had some.

A clear path to the elevators opened to his left, so Joaquim thanked the woman with a nod and slipped off the dolly near a videoboard. A few tourists gawked at an update on the sandstorm that had hit late that afternoon, the reds and oranges swirling on the replays. Opposite the elevators, Joaquim leaned for a moment against the pitted glass windowall where the stars shone through. Then he took the express tube to the top of the hub.

At the tube exit into the hospital complex, a woman stopped him and tugged him over to where the body of a child lay slumped against a partition. "The boy died before I could get him to the doctors, Senhor," she said urgently. "But *you* can save him." She'd recognized Joaquim as a mnemoniphage, spotting the brown insignia on his lapel. "Please, save him, Senhor," she pleaded. "He was so precious."

Joaquim shuddered. "I am under contract to the colonial authorities," he said stiffly, through clenched teeth. "I can only preserve those important to the colony's survival."

"He's all I have, Senhor! My husband was killed in a mining accident."

Joaquim shook his head blindly and walked away, pushing past the woman, who began to wail. He empathized with her, for he'd lost his own father to the harsh surface of Mars, but the fear in his gut paralyzed him. He resented his duties as a mnemoniphage, hated the horde of strangers bottled and fizzling in his skull.

He also faced a far more pressing duty.

Celina Cristobel was dying. Family tradition demanded that he preserve her. But Joaquim knew that he could not.

Joaquim turned from the view of the flood-lit towers outside and stared at his mother in the hospital bed, reading the signposts of her frailties: the thin white hair, the purse-stringed wrinkles about her slack lips, her shallow breathing, the big blue vein that throbbed on her neck like a newborn butterfly pumping up its wings.

Typical, he thought. Medical techniques improved, but a goddamn hospital bed always remained the same. This one was fundamentally the same as the dozens of others in his total collective memory, in the experiences of the mnemoniphaged individuals that trailed back in his mind to the late twentieth century. This bed had built-in videoboards to display spectroscoped biochemical levels and other medical data, but it also still featured ugly chrome railings, an uncomfortable plastic mattress that let the patient slide, and snow-white linen tucked tight enough to pass military inspection.

The hospital itself presented an appearance of great order and efficiency, but at heart it was no different from past facilities in Joaquim's memory. In spite of the high-tech gloss, the halls still smelled of antiseptics and toilet bowl chemicals, and postcard holograms of the Martian sunrise hung askew in the same spot in each identical room. A radio left on for an insomniac fizzled with static, giving off faint riffs of great composers like Philip Glass and Villa-Lobos, ground to a mu-zaky pablum. Technicians pushed equipment about on rollers that were just squeaky enough to wake only those patients in dire need of rest. Joaquim looked to Celina's arm where it rested on the cowling, noted a black and blue bruise. Shit, the nurses might be as highly trained as advertised, but they could still botch a probe with an IV needle. All that seemed missing was a leaky faucet, though he imagined that it also must exist here somewhere, perhaps dripping in the dark recess where the sink retracted beneath the bed structure.

"Jake," his mother said. "Are you there, Jake?"

Celina spoke as if cotton filled her throat, preventing each word from forming, leaving the component sounds of his name to rattle against themselves. She drifted back to sleep, her mouth falling open beneath a hooked nose and pale cheeks. Joaquim sighed, then repressed a shudder. He'd look just like her someday.

"I'm here, Mamacita," he whispered as he sat beside her.

Joaquim gazed out the tinted windows again at Mars, past the compressor towers that extracted water from the carbon dioxide atmosphere above Mangala Vallis, past the confines of the crater base. Two solar-powered dirigibles outlined in red and blue lights were returning from a trade mission to the canal colonies near Olympus Mons. The slug-like ships resembled pupilless eyes set in stars and rimmed with foxfire. Night had become a funerary mask.

They're probably low on energy, he mused. But wasn't everyone? He'd been up with Celina since early evening, and he'd worked through the previous day cycle at the labs, testing a new ice sample. He was bone-ass weary. Plain and simple. And Celina? Her vital signs showed nothing acute, yet something seemed to have given way inside her, a core had collapsed, and weariness radiated through her greyed skin. Despite her adventurous self-image as a Martian *posseiro*, a handy pioneer scratching out homesteads in a vastly different kind of Amazonia, she had finally run out of juice. Suddenly, in a vivid stab of sound and light within his head, he was gripped by a memory from one of the first colonists, a memory of that colonist's frozen death down in the Big Feather channel of Mangala Vallis. The woman's battery pack had run down, the suit had stiffened, and time itself had seemed to alter, slowing down until it became fixed in stone, like the great channels carved by ancient flash-floods along the red plain. He nodded his head. The import of this memory of the woman's death was not lost on him. Celina was near the end.

Joaquim leaned over to check the green needle on the battery yoke for her LVAD heart assistant. It showed a full charge, no doubt it was functioning perfectly within her left ventricle. He leaned back in his metal chair, an uncomfortable thing that he'd grown so accustomed to during his long hours here that he'd forgotten about it and imagined himself sitting on air. He noticed the time on the LED display above the door. His night crew at Geolab would be getting off shift in a few minutes. He glanced at his briefcase near the door. It contained a ton of work he'd ignored while sitting with Celina. At Geolab, Joaquim studied plugs that had been drilled from the Martian North Pole before it had been melted with an orbiting mirror . . . a strategy that terraformers hoped would chain-react into a greenhouse effect. His specialty was extinction theory, so he tested the plugs for striations of cosmic dust, signs of the cometary swarms that pelted the solar system every twenty-six million years—a possible factor in the mass extinctions of Earth species. His father, Paulo, had been a groundbreaker in this field, and Joaquim preserved his storehouse of insight and knowledge.

As he shifted in his seat, his joints popped.

He wondered why he felt so old.

He was barely twenty-one, yet he encompassed the feelings of a centenarian . . . so he knew the answer even as he thought the question. He'd inherited the mnemoniphage gene that allowed him to assimilate, to gestaltically experience the dead. The lives of many Cristobels survived within him, and they in turn—as mnemoniphages—held many others. These ancestors spoke to him, whispering secrets that might otherwise have died with them. They sifted through his brain like windblown sand filling the cracks in the Mangala basin. His father Paulo especially, since Joaquim continued with Paulo's studies. Who wouldn't feel old?

And what secrets, he wondered, would be lost when Celina was gone, what insight about their origins and extinctions, or their home on the red planet?

She seemed too fragile a package to hold much . . . yet even without her own root system of ancestors, she was a universe waiting to be explored. Joaquim remembered what she had said once to Paulo, before he had died in a storm accident and had been assimilated in a truly painful mnemoniphaging for Joaquim. It was a confused memory, combining his own viewpoint with the viewpoint of his father, yet the truth of it still touched him as it had touched them both then for a bare moment.

"It's such an *easy* thing for you to die," she had said. "Because you will live on."

Joaquim rubbed his eyes. A numb line ran straight through his head, above his right eye and the bridge of his nose, and his exhaustion urged it to diffuse and spread throughout his upper torso. He felt that if he were suddenly turned inside out, they'd find his blood and organs and bones reduced to a thick goo. He should have been alert for his mother, reliving their good times, yet instead he allowed a bland garble of thoughts to branch through his head—musings on beds and hospitals, on his work, on people past. He knew her time was short, yet he found no strong emotion within him to counter the dull reality, no cause to rant at the universe. Too much bad blood had existed between them in recent years, much of it centered on his decision to continue in his father's footsteps. Besides his passion for science, Paulo Cristobel had been fanatically dedicated to his role as a public mnemoniphage; and, despite a personal aversion, Joaquim had succumbed to political pressure and agreed to provide the same service for Rio Base, acting as a human library. His mother would not accept this. She grew callous toward Joaquim, hardened by her bitterness over the last, lonely years with Paulo. Joaquim was wounded. He allowed the bitterness to work on him also. It became increasingly difficult to separate the tender moments with a younger Celina from the troubled, embittered moments of the present.

"Jake?" She opened her eyes and leaned her head toward his side of the bed. "Do you have it with you?"

"Yes, Mamacita. Safe in my pocket."

He peeled the velcros on his right shoulder sleeve and removed a small corduroy case whose green nap had been worn smooth with decades of use. Celina's eyes widened for a moment, and then she succumbed to a fit of coughing and lay back on the bed, staring at the ceiling with a glazed look. He gripped her ankle, as if to hold her from drifting away.

"Good," she said with a cough. "I want you to remember me with all the others."

There was a taunting, vicious undertone in her voice that gave her words a chilling ring. Joaquim realized that this was her final weapon against him, a blade of irony to be twisted in his gut. He'd have to absorb her life into his, literally swallowing the totality of her bitterness. Then he would see *himself* through *her* eyes. He'd experience all the times she thought he'd wronged her, from *her* point of view, and suffer all the accompanying pangs of guilt that he'd experienced when he mnemoniphaged his father. Acids roiled in his stomach like thunderheads, spitting lightning. He imagined the shock to his system, the dizzying double-image shift in his awareness.

He almost told her then that he couldn't do it.

Celina groaned and closed her eyes. He looked away, focusing on the case in his hand. He undid the antique zipper and unfolded the two halves in his palm. How he hated and feared the devices within. Just as Celina did, but for different reasons.

"Tell me about them," she pleaded. "They were your father's most prized possessions. The bastard."

Joaquim looked up sharply. She had surprised him; something he had not thought her capable of anymore, for he considered these last hours to be inexorable—choreographed and rehearsed by the wealth of similar memories in his mental library of death scenes. She hadn't opened her eyes, yet she'd known what he had done. Did she hear the minute whisper of the brass teeth as he unzipped it? Had she undergone a heightening of perception as she approached oblivion? As Joaquim's father had. Paulo Cristobel had felt like that when he lay broken in the sandstorm, his essence draining away into the red sands. He'd sensed some underlying rhythm, some pulse-like drumming in the storm's heart throbbing around him. The ebb and flow of entropy had coursed through him.

Celina interrupted his speculations.

"Please, Jake. Like you've described them before."

"Sorry. It kind of gripped me there for a second. The sight of it, I mean."

"Ah, yes," she said. "It always did your father. Just a glimpse of his tools sent him back into his other selves. To *his* father, and his father's father. A backward vision. It was like a drug to him.''

Celina placed both hands on the cowling over her chest and began to stroke the twisted arthritic fingers of one hand with those of the other, as if folding down the curled edges of hard copy as it fed off a computer printer. Up until this final hospitalization, she'd retained a position, at least part-time, as an information processor for the colony's weather watch.

"The kit contains five things," Joaquim began. "Two ampules of neurotrans stimulator. There's a pocket for a third, but I took that a half hour ago at your request. There's a circular mirror, modeled after an outmoded surgeon's headpiece. To illuminate the work.''

He sensed Celina's impatience, and he found a perverse pleasure in dragging the description out.

"There's a battered gold tube used to suck up the necessary cells . . .''

"Jake?''

"Yes, Mama. I know. Father treasured this.''

"How silly of me. Of *course* you know. You really *know*. But do you remember *yourself* how he'd wear it in his lapel? When the women would say 'There goes Paulo,' he'd puff out his chest and swagger. He looked so handsome.'' Suddenly her voice faded. She grew still. "Now the drill.''

"It's hand-cranked, with a diamond tip. The tiny steel works are well oiled. And the handle.'' Joaquim realized that this was the part of the description she had waited for, the part of the litany about the handle.

"On the handle," he continued, "is a smooth round ball of hard brazilwood, from great-grandfather's home in the Amazon. It is well worn, oiled by the skin of many hands. The wood's stained pink from . . .'' he hesitated. "The blood. Grandfather's is part of that, as is father's.''

She sighed, and it sounded like a small animal escaping in a flurry of feathers, like the whir of the hummingbirds and macaws kept in the colony's vast aviary. Joaquim held up the drill for his own inspection.

"It's a cranial drill, for making the incisions.''

Celina said nothing. She no longer seemed to breathe.

Joaquim held the mirror from the kit above her slack lips. No vapor exited. He sat unmoving within the exterior silence all around him. A bubble of grief floated within his throat, and through his head rose the unbidden memories of a hundred other deaths.

Later, after the night nurse had attested to Celina's brain death, he placed his mouth upon his mother's mouth and drew her last air. As he held it, knowing he must hold it until his lungs throbbed and burned, he realized how fitting it was that she had departed during the description of the mnemoniphage tools, the simple instruments that would assure her of an immortality of sorts. Yet he cursed himself for yet another wave of indecision about continuing the ritual. Was he too bitter towards Celina, and too fearful of her memories, to really go through with mnemoniphaging her? Perhaps this doubt was also choreographed, but he'd expected better of himself. He shrugged in resignation, exhaled in a gasp, and continued with the ritual.

"Celina Cristobel. By the code of the mnemoniphage I must request permission of your surviving heirs to perform this rite." He accepted her silent approval and added his own. "I give permission."

Joaquim gritted his teeth and started the drill-bit turning. He was stubborn, a condition Celina had called "a vein of silver shot through the soul," yet despite this, and the patina of cool he tried to maintain about everything he said or did, the guilt was beginning to eat at him. A few tears forked like the traceries of a bayou along his cheeks.

He drilled into Celina's skull and penetrated the brain. His throat constricted as blood welled onto his fingertips and the drill's wooden knob.

"Here is the exit of life." Each word escaped as slow as a gas bubble rising through lava. "The portal. The path. The gateway of pain."

Instead of putting the gold tube between his lips, though, and sucking out brain tissue as the ritual demanded, he pushed the tube into the incision in her skull, forcing tissue into the tubing. He replaced it in his kit, along with the drill.

"Now we are mingled," he said, though it was a lie.

At the Geolab transportation garage, on the outer ring, he filled out triplicate forms for a rover, punching in the answers on the comptroller's screen. He wedged himself carefully into a "skinnie," a pressure suit with a flexible armor which tightly adhered over his lab coat. As he was adjusting the neck seal the comptroller returned with a hard copy for his signature.

"Dr. Cristobel, the purpose of your mission is listed as . . ."

"Mnemoniphaging!" His voice blared out in anger, startling him as well as the young woman. He could not cope with bureaucracy at a time like this. "Is there anything wrong with that?"

"Yes, well, geosurveys are the only authorized uses for these vehicles. You should sign out a general excursion rover from the base government." Her black eyes narrowed in challenge. She knew that he knew that the touring visitors had those rovers booked to the limit.

He cooled. Now he sensed that there was a grudge involved here somewhere. "Miss, this is essential to my present work as well as my future state of . . ."

"I understand," she said, waving the papers at him. "But regs are regs."

"I have authority." He began to heat up again. "I'm under contract by the colonial administration."

"Oh, I know that. You told my mother that earlier today when you refused to help her." The woman's voice hissed with repressed vehemence. "You must remember that? The young boy?"

Joaquim tensed. He now knew the extent of the game she played against him. "For that, I'm sorry."

"But regs are regs, right?" She smiled triumphantly.

He nodded, knowing that she'd boxed him in.

"Look," he said. "Why don't you call this requisition whatever you like. Then later you can have a try for my neck over it. But I *am* taking the vehicle."

He watched surprise wash over her face, then a doubtful look as she squinted at him, and he felt as if he'd missed something important. He knew then that he had to get moving. Until he could get away by himself, and resolve this crisis over Celina, his actions would become more and more erratic, more out of control. She was still watching him. When he snapped his helmet in place, she flipped up the visor to speak to him.

"Have it back by 0900."

He nodded, resealed the visor and wiggled in behind the wheel of the rover. He eased the cab bubble down and punched in the vacuum seal. As the woman raised the inner door to the exit lock and he drove in, he saw relief on her face. It mirrored the mix of emotions within him. He just wanted to get *away*. He had a vague plan for burying the small bit of Celina he carried with him. He'd drive out to her favorite climbing spot near Rio Base and release it to the changing chemistry of the sands.

Joaquim steered the rover out of the lock and up the crater rim that surrounded Rio Base. As he mounted the plain above Rio and the main channel at Mangala, he passed two cumbersome ore caterpillars moving down into it toward the feather channels that branched away on the opposite side. The plain, which ended at the scarp of Mangala, was strewn with boulders and mini-craters, and winds whipped dust about his already-pitted windshield at speeds of thirty to forty knots, a calm morning in comparison to the three-hundred-knot intensity of the afternoon before. The sun turned the horizon into a raw wound behind the silhouettes of volcanoes slumbering in the distance. Joaquim polarized the windshield, and it was as if the whole planet had been developed in a photochemical bath: the pock-marked plains, the blast craters, the deltas etched in bedrock, the shifting dune crescents. The world bled red on red.

At a steep cliff near the convergence of Big Feather and the main channel, Joaquim eased the six-wheeler along the cliff edge until he reached Skaros. This curious wind-carved promontory had been a favorite climbing spot for Celina, who had once been the best free-solo rockclimber on Mars. It offered a superb overlook that rivaled the Grand Canyon or Olduvai Gorge on Earth. Back away from the channel, he could make out the details of Rio Base, enhanced by its growth of morning shadows. The base looked like a series of puzzle rings, linked and buried in sand to shield them from solar and cosmic radiation. At the center, the hub poked up like a teed golf ball, with the hospital along its equatorial girth.

She died there, he thought.

Joaquim checked the atmosphere in the cab, unclipped his left glove. He separated the seam on the shoulder of his suit and fished inside his lab coat, then inside the tool kit for the tube containing her brain tissue. His hand shook as he held the tube. If he let Celina go unpreserved, then his children and his children's children would lose a link in their family tree. And a key perspective on Martian life. He closed his eyes and drew a soft blob of her brain tissue into his throat, working to produce more saliva, swallowing. He couldn't deny her, as he had the woman with the boy. He closed his eyes and steeled himself against her onslaught.

Later, with the outside temperature spurting to minus 10, he adjusted his suit environment, climbed out of the rover, and began to free-solo up the face of Skaros. The neurotrans drug, now that it was combined with Celina's cortical cells, torched his nervous system. Memories began to pop in his head like flash bulbs. He climbed faster, clawing his way up a vertical crack until he reached a lip of rust basalt about three hundred meters from the base of Skaros. He sat with his back pressed against the sheer rock. There, at last, he opened his mind wide to a flood of images that boosted the noise level in his head, adding themselves to the countless information bits already stored there. His scalp prickled. His ears seemed to radiate heat. The top of his skull went numb.

Voices spoke a slush of random phrases that buzzed in an imaginary line between his ears. Many Joaquim recognized as people he had preserved during his work at Rio Base, while others were kin, like his father, whose experiences were colored with images of ancestral homes, Brazil, its people. The ebb and flow took Joaquim along a branching and rebranching series of lives until the drug no longer controlled the flow.

Celina's voice burst open within him, releasing the time-delay pills of her memories. For awhile, they dominated everything with a fresh perspective. Then the two sets fused and the noise rose in crescendo. He imagined it as a vast orchestra of strange instruments that imitated the human vocal apparatus, which then mingled with counterpointal songs. He twitched inside his suit, a seizure of almost epileptic intensity, yet his body responded with the trained instincts of a climber and he held on. A slow orgasm of sound melted through his head, topped by a familiar call. *"It's such an easy thing to die."*

Joaquim no longer heard a bitter quality in Celina's voice. The assimilation had ended. He was no longer distanced from her by his own fears and guilts and problems. He accepted her.

When he stretched, finally dampening the voices into a background murmur, the sun freed itself of the mountain tops and the thin atmospheric haze to illuminate Mars in full. It painted Mangala Vallis in a seemingly-endless pastel of ochres, purples, and reds. Joaquim's mind seemed as clear as his view. The moment matched none among all those he stored, yet it held an implication with meaning for them all—a look at the role of his kind over the coming centuries.

One day, he realized, humanity would be born with its heritage in place, with its past melded into the present in a unity as subtle as these dawn colors. *Everyone* would be a mnemoniphage. Everyone would see back to the very first of their kind, like his father, like himself. They would all possess this strange kind of immortality. Until the cycles of extinction rolled against *them* as well, and they *all* passed the way of the crinoids and the coccoliths and the dinosaurs. Until then, he reasoned, there was plenty of work to do.

Joaquim picked up a thumb-sized chunk of basalt and flipped it out from the rock cliff, watching it fall until it shrank to nothing against the mottled background of the channel below. He felt strength return, overcoming his weariness. Celina was a part of this world now, part of its legacy, and, despite the pain her memories would bring, part of him, too. Joaquim had never considered himself truly alone, and he felt even less so now. He picked up another wedge of rock and tossed it.

The voices within him spoke. *There's one for you, Celina.*

Later, someone stopped a rover near Skaros and radioed to Joaquim about a dustgale due that morning. For a moment he was mesmerized by the woman's tiny face behind the red-tinted bubble of the cab. Would he preserve *her* someday? Who else would be bound with him and Celina in the web of the future?

The woman asked if he was well, and Joaquim assured her that he was fine. He said he'd keep in touch with the base weather watch and be in before the storm. She started up and rolled over the rough terrain toward where Rio spread in the distance, a hive mound surrounded by caterpillars and insectoid dirigibles.

Joaquim turned and set himself for the slow hand and foot descent down the rock wall to his rover. His muscles flexed within his suit. Further within, the rhythm of his people seemed to pulse in his veins. A musical tempest moving with an unknown yet irrevocable purpose.

Joaquim moved with it.

THE GREAT MARTIAN RAILROAD RACE

Eric Vinicoff

"The Great Martian Railroad Race" was purchased by Gardner Dozois and appeared in the August, 1988, issue of IAsfm, with an evocative cover by Gary Freeman and a striking interior illustration by Bob Walters. This is Vinicoff's only sale to IAsfm to date, but it was a memorable one; in it, Vinicoff spins the clever and suspenseful story of entrepreneur Timothy Lo, who thinks that he knows just what the developing Terran colonies of the Red Planet need—a railroad! Now all he has to do is to convince everyone else . . .

Eric Vinicoff began writing in 1975, and has since sold over forty stories to science fiction magazines and anthologies. He is a particularly frequent contributor to IAsfm's sister magazine, Analog.

"What this planet needs, Candice, is a railroad."

Timothy Lo made the comment as he walked through the deboarding tube toward the terminal. He made it to his personal assistant, a cryogenic Danish beauty. They were alone in the tube, since the shuttle captain had escorted them to the airlock ahead of the less important passengers.

"You've certainly found the right setting for your venture," she said. "You won't need your rose-colored glasses."

His glasses were thick and clear. But the afternoon sky outside the tube was a gently luminescent pink. A small bright sun sent rays skittering across the rippling ice fields, glazing the metal of the port facilities.

They were still adjusting to the surreal experience of walking in the .38 *g* when they reached the terminal. "Look sharp," he told her. "The curtain is going up."

A reception committee was waiting in the almost-empty concourse. Masa Kobiashi, the CEO of the North Polar Consortium, stood in front of a row of vice-presidents. "Six VPs," Timothy Lo whispered. "They aren't sure they want in, but they are taking me seriously."

The Consortium contingent bowed in unison; he bowed back. Candice had slipped into her role of minor functionary and nonperson.

"Welcome to Mars, Mister Lo," Masa Kobiashi said. "I trust your trip was enjoyable?"

"Very much so, thank you."

"I've arranged suitable quarters for you at the Residence. You've been cleared through United Nations Customs, and your bags will be forwarded. Shall we go?"

"By all means."

Three limos were parked in front of the terminal, their open doors suckled by entry tubes. A spacecap in a snug JSL red-and-white marssuit was tending the tubes. Without the suit he would have been rather uncomfortable. The air pressure was less than one percent of Earth sea level, with very little oxygen, and the temperature was a balmy −115 degrees.

But the entry tubes were an extension of the friendly environment senior execs preferred, and so were the stretched Toyota Ultimas with their fat traction tires. Timothy Lo settled into a conforming seat in the first limo, beside Candice and facing Masa Kobiashi.

"We can take the long way around," the CEO said, "if you care to see more of the Consortium."

Timothy Lo smiled. The most important businessman in the solar system didn't offer to play tour guide idly. "I do indeed."

Masa Kobiashi touched a button. "Take us out Radial Two," he told the autocon, "then left on Circum Seven to the Consortium Administration Center. Residence, level six."

As the limo pulled away from the curb, the flagship leading the fleet, Timothy Lo took a comprehensive look at the port.

At first glance, it resembled the contents of a toy chest scattered across the ice. Then the pattern and scale emerged. A ring of buildings, shipyards, and storage tanks enclosed dozens of cradles. Highways and pipelines ran into the tundra, linking the port to the company complexes. The spaceships were shiny silver globes, ranging from the passenger shuttle that loomed over the JSL terminal to the really big cargo drones. He was impressed. Wealth was his religion, and he liked his temples grandiose.

Masa Kobiashi noticed his interest. "North Polar Port handles more tonnage than any other facility on Earth or Mars. Raw materials from the belt and Jupiter's moons, manufactured goods to Earth, petrochemicals and organics from Earth, and supplies to the miners."

"With the Consortium making a tidy profit on each leg," Timothy Lo observed. "Likewise EIP at the South Pole. I'm curious how Mars managed to become the hub of space industry?"

"Well, for one thing, it's closer to the mining activities than Earth is—close being a relative term involving escape velocities as well as distances. But the main reason is all around us. Look over there."

The highway cut laser-straight through the uneven terrain; they were sharing it with a lot of vehicles, mostly trucks. Off to the right a metal globe at least fifteen meters in diameter was rolling across the ice. It reminded Timothy Lo of a snowball, because it left a path of bare rock behind it. There was a Komatsu logo on its side.

"A water collector," Masa Kobiashi explained. "A robot drone, of course—there are hundreds of them working the cap. Water to drink, water for industrial use, oxygen to breathe, and hydrogen and oxygen for rocket fuel. More than we'll ever need. That is why we're here.''

Masa Kobiashi suggested drinks, and they gave their orders to the bar. When they had glasses in their hands the CEO said, ''You've come a long way on an interesting errand, Mister Lo. But maybe an impossible one.''

''It's eminently possible. You think so, too, or one of your VPs would be making meaningless noises to me now.''

Masa Kobiashi frowned momentarily at the crudeness. ''Your reputation precedes you. You've been successful in the investment business due to good judgment and, ah, creative techniques. Your current net worth is in excess of two hundred million dollars. But you've never operated a railroad.''

''My compliments to your espionage network. Speaking of which, isn't it safe for you to conduct business in your office?''

Masa Kobiashi decided to be amused rather than insulted. ''You may be right—one never knows for sure. Let's return to the topic of railroading, shall we?''

''Let's. I've never operated a railroad, but I've hired some people who have.''

The limo curved left onto another highway, skirting an arched entrance that read: FUJI CHEMICALS CORPORATION. Beyond the archway a fantastic jungle of gleaming towers, tanks, pipes, and other shapes seemed to grow out of the ice.

''I think you've underestimated the engineering challenges involved in building your railroad,'' Masa Kobiashi said.

''How so?''

''The straight-line distance from pole to pole is 10,700 kilometers. Your route will have to be even longer, to avoid volcanoes, canyons, craters, and dust lakes. You'll have to lay track on permafrost. Then there are the sand and dust storms, with winds up to two hundred KPH. Martian dust is very fine. It gets into everything, and has an unfortunate effect on moving parts.''

''Engineering problems can always be solved. That's what engineers are for.''

They passed another entrance: NISSAN CORPORATION. Long, low buildings surrounded a terraced pyramid. ''The car parts factory is fully automated,'' Masa Kobiashi explained. ''The central structure is an arcology for the administrative and maintenance personnel. What makes you think we need a pole-to-pole railroad?''

''The North Polar Consortium consists of forty-six Japanese firms in a wide range of industries. The European Industrial Park isn't much smaller. You could be doing a lot of mutually beneficial business, if it weren't for the high cost of shipping by cargo drone.''

''We did our own study of the potential trade. While substantial, it wouldn't justify the massive capital outlay needed to build such a railroad. How do you intend to make a profit, if I may ask?''

Timothy Lo smiled. ''I've seen your study. All I can say is maybe you looked at the venture too narrowly.''

''My compliments to *your* espionage network. So you hope to sell the Consortium a share of this railroad?''

''No.''

''No?''

''It's going to be my railroad,'' Timothy Lo said firmly. ''I've arranged financing with a group of banks, but they need loan guarantees way beyond my own holdings. I want the Consortium to be my cosignatory, in exchange for very favorable terms in our shipping contracts.''

''The benefit you offer hardly matches the risk we would be taking. I don't see how I can recommend it to our members.''

Timothy Lo didn't respond for several seconds, then spoke in a level voice. ''If I go bust, you get the railroad.''

The Nippon Atomics entrance had a gate and a tall security fence. In the distance nine ominous white hemispheres rose above the complex, venting pale stream.

Masa Kobiashi was looking at him intently. The CEO thought that he was a fool, destined to fail. But was he a capable enough fool to build the railroad first? If so, the Consortium would acquire it at a bargain price.

''I think something can be arranged,'' Masa Kobiashi said at last. ''When you're settled and rested, would you be willing to explain your venture in detail at a meeting with my department heads?''

''My pleasure.''

''There is something you should know. You aren't the only person to approach us about a pole-to-pole railroad. Shortly after I received your prospectus, I was contacted by an Irish businessman named Michael Killeen.''

Timothy Lo's face went blank. "I've never heard of him.''

"His proposal was remarkably similar to yours.''

"Thanks for telling me—seems I have some housecleaning to do. May I ask why you aren't talking to him instead of me?''

"He has ties to EIP,'' Masa Kobiashi replied. "He's there now, probably trying to negotiate a financial package.''

"I see. If there's going to be a railroad, you don't want to be at the short end of it. Well, rest assured, there will be a railroad. Mine.''

The UNSA didn't rate space in the United Nations compound; it had been exiled to three floors of an unassuming downtown office block. Timothy Lo sat in Director Obomi's anteroom while that official showed proper contempt for businessmen by making him wait. Beside him Candice was synopsizing reports in her hand computer.

"Mister Lo, the director will see you now.'' The secretary gestured to the inner door.

The office of Idi Obomi, Director of the United Nations Space Agency, wasn't very impressive even by bureaucratic standards. He rose from his desk wearing a colorful Mali tribal robe and a phony smile. "Good afternoon, Mister Lo.'' They shook hands. "I'm sorry about the delay. Thanks to the budget cuts everyone here is doing the work of three.''

"That's quite all right. I appreciate you taking the time to see me.''

They sat. "Your notion is very imaginative,'' the director began. "But I doubt this agency can authorize the territorial grant you're seeking.''

"Why not? Legally it's no different from the grants you made to the Consortium and EIP.''

"The United Nations holds the solar system in trust for the benefit of the human race, and the UNSA acts as trustee. The polar grants were made to open Mars for exploration and exploitation.''

"That's exactly why you need my railroad. Right now there are two polar enclaves, your Lowell Research Station, and a lot of empty planet. I'm sure you can see the potential in having rail access to 11,000 kilometers of Mars.''

"If you were just asking for the right-of-way along your

route, that could be arranged. But why do you need alternating five kilometer squares beside the right-of-way?''

"To make the venture financially viable. Some of it will be used for stations and other railroad facilities, the rest will go on the market.''

"You expect the United Nations to give you 55,000 square kilometers of land so you can turn around and sell it?''

"Right now nobody wants the land. Except at the poles nothing on Mars is worth the cost of getting to it. When property values go up due to my railroad, why shouldn't I reap some of the benefit? Remember, the *other* 55,000 square kilometers along the line will belong to you. You'll come out way ahead.''

Director Obomi developed a facial tic at the thought of more revenues for the UNSA to spend, but he was still reluctant. "Your proposed grant is bigger than both polar grants combined. It would be very hard to justify to the Secretary General, particularly after the media got hold of it.''

Timothy Lo shook his head. "I share your vision of humanity's destiny in space. It saddens me to see that vision treated so shabbily.''

"What do you mean?''

"You do wonders with limited resources, but you could do a lot more if you received proper support in the General Assembly. Small minds can't see how important your work is. Well, my railroad is going to open up a new frontier. Frontiers mean people. People pay taxes, vote, and need public services. You'll have to have a bigger budget, more staff, and,'' Timothy Lo's eyes flicked around the austere surroundings, "a suitable headquarters to handle your increased responsibilities.''

When Timothy Lo left a few minutes later, a sincerely smiling Director Obomi walked him to the door. "I'll call you when I have a better idea where we stand.''

"Thanks. It has been a pleasure.''

There followed several weeks of planning, organizing, and very discreet bribery. Finally the call came.

"Good news, I hope?'' Timothy Lo asked.

"Yes and no,'' Director Obomi said. "The United Nations Space Agency is prepared to authorize your grant, in exchange for transportation service to Lowell and any other facilities we establish.''

"What's the bad news?''

"We've received a similar application from the Ulster-Mars Railroad Company Ltd."

"Owned and operated by one Michael Killeen?" Timothy Lo asked through gritted teeth.

"I believe so. We're required to treat both applications equally, so we've borrowed a precedent from history. A railroad race."

"A what?"

"Curiously, you both proposed the same route," Director Obomi answered. "The equipment will be standardized. You'll start from the North Polar Consortium, and Ulster-Mars will start from the European Industrial Park. You'll build your rail lines until you meet. The more kilometers you cover, the more grant territory you get."

Timothy Lo didn't say anything for several seconds. "Who suggested this piece of fiscal insanity?" he asked at last. "Mister Killeen? I don't even know the gentleman, but I'm beginning to dislike him intensely."

"I'm sorry you're taking such a negative attitude," Director Obomi said stiffly. "Please come to my office Thursday morning at ten for a full briefing."

The Adachi Company complex was a cluster of reinforced glassite domes of a size possible thanks to the low Martian gravity. Hida Adachi's office occupied the top floor of the central dome, with a 360 degree view of the floodlit complex. The night was crowded with stars, and Phobos was rising in the west. Timothy Lo enjoyed the view while Hida Adachi settled behind his desk/monitor station. The office was a reflection of the Adachi Company; big, successful, and very high-tech.

"Welcome, Mister Lo," Hida Adachi said. "I'm honored to meet you. And fascinated, I might add. Your railroad is the most exciting project here since the founding of the Consortium."

"Thanks. It's a unique opportunity."

They chatted pleasantly for a few minutes, then Hida Adachi asked, "Is there some way the Adachi Company can help in your great project?"

"As a matter of fact there is." Timothy Lo slid a memory disk across the brushed steel desktop to Hida Adachi. "The details of what I need are in there. Shall I give you the general outline?''

"Please."

"The Consortium doesn't think a railroad can be cost effective, but its calculations are based on building a lot of automated construction equipment. There's another way to go. Human labor. Thanks to the UNSA I have to lay track as fast as I can, so I'm hiring a five thousand man work gang.''

Hida Adachi was used to big numbers, but not of that sort. "How can you possibly afford such a large work force?" he blurted out, his curiosity overcoming politeness. "Employees are even more expensive than machines.''

"Not necessarily," Timothy Lo replied. "I've arranged to import five thousand Chinese peasants and their families. The Chinese government was glad to cut a deal—the birth control program hasn't been going well. They will be shipped here in cold sleep.''

"But . . . why would they be willing to leave their home to come to this inhospitable place?''

"For land. They're farmers whose farms were taken over for government collectives. I'll be paying them in acreage instead of money.''

Hida Adachi laughed. "Forgive me, but the notion of peasant farmers on Mars is hard to take seriously.''

"It shouldn't be. You put a dome like this one over some land. Fill it with air—oxygen from water, nitrogen and carbon dioxide out of the atmosphere. Run a line from a community reactor for heat and electricity. Melt ice for water or pump it out of the ground. Grind rock, and add some organics to make dirt. Stock it with plants and animals adapted to Martian conditions. You have a farm.''

Hida Adachi thought it over. "The technical problems are more involved than you imagine, but not insurmountable. I'm sure we can build your farms for you. By mass producing them we should be able to make the price per unit very reasonable. But will you be able to afford five thousand?''

"You misunderstand me," Timothy Lo said. "I'm not in agribiz. You'll be selling them directly to the farmers, and running the power/water/air distribution business.''

"That is absurd! They won't have any assets. How will they pay?''

"On credit, to be repaid with interest from the proceeds of crop sales. Food for the thirty-thousand-plus Consortium personnel around the solar system, who must be getting pretty tired of flavored algae." Timothy Lo shuddered. "And industrial organics that the Consortium now has to import from Earth or do without."

"What recourse would we have if a farmer defaults on his loan?"

"The tenacity of the Chinese peasant farmer is legendary. The whole family will work like slaves to keep their land. In the rare default, you can dispossess them and sell the farm to someone else."

"That is rather inhumane policy," Hida Adachi commented.

"I'm a railroad builder, not a philanthropist. When you review the complete package, you'll find that the projected long-term profits are very impressive."

Hida Adachi didn't seem impressed. "Even if we were interested in such a speculative market, we would require substantial down payments."

"I'm sorry to hear that," Timothy Lo said. "I guess I'll have to do business with EIP."

"I beg your pardon?" Hida Adachi leaned forward in his chair.

"Black Michael Killeen stole this idea from me along with the others. He's hiring five thousand Irishmen, Northern Protestants who aren't happy with the reunification. Verlagsgruppe will be building their farms, and more customers would mean more profits. I suppose that explains why Herr Zisser wants to meet with me."

Hida Adachi frowned thoughtfully, then put on a smile. "It would be unfortunate for our new neighbors to have to depend on goods and services from so far away. Let me study your proposal. Would it be possible to see you again in a few days, before you contact Herr Zisser?"

"Certainly."

Timothy Lo peered through the cockpit bubble at the activity stretching across the rock-strewn plain. Four hours ago the ATV had left the advance camp. At first the only human presence had been survey and geology crews, but gradually the terrain had become busier.

"ETA three minutes, sir," the autocon reported cheerfully.

The sausage-shaped ATV wove awkwardly through trucks and other vehicles on the access road that paralleled the roadbed. Work crews in color-coded marssuits swarmed everywhere. The access road was evolving from a raw path into the Pan Martian Highway. The roadbed was being cleared, excavated, poured with gravel-like ballast, and graded.

"It seems very well organized," Candice said.

"It had better be," Timothy Lo replied. "I don't like the reports I'm getting from down south. Black Michael's gang is laying over thirty-five kilometers of track a day."

His eyes kept wandering to the exotic scenery. In the distance the jagged rim of a broad crater dominated the plain. The pink sky was turning sunset-red, and a wind kicked up swirls of dust.

"Here we are, sir," the autocon reported.

Three portable domes had been inflated near the access road. The ATV parked in an informal lot beside the "construction shack." A sign over the shack's airlock read: NORTH MARTIAN RAILROAD COMPANY CAMP NO. 38.

Two people were emerging from the airlock. Timothy Lo and Candice put on their helmets, waited while the autocon evaced the cabin, then climbed down to the frozen ground.

"It is good to see you again, Mister Lo," the smaller of the two said on his com channel. They shook hands.

Long ago he had realized that, while menials were interchangeable, having the right people in key positions was essential. He had discovered Doctor Seuki Nakano languishing in the Consortium's engineering department, a victim of the traditional Japanese reluctance to promote women. Now she was his Chief Engineer, doing the work of two for a fraction of the salary of one, and grateful for the opportunity to prove herself.

"Likewise," he replied. "I want you to know I'm very happy with your work. Don't worry about this visit—Candice isn't carrying my black hood and ax in her purse. I'm just here to watch my railroad being built."

Doctor Nakano had no sense of humor, but she laughed dutifully. "You timed your arrival perfectly. There will be something well worth seeing in a few minutes. Would you care to join me on my inspection turn?"

"By all means."

They set out toward the roadbed, and Candice and Doctor Nakano's translator/bodyguard fell in behind them. Halfway there a piercing siren came from Timothy Lo's helmet speaker.

"Shift changes are sounded on all channels," Doctor Nakano explained. "We had better move aside to avoid being trampled."

Floodlights on tall poles woke in unison, pushing back the gathering darkness beyond the camp, access road, and roadbed. Work crews poured out of the residence domes and trotted by in ranks. Timothy Lo switched his com through a few work channels. The babble of orders and conversations was in a variety of local dialects, many unintelligible to him, plus a quickly developing pidgin.

Soon the relieved work crews jogged past heading for the domes. "How are the workers holding up?" he asked Doctor Nakano.

"Amazingly well. I thought we would have serious labor trouble over the twelve-hour shift schedule, but they seem to have accepted it."

"You would understand why if you knew more about the working hours of a peasant farmer. They want to finish the job as fast as they can, so they can get their families out of cold storage and start farming."

Doctor Nakano made sure they were on the private channel. "The UNSA observers have been complaining about the opium and prostitutes. They want us to stop providing them."

"The job will be done long before the UN can pass a law. Meanwhile we get a contented work gang."

They stopped at the edge of the construction area and watched. Two tanker trucks were crawling side-by-side on the roadbed, spraying a liquid into the ballast.

"The sealant creates rigidity with sufficient give to resist seismic shock," Doctor Nakano explained. "It also insulates the track base from the permafrost. The only good thing I can say about permafrost as a platform is that it is marginally superior to dust."

A knot of frantic activity was approaching along the roadbed from the north, becoming clearer as it got closer. Flatbed trucks carrying prefab track sections were pulling off to the side of the access road. As each one stopped, a work crew materialized and manhandled the section into position, a feat that would have required cranes on Earth. The foreman ran around and gestured wildly. Everything was happening in an eerie silence.

The sections reminded Timothy Lo of his model train sets. A base of beams and ties was anchored in the ballast, and the two elevated guideways sat on rows of supports. Each guideway was a rounded alloy strip two meters wide and a half meter thick.

"In six weeks Hitachi will be delivering the first cars," he said. "I can't wait to see one of my trains gliding along that ribbon at three hundred KPH."

"It will be a beautiful sight."

Workers began bolting the sections together. Engineers moved along the track, making electrical connections and using lasers to align the guideway sections.

The trucks and tools and hundreds of workers never slowed. They were a colony creature, constantly fed, excreting track. North Martian was busy along 1700 kilometers of the line, but this was the focus.

Timothy Lo watched raptly as his railroad raced south.

"I'm glad to see you're all enjoying yourselves," Timothy Lo said, his voice amplified by the podium. "The next time you drop by, the drinks and tickets won't be on me."

Consortium execs, UN officials, celebrities, media reps, and potential customers jammed the new North Martian passenger terminal adjoining JSL's. The loud cocktail party babble subsided as they turned to listen.

"Don't worry—I'm saving my speech for the ceremony. But I do want to say a few words. Really just one word. Thanks. Thanks to everyone who helped build the North Martian Railroad."

His audience applauded. He smiled broadly and looked over their heads, through the tall windows. There had been some recent additions to the port; the North Martian headquarters buildings, the yard and the sidings to the port facilities.

"There's one more thing I want to say. ALL ABOOOARRRD!"

North Martian conductors in sharp black uniforms began ushering the passengers through the row of entry tubes.

Except for its flat nose the Deimos Express was a standard

maglev train, a descendant of the original Transrapid 06 design
that the Japanese had bought from the Germans. The cars were
gleaming aluminum and glassite. Below them, sideways-on,
U-shaped skirts wrapped around the edges of the guideway.

Candice had gracefully collected Director Obomi, Masa Kobiashi, and the rest of his special guests. "Director, ladies,
and gentlemen," he said, "we're going to have the best seats
on the train. This way, please."

His private car was at the front end of the train. Like all of
North Martian's passenger stock, it was a double-decker. The
observation deck was styled like an Orient Express parlour car.
Stewards showed his guests to their seats, while he settled into
his and put on a throat mike.

"Welcome aboard the historic inaugural run of the Deimos
Express," he said, and his voice rang throughout the train.
"True, we've been operating on the northern part of the line
for several months. But this will be the first train to travel from
pole to pole." Unless Ulster-Mars' Sidhe Express arrives here
first, he didn't add.

A feminine pseudovoice interrupted him. "The Deimos Express is now departing North Polar Port Station."

There was a barely perceptible moment of rising, then the
train pulled out of the station. It accelerated smoothly, silently,
and without vibration. The guideway banked for curves, off-
setting the centrifugal force.

"Unlike the usual maglev system," he continued, "we're
suspended above the track by magnetic attraction instead of
repulsion. The magnets on the lower U-skirt arms are pulled
up close to the ferromagnetic armature rails on the underside
of the track. More magnets in the bend of each U keep the
cars in lateral position. Traction and braking are by linear
motor, reacting with a long stator in the track. The power comes
from nuclear generators at the stations."

The train was rushing across an uneven ice field, gaining
speed. The Sony electronics complex appeared off to the right;
it swelled and shrank in seconds. The track passed over highways and other obstacles.

"Our freight trains are fully automated, and our passenger
trains carry only a service staff. Sensors in the cars and the
track keep the computers informed." He sighed theatrically.
"I always wanted to be a train engineer. Now I own a whole

railroad, but there aren't any engineers or engines anymore.''

The Consortium was quickly being left behind. The tundra blurred close to the train, and the tenuous atmosphere whined faintly as it was pushed aside.

''All of which is to say you're traveling on the finest railroad ever built. So relax and enjoy the ride.''

The stewards began serving drinks. Personal service was a throwback to an earlier era, but North Martian had access to a vast pool of inexpensive labor.

Timothy Lo looked at his watch and smiled. He knew what was coming; the reactions of his guests should be interesting.

What came was a northbound freight hauling meat and produce to the Consortium. It hurtled toward them at a relative six hundred KPH. Only at the last split-second did it seem to move aside, a flash of silver less than three meters beyond the double panes.

The reactions were interesting.

''There's really no cause for alarm,'' he reassured them as the stewards cleaned up a few spills. ''You traveled quite a bit faster on your flights from Earth, and these trains can't jump the track.''

The passengers divided their time between socializing, admiring the scenery and enjoying the civilized comforts of the Deimos Express. The dining/club cars did a brisk trade all evening. Eventually the passengers retired to their sleeper compartments.

Sunrise found the train gliding through a dune field which reminded Timothy Lo of Death Valley. Sand had been piled in wave patterns inside cracked obsidian craters. Then came low, raw hills. A reddish-brown plain. Volcanoes, some of them active. A trestle over a canyon cut by ancient water. The face of Mars was an unending entertainment.

The train slowed going through the towns, so the passengers could get a good look. They were all pretty much the same. A North Martian station, a UNSA Civic Center, an Adachi Company plant and a mall were surrounded by dozens of farm domes. Beyond them was a ring of new construction. Trucks, bicycles, and brightly marssuited pedestrians shared the streets.

''Most of the farmers are doing well,'' Timothy Lo told the media reps. ''Immigrants are arriving in increasing numbers. Consortium members are already selling to this growing market, and Earth's consumer industries are establishing a beach-head. Banks are opening with capital to invest. I foresee a grand future for this new frontier.''

He spent most of the trip tending to business. He consoled Director Obomi over the myriad problems caused by the UNSA's rapid expansion. Masa Kobiashi raised the subject of certain mineral deposits which could be profitably mined if North Martian would extend branch lines to them. A hotel operator was interested in building tourist meccas at Olympus Mons and the Equatorial Rift. All sorts of people were scenting a boom and wanted in. He encouraged them.

Shortly after three P.M. the Deimos Express arrived at Promontory.

"Promontory," Timothy Lo announced proudly, "is where the North Martian and Ulster-Mars lines meet. It's six hundred and forty-four kilometers *south* of the equator. It's also the only town without a Chinese or Irish name."

The train eased past the big North Martian station with its yard and maintenance sheds, and stopped at the center of town. A portable dome sat beside the tracks. Beyond it another train was parked on the northbound track, similar in design but wearing the Ulster-Mars logo.

It took awhile for the passengers to deboard through the front entry tube, but soon they were mingling under the dome with those from the Sidhe Express. When everyone was seated the ceremony began.

Timothy Lo sat on one side of the podium platform with North Martian's officers; opposite them were Michael Killeen and his key people—all of them Killeens. Ulster-Mars had the biggest family payroll on the planet.

Director Obomi made a reasonably brief welcoming speech, then drew his audience's attention to where the two lines came together. They had been linked and tested for weeks, but no train had yet crossed the intangible barrier. A North Martian and an Ulster-Mars worker stood on the track base. At Director Obomi's command one placed a superfluous gold-plated spike and the other sledgehammered it home.

When the applause died down there were more speeches. Then everyone drifted toward the bar and buffet, the chairs were removed, musicians took the platform, and the first annual Golden Spike Gala got underway.

As soon as he could slip away without being noticed, Timothy Lo went back to his private car. He sagged bonelessly in an observation deck seat, smoking a rare festive cigar and watching a meteor streak across the evening sky.

"A nice little train you have here, Mister Lo."

He swiveled the seat, and saw Michael Killeen standing by the stairway.

For several moments they looked at each other without speaking. Then Timothy Lo said, "Make yourself at home, Mister Killeen. The booze is to your left."

Michael Killeen poured himself a drink, and brought it over to the seat across from Timothy Lo. "The Rail Society meetings have been duller for your absence."

"Alas, being seen together would be bad for our arch-enemies image. Speaking of which . . ."

"Put your mind at ease. No one saw me come, and no one will see me go. Not that I'm really convinced we needed this fake race."

Timothy Lo admired the glowing tip of his cigar. "You have a charming innocence, old friend. Misdirection is the key ingredient in any great con. If the railroad could have been sold on its merits, it already would have been. Whereas a fight over something tends to increase its perceived value."

"Innocence, my assets!" Michael Killeen grumbled. "At any rate some self-congratulations are in order. Even if they figure out what we're doing, they can't back out now. They have too many chips on the table."

"We're over the hump," Timothy Lo agreed. "Now we have to nurture the boom so it doesn't go bust. Mars has the resources to support a population of millions, and it's going to. We'll lay a lot of track, develop a lot of land, and build our empires."

He looked at the lights of the town. Tonight they were just a handful huddled together in the middle of the empty darkness. But every night would see a few more, spreading out a bit farther. "It's like I said all along. What this planet needed was a railroad."

ALL THE BEER
ON MARS

Gregory Benford

*"All the Beer on Mars" was purchased by Gardner
Dozois and appeared in the January, 1989, issue of
IAsfm, with an illustration by the late Hank Jankus.
Benford published a string of strong stories in IAsfm
during the 1980s, all of them marked by that mixture
of humanistic insight and shrewd technological speculation that has always been his forte. The story that
follows is no exception, as he takes us along on a
near-future expedition to the Red Planet—one that's
going to run into a few surprises . . .*

*Gregory Benford is one of the modern masters of
the field. His 1980 novel* Timescape *won the Nebula
Award, the John W. Campbell Memorial Award, the
British Science Fiction Association Award, and the
Australian Ditmar Award, and is widely considered
to be one of the classic novels of the last two decades.
His other novels include* The Stars in Shroud, In the
Ocean of Night, Against Infinity, Artifact, *and* Across
the Sea of Suns. *His most recent novels are the best-
selling* Great Sky River, Tides of Light, *and* Beyond
the Fall of Night, *which he coauthored with Arthur*

*C. Clarke. Benford is a professor of physics at the
University of California, Irvine.*

Bradley Reynolds climbed into the crawler's cabin. He always
had trouble closing the lock door but he got it sealed finally
and ran his gloves over the lip of the collar to be sure it was
lined up and smooth. Then he walked over to the work bench
and sat down without saying anything. The crawler growled
and surged forward.

"Beer?" Lev Stelonski asked.

"A little early in the day," Bradley said.

"Is already poured." He handed Bradley a beaker filled with
amber fluid and no foam on top.

Bradley laughed. "Looks like my whole ration."

"Liter extra today."

Bradley put the beaker down carefully. The crawler rocked
and some beer slopped out. It fell slowly in the low gravity
but he could not catch it. Wellen, who was driving the crawler,
said without looking around, "Get to it."

"You stop, we work," Lev said evenly.

"You can do the setup while we're movin'," the driver said.

"And we can spill the beer, too. Please to slow down." Lev
raised his eyebrows at Bradley.

"Wait'll I get through this dry wash."

Bradley picked up his drink respectfully and caught some
beer just as the crawler lurched. He was damned if he was
going to let any more spill. It would make Wellen smile and
maybe say something and then they would get into an argument
again. Bradley had promised himself that wouldn't happen
anymore. He was senior here and should stay out of minor
scrapes. The hierarchy of the expedition had loosened a lot but
he should not let it go completely slack.

Out the broad windshield of the crawler he could see the
canyon open up before them as they came out of the little side
arroyo. Pink and brown stains in the sandy soil stretched away
into the distance. This part of the great Valles Marineris com-

plex had plenty of signs that looked like water erosion. But no water.

Wellen stopped and killed the engine. The second crawler sat in a gully up ahead waiting for them. "Okay, got it set?"

"In time," Lev said tensely.

Lev took the cylindrical sample holder from Bradley and put it into the biological diagnostic booth that ran halfway along one side of the crawler. Opposite the booth was the main equipment locker. In the back were the bunks and head and kitchen. Everything had a thin film of dust over it but nobody cared about that any longer.

Lev prepared carefully for the test. No matter how many times he did this the biologist methodically went through each step. A shortcut could mess up the whole thing.

The inside of the bio booth was at Martian pressure, about one percent of an Earth atmosphere. That made the fixed gloves in the side of the booth stand out straight, as though an invisible man were trying to reach in toward the shelf of bottles and flaskware. Lev opened the sample holder using the gloves.

"Looks like same consistency as before," Lev said.

"Clay with some sand," Bradley said.

"Hard boring?" Lev spread some of the flaky soil into a receiving port.

"First meter came easy."

"As before. The top layer was washed here."

"By water," Wellen said.

"Or by mud flows," Lev said automatically.

"Or blown by wind," Bradley said.

It was an old argument. Some sites looked to Wellen, the geologist, like classic river valleys. But the rutted land had been carved billions of years ago and then the atmosphere had been heavier. Earthside studies showed that a brief Eden might have flourished for a while. A Mars of streams and lakes and molecules fumbling to find each other and build something bigger. Certainly there was not much water left now and the atmosphere outside was nearly pure carbon dioxide. But most of their expedition favored the water explanation even though there was not even much permafrost left in these deep, dry chasms.

"Good beer." Bradley sipped some more, taking his time.

"I learn," Lev said proudly. "Slow but I learn."

Making beer from their food stores had been his idea. He had smuggled the yeast on the expedition and experimented with it during the eight months voyage. They recycled their water and the brewing concealed the processing tastes. It was the best possible morale booster in a world of stinging aridity.

Lev's hands moved expertly with the sample, not rushing. He divided it and put five little piles of the crumbly soil into small vials. Then he fed them one by one into the bulky gas chromatograph.

Bradley looked out the windshield at the sheer cliffs that rose in the distance. Pink dirt, pink sky. A blue-black tinge deepened the pink further up. The white dot of Deimos hung near the horizon.

As Wellen watched Lev's work his angular face was pinched with irritation. Bradley had not seen any other expression there for days.

Lev said, "Organics again."

"How much?" Wellen demanded tightly.

"Two hundred forty-three parts per billion," Lev read off the digital display.

"Huh," Wellen said. "Less than last time."

"Within the error bars of the diagnostic," Bradley said evenly.

"But less," Wellen said.

They had been following the concentration of organic molecules for weeks. As they came down into the great rift valley the concentration of organics slowly increased.

"What'd you see?" Bradley asked.

Lev shrugged and read off the screen. "Formate. Amino acids. Same as before."

Bradley nodded. These could easily have come from the peculiar, virulent peroxide chemistry of the soil. Like the results of the earlier unmanned Aero probe, they suggested more complex organics could form. But where?

"Look," Wellen said sharply. "We're dippin' around here. Should head straight for the valley floor."

Bradley pointedly ignored Wellen and looked at Lev. "How far down were the organics?"

"Few centimeters."

"Nothing deeper?"

"No."

"Like last time," Bradley said.

"We're following a trail that's petering out," Wellen said.

"We're being systematic," Bradley said.

Wellen said sarcastically, "I say we *systematically* head for the Herbes Chasma."

"We went over that," Bradley said. He looked levelly at Wellen for a long moment.

Wellen snorted and shook his head. Their long expedition was coming to its end and they had little to show for it. Wellen said, "Let's goddamn well get movin' then," and started the crawler engine.

Wellen sped up quickly over the dry wash. Their big tires spewed dust into a filmy curtain behind them that settled slowly. Bradley drank some more beer, telling himself he was just making sure it did not spill. He wanted to drain the beaker. Anything to get the alkaline tang out of his mouth. He knew the taste would come back though as soon as he inhaled any of the dust that had worked into everything.

Lev pulled his hands from the gloves and took his own beer flask from its wire rack.

"Like this better?" Lev asked.

"Yeah. Darker." Bradley brushed some pale dust from his black pressure suit.

"A different yeast culture. I tried something like it at the Institute when I was a student. Bought from Austria."

"Sold it, too, I'll bet."

"Of course. Was the first good thing I got from *glasnost*."

"You used the money to buy another Lenin poster?"

"No, rock records. The metal heavy kind."

"Heavy metal."

"Loud, I did not like."

"You'd have been happier with Lenin."

"No, the records, I bought them in Moscow, sold for twice the price in Kharkov."

"Admirable." Bradley cradled his beaker as they rolled over a rise and came down into a broad gully.

"Looks good here," Lev said distantly.

"Same as yesterday."

They joined the other crawler and the two churned abreast along the wide valley. Stone ramparts reared at the northern and southern horizons. They were making slow progress down a tributary that finally would neck into the deepest parts of the great Martian rift canyon. Wellen wanted them to take a short route through to Hebes Chasma. That was the last major site they could visit in the time remaining. It had a central plateau which from orbit looked like the rippled terrain left when a lake dried out. But the biologists wanted to cover a wider track.

"Funny, y'know," Bradley said in a hushed voice. "We spend thirty billion dollars and come all this way and we don't get anymore than the Aero rover did. Organic molecules and sand."

"Not funny," Lev said.

The next sample point was in a stream bed that swept out of a side arroyo and fanned into the main valley. The stark iron-dark strata here jutted up into a shimmering pink sky. Thin yellow dust moved at high altitude like lace.

Bradley took the core sample again. The work of turning the screw of the borer made him sweat. It was better that way because the work kept the piercing cold out of his arms and legs.

He wore a black sheath very much like the wet suits used in ocean diving and with his breathing mask it made him look a lot like the creature from the black lagoon. He liked the image. Mars, he had said on one of the PR 'casts to earthside, was a place suited for monsters—so he might as well look like one. In fact only hardy lifeforms like lichen and humans had any chance here. But there were certainly no lichen and probably never had been.

When he got the sample inside Lev performed his usual careful analysis. Wellen started up again and the crawler's steady purr lulled Bradley. He sat for a while and let the crawler rock him and daydreamed not about women but about going for a swim in big rollers off Australia. Lev's startled outburst made him blink awake.

"You broke the seal!" Lev said.

"What? No I didn't." Bradley looked through the transparent booth canopy at the neatly arranged samples. "What's wrong?"

"It's contaminated."

"What with?"

"Small peptides. And some iron-binders, looks like."

"Um." Bradley tried to remember if he had made any slips. Those were both complex organic molecules that were present in even a small flake of skin or gob of spit.

"Let me look closer," Lev said. He moved his working capsule to the scanning electron microscope and punched in commands, studying the screen. Bradley had tracked in more dust and the acrid tang stung his nostrils. He thought about beer.

"Cells! There are cells in this."

"Huh? What level?" Bradley asked.

"First few centimeters off the top."

They looked at each other. Bradley said, "Try further down."

He sat pensively as Lev methodically tested the other small vials. Each went under the microscope and then into the gas chromatograph. A digital plate showed the organic compound concentration: 236, 248, 197, 214.

"None of the others has any cells," Lev said accusingly.

"They're only in the surface layer?"

"Yes."

"I didn't do anything different this time."

"Try again."

"Okay. Stop, John."

John Wellen was irritated to lose the time. He muttered to himself and grimaced.

Bradley took more care and got a second sample from a low, sandy spot. He walked around the area looking for unusual signs but saw nothing special.

When he got back inside Lev said, "I did some more runs on the scanning 'scope. Still look like cells. Chewed up by peroxides but cells, yes. Damage is bad but some might be refractile bodies."

"What's that?" Wellen asked.

"Spores, maybe," Bradley said cautiously.

This time Lev carefully checked the seals on the translucent sample cylinder. He took a long while making his measurements and then looked under the microscope.

"Still there," he said flatly.

"Not my fault," Bradley said evenly.

Wellen said sharply, "Come *on*, Reynolds. You botch up two pickups in a row—"

"What kind of cells are they?" Bradley asked Lev, ignoring Wellen.

"They have some common bacterial features," Lev said.

"I took that sample canister from the rack outside. It hasn't been in here for days."

"Should be clean, then," Lev said.

"The UV outside would zap any ordinary bacteria from us, right?" Bradley asked. He was backup bio officer but his real area of competence was astronomy and he felt a little unsure.

"Of course. But we try again."

"Hey," Wellen said, "*you* go get this one, Lev."

They moved on a few hundred meters. Lev took elaborate precautions. Wellen tapped his fingers on the dashboard of the crawler and watched the sky darken as night came on.

A long silence hung in the crawler. Lev looked up from his microscope screen.

"They are here. Cells. Not ours. Of that I am now sure."

The team from the other crawler came to the celebration that night. Lev opened more brewing bottles and they had pungent beer with their food rations.

"Here's to life on Mars," Wellen toasted the five others.

"Besides us," Lutya Karpov replied. She was the commander of the other crawler and had a solemn air even while enjoying herself.

"To us, too," Wellen said.

"To us, the highest lifeforms on Mars," Bradley answered. "Maybe."

"These cells, they live in peroxide soils," Lutya said. "They scavenge for the little drops of water mixed in the grains. *We* cannot do that."

"Don't want to," Bradley said. "That's what makes us higher lifeforms. Judgment."

Wellen asked, "How long you figure those cells been dead?"

Lev rubbed his long nose. "Could be many, many years. Dead is dead. Doesn't change much after."

"What'd Earthside say?" Wellen asked.

"They think my binding stain test of the cells is—what is your word?—'indicative.' Very cautious."

"Of what?" Bradley asked.

"Of nucleic acids," Lev said. "But is same as our DNA? We cannot tell."

"And why?" Lutya asked, sipping her beer and absently scratching. There had been no time today for even the sponge baths.

"The peroxides in soil, they have degraded molecular structure. Muddied the waters, the Americans say."

"Only there's no water here," Bradley said. "I took the boring pipe as far down as it'll go."

"Cells come from elsewhere," Lutya said.

"Must," Lev said.

Lev had beamed his results up to the other five members of the expedition. They were heating the Phobos rock to extract water as reaction mass for the return voyage. They had dropped everything and run analysis on Lev's scanning electron microscope data. There were more tests Lev could do and everybody needed time to think. Better samples were more important than any amount of theory, though. Lev's data, squirted to earth on laserlink, now made every biologist alive a potential kibbitzer. Clearly, Bradley saw, all this was making Lev play his game close to the vest.

"Caution," Bradley said, clinking beakers with Lev.

Lev nodded. "Caution, much caution. Wish we had vodka. Proper toast requires vodka."

Wellen said, "Beer disguises the Martian taste better."

"Peroxide residue," Lutya said. "I wish I could find a way to take it out of our water."

"How high did you run the last batch?" Wellen asked.

"Four hundred twenty degrees Centigrade," she said precisely.

"Damn! Should do it," Wellen said.

Bradley listened to the continuing talk about Lutya's water extraction rig. The tangle of pipes and solar panels on top of the other crawler heated up the soil and got about one percent water out. The few extra liters per day were a precious addition to their meager ration. That also gave them something to talk about besides the continual problem of the smell from the john. Every other topic of discussion had long been exhausted.

"Another toast," Wellen said. "Fill your glasses."

This took a while and then he said, "To the Vikings."

"Viking, 1976," Lev said solemnly.

Bradley said, "Smart little probes. Got the chemistry right but said there were no organics here. Half credit."

Lev said, "And I propose also, to Mars One."

"Mars one what?" Wellen asked.

"First work of humankind to touch Mars. In 1971." Lev grinned.

"Doesn't count," Wellen said. "Crashed, didn't it?"

"Yes. Still, it came," Lev said.

"Good point," Bradley said. He automatically backed Lev against Wellen.

"Didn't *do* anything," Wellen said edgily.

Lutya lifted her beaker. "Then I propose, to Mars Three."

"Another smashup?" Wellen asked sarcastically.

"Landed fine," Lutya said. "And sent data for twenty seconds."

"Terrific," Wellen said.

Bradley asked, "How about Mars Two?"

"Lost," Lev said. "Probably missed making orbit."

"How many times you guys shoot at this place?" Wellen asked.

"Seven times," Lutya said smoothly. "But was Viking that triumphed."

She was the diplomat in the crew and knew how to soothe Wellen. They were all getting short-tempered as supplies got low and they found nothing beyond the organics they had already known about before they arrived. And the increasingly anxious voices laserlinked from Earth through Phobos only irked them further.

Her job and Bradley's was to be sure none of this boiled over into outright conflict. Bradley allowed himself a moment of amused speculation. There had been some talk that she was supposed to soothe the Soviet half in more important matters but there had never been any plausible way it could have worked. There was never any time when she or Faye Nguyen, the American woman who was now up on Phobos, was alone with any of the men. Still, it was something to think about. Bradley had run through the predictable fantasies but finally had found that he preferred thinking about some women Earthside. The compacted spaces of the main module and this crawler had leached his animal spirits thoroughly. Or maybe it was the peroxides.

"How many times you hit?" Wellen asked.

"Three. Mars Six had retrorocket failure," Lutya said with a shy smile.

A low moan swept through the crawler cabin. "The old man of Mars," Lev said.

The winds came up at night here in the canyons. They moved at several hundred kilometers per hour but with the low atmospheric density there was no danger of blowing a man over. It did sound deep bass notes, though, an eerie mournful voice.

"Maybe the old man ate your probes," Wellen said.

"Did not eat Aero," Lev said.

Wellen nodded. "To Aero," he toasted.

"Without whom," Bradley agreed.

He did not like to let national antagonisms start up even in the mildest way. He and Lutya were nominally in charge but they all knew the expedition rested on a fine balance of co-operation.

The Soviets had paid the big chunk of the bill to get here. They alone had the boosters to place large masses in Martian orbit. They had sent the Aero probe lofting over the sands of Mars in the 1990s.

The design was ingenious, a sealed helium balloon with a larger *montgolfiere* below. The *montgolfiere* was a black hot air balloon open to the Martian atmosphere. With morning it absorbed solar infrared and rose, pulling the bottom payload off the ground. The two balloons rode the winds until sundown, when the *montgolfiere* deflated, lowering the detection package to the surface where it could process more soil samples.

Aero had made seven such touchdowns before a duststorm punctured it on a cliffside. It found organic molecules at two sites. The soil chemistry showed tantalizing hints of biochemical processes at work. Ambiguous, but far more promising than the Viking results of the 70s. And that had been enough to inspire a manned expedition.

Appropriately, Aero was conceived by the French, the pioneers of balloon flights a century before. The Soviets helped build Aero and flew it to Mars, beginning joint national explorations. Now came the big gamble, the manned expedition. A gamble that wasn't paying off.

"The past," Lev said solemnly, "conditions the present. May our great countries find the end of our conflicts, on the

sands of a world named for war.'' They all nodded. Periodically
the Soviets solemnly invoked *mir*, peace, as the underlying
reason for this expedition. Bradley knew he had to pay the
proper respects. He had spent two decades helping NASA pull
itself out of its long slump and this was the biggest event of
his generation. Without the Soviets it could not have happened.
Still, he didn't give a damn about politics. Or about interna-
tional relations or peace or providing the right symbolism for
the laserlink appetite. He wanted to find life here. Period.

''*Mir* and *svoboda*,'' he said.

Lev smiled at the little joke. ''*Svoboda* means freedom.''

Bradley grinned and spread his hands expansively. ''Here,
comrades, we are free to find what we can.''

''And find it quick,'' Wellen said.

''Someday this'll be Martian Arches National Monument,''
Bradley said.

''For tourists?'' Lev stopped beside Bradley and reconsidered the stunning sight.

''Sure. Life corrupts everything.''

Across the broad stream bed swept eight thin stone arches.
They were volcanic tubes, Wellen said, black and crusted.

A hundred meters long, impossibly spindly, like a sketch of
a proposed bridge. The soaring black lines stood starkly against
the ruddy landscape. The same light gravity that had permitted
this gossamer stretch of stone let Bradley skip easily down the
slope. He jumped but could not reach the lowest black arch.

''Walk up it,'' Lev called. ''Like a bridge.''

Bradley shook his head. ''I shouldn't have tried. What if
my weight breaks it?''

''They are nearly four billion years old,'' Lev said. ''They
have withstood more than a boot.''

''Four billion?''

''So Wellen says.''

Bradley looked over the soft pinks and mottled greys of the
wide valley. They could not see the canyon ramparts now. The
valley was hundreds of kilometers wide, a lowland refuge from
the pervasive bleached aridity. The great cut that wrapped
around a third of the planet had sections three times deeper
than the American Grand Canyon. Yet it was vastly ancient
and had stood this way for nearly as long as life had crawled

on Earth. "Even more reason not to break them," he said.

Lev said, "And more the reason to find what lived here then."

"How about those micromats you found?"

Lev shrugged. "Microbial fossils, I thought. Now I am not so sure."

"Take more samples."

"That is not problem. Hard to tell if mat is trace of fossil life. Could be merely meaningless blob inside rocks. Too many chemical events can mimic the biological."

"But if they *are* . . ."

"Yes. Ancient life. But mats are hard to identify even on Earth, where we *know* there was life. Such studies take time."

"Only got two days till pickup."

Lev sighed. "All the cells we have found are dead. Perhaps they came from a watery zone."

"From the poles?"

"I hope not." They were all tired from the incessant moving. Bradley had driven all night. The density of small cells increased slowly as they approached Hebes Chasma. Most were windblown, Lev and Lutya had decided. From where?

"Still not much permafrost around here," Bradley said. "Maybe Chasma's got more."

"An oasis?" Lev looked up at the dark bowl of sky rimmed by pink.

"The cells couldn't live here anyway, you said."

"Yes. Too high a peroxide content to these soils. And it is difficult to test their age. They cannot be as old as these arches, however."

"Even so—"

"Yes. Even so, life on Mars. Hooray. But when?"

They came down the wide wash into Hebes Chasma on the last day. The mission had been planned with some slack in it but that was all gone now. The pickup rocket would have to land here within hours.

It was not a bad site. The grand Valles Marineris walls were hundreds of kilometers away, no threat to the lander's navigation. The sandy banks were rippled and undulating. Morning frost gave a light white touch to some ruddy rocks. It would evaporate within an hour.

Soil water content was higher here, but still more arid than the driest site on Earth, the valleys of Antarctica. Bradley reminded himself that some of the early Viking detectors had registered nothing living when the Americans tried them out in Antarctica. It had been years later that biologists found bacteria and algae thriving there in the moist, minute spaces between mineral grains, deep inside rocks.

"Almost like Siberia," Lev said beside him.

They rode in the roof chairs atop the crawler. They faced an eight-month voyage in a capsule now and wanted openness.

"Colder."

"Yes. But even in Siberia, believe it or not, we have human beings."

The crawler swayed as Wellen drove forward at top speed. Bradley said, "But many do not wish to be there."

Lev laughed. "That was the old Soviet Union."

"What was that you said a couple days back? 'The past conditions the present,' I believe."

"I can tell you for sure we will not turn Mars into a prison colony."

"I wish I could promise we won't let tourists carve their initials into those arches."

"Still you will try."

"Yes."

"We have a treaty, then."

"Agreed. No tourists, no prisons."

Lev hugged his coat tighter over his pressure suit. The crawler's speed brought biting cold. "Very solemn treaty."

"Deserves a beer."

"Indeed. I suggest we drink our reserve well before the lander crew comes."

"Very wise."

"Another historic agreement?"

"Yeah, the First Martian Beer Protocols."

"We are being diplomatically silly."

"Of course. All diplomats are."

Bradley knew how to read Lev's tension in the little jokes, the tightened voice. The cell count was rising rapidly as they lumbered through the rolling plains. Each halt brought a higher count. But the cells were still dead. Outcasts from some primordial Eden.

If there were some oasis where primordial Martian life clung to a last vestige of moist wealth, it had to be near here. Winds had scattered it far down the great valleys. Cold and ultraviolet had killed the cells as they blew in the thin, hard gales.

Phobos came up fast in the west. Its pinhead disk swept visibly through the pink rim and into the dark center of the sky. It seemed to be rushing.

On its next pass the lander would detach. The lander's tanks were filled with water harvested by cooking the grainy Phobos rock. They were clinging to the land here, stealing from the scanty Martian reserves of moisture. Life had to, whether cells or humans.

Lev said distantly, "Phobos means fear, yes?"

"Think so."

"And Deimos?" He gestured at the starlike point, brighter than Venus.

"Demon? No, terror."

"Attendants to the god of war."

"Fearsome names," Bradley said.

"A fearsome and deadly place."

"Maybe we should rename Mars."

"To what?"

"How 'bout *Mir?*"

Lev chuckled. Bradley kept surveying the landscape that lurched past. They might be able to spot something from up here. Algae, discolored soil. He watched and gave Lev time to come out with it.

"The final laserlink report is in," Lev said.

"Uh huh." Bradley watched the horizon.

"The cellular structure is in line with evolutionary theory."

"Which means?"

"Simple structures. Same principles of morphological function."

"Seems reasonable."

"Without the samples themselves they cannot tell much, of course."

"Wish we had a DNA reader." They had carried one on the landing at the south pole. There was more permafrost there but no organic compounds at all. To range further in the crawlers they had cut their weight and left the bulky DNA reader. There was a backup on Phobos.

Lev said, "I think the underlying structure will be very different. I am eager to look more deeply."

"Wish we had more equipment. And time."

"These cells, they must have adapted to arid and peroxide-rich soils. They must use very different metabolic pathways, be very UV resistant."

"Let's hope there're some still alive up ahead."

"There are faint similarities, I believe, to *Bacillus subtilis*. That is a spore-forming bacterium found in soils."

"Not surprising. Evolution forces similar adaptations."

"It is good news in a way."

"How come?"

"Such cells imply significant development in at least a rudimentary biosphere. They are rather more advanced than theory supposes the very first life would be."

"That's the clay theory, right?" Bradley shaded his eyes against the sun's hard glare. There was a blue-gray hill to the right that looked unusual. Algae? He held his breath for a long moment.

Then as they approached he saw it was a trick of the lighting. With no ozone layer Mars let through all the ultraviolet and the hard blues played with colors. Their pressure masks had UV filters to protect their eyes. The dead cells could have used such help. Maybe there were caves with natural aquifers that sheltered them up ahead, though.

Lev shrugged. "Elementary self-replicating crystals might have begun in clays, yes. A theory appropriate for Mars, perhaps."

Wellen's voice broke in on radio. "Touchdown's in seven hours, guys. I'm gonna gun this up faster."

"Go ahead," Bradley answered. Wellen had never taken orders from him well but now they all agreed. Their final goal was the deepest part of Hebes Chasma, over a hundred kilometers ahead. Permafrost was probably closest to the surface there. Atmospheric pressure was higher. The lander would come down there, right in the middle of what they all hoped would be the oasis.

"Something." Lev pointed.

It was a long way off. Darker soil and a slight bump.

"Go left," Bradley told Wellen over radio. "See it?"

"No." The crawler turned.

"More left."

"Gotcha."

"Careful."

They lumbered down a gully and across a flat wash of gravel. The mound ahead was a few meters high and the soil nearby was light brown. They came up on it fast.

Lev got down first and approached the stained ground. The patch was about as big as a soccer field. Lev stooped to take a sample.

Bradley kept walking. His boots came down on the stuff and made deep prints into the tan sand below.

"No! Stop!" Lev shouted.

Bradley kept going without any clear idea why. Life. He wanted to see it, to touch it. Life. The alien. He was breathing hard.

"You contaminate it!" Lev shouted. He started toward Bradley but halted at the edge of the stain. "Come back!"

"No . . . no." Bradley's throat was tight and he could not get more out.

The mound was about a third of the way into the stained area. The brown color was deeper there, the deepest of all.

"That is most probably the aquifer," Lev called over radio.

"Yeah," Bradley said numbly.

"A water source. That is what we sought."

"Maybe."

Bradley reached the mound and kicked at it.

"My God, Bradley! Leave it alone!"

"We haven't got time."

"No! Don't disturb the layers!"

His boot hit something hard. He kicked again and heard a metallic clank.

Wellen called, "Bradley, what in hell are—"

He got down on his knees and pushed away the sand.

There was a smashed cylindrical body with lots of struts and bolts around it. Oxidants in the soil had rusted the thin metal.

There was a date in Roman numerals: 1971.

Bradley looked up into the dark sky and saw a single wisp of cloud. He sighed and gazed down at the garden of Eden rusting in the dust.

Lev came to a halt beside him. Wellen was shouting something but Bradley did not answer. Plenty of time to talk later. Eight months of talk.

He jumped on the thing. Lev had brushed more soil away and Bradley kicked hard at the struts. The metal split and the little lander legs bent.

Nobody said anything. Bradley kicked it a last time and stepped back, puffing.

"What's the Cyrillic script say?" he asked at last.

"Mars One."

"*Bacillus subtilis*, huh?"

"In the early days of our program . . ."

"Yeah?"

"There was a common assumption. That the passage through the interplanetary medium would sterilize the probe further." Lev's face was pale and etched by deep lines.

"In case your lab sterilization didn't get everything?"

"Yes. In the loading, the waiting on the pad, there are opportunities, however small, for a leak."

"Yeah." Bradley made himself breathe normally.

"And we hurried."

"To get here."

"Yes."

"You made it all right."

"An error."

Wellen said, "Your goddamn carelessness!"

"It was . . . a different time."

Wellen shoved Lev aside. "All this wasted! Come so far, and *you* messed it up before we even had a, had a *chance*—"

Bradley grabbed Wellen's shoulder and gently pushed him away from Lev. "He's right. It was a different time."

Wellen's eyes were big. "But, but they—"

"Listen to me," Bradley said. "It was a human kind of error. That—"

"Yeah, *their* goddamn mistake." Wellen shoved Lev again. "We oughta—"

Bradley stepped between them. "And *humans* made the error. *Humanity* made it. That's all that counts now."

Wellen stared at Bradley and Lev for a long moment, breathing hard, his mouth compressed. "Damn!" He kicked the probe savagely. "Damn!" He glared at them again and then whirled and stalked off, his gloved hands knotted.

Silence. Just the wind brushing them with its small dead voice.

Bradley said, "Well, you were first all right. You were first."

Lev could not take his eyes off the battered metal. He was dazed.

"Let's go," Bradley said.

"What?"

"Let's go inside. Samples we can take later."

"Well, I . . ."

"No, no, my friend. Come inside."

"For . . . why?"

"A toast. We will drink a toast to Mars One."

Lev said carefully, "All right."

"You said it before. The past conditions the present."

"We have to be sure . . . this incident . . ."

"The past isn't everything. It's just prologue."

"I hope . . ."

"Sure. Sure."

"Bradley—"

"Come on."

"We . . . we will never *know* now. Not for certain."

"Yeah."

"The others. Mars Three, perhaps more. The entire planet could be contaminated."

"Yeah. Even if there are fossil mats left, this'll disguise them."

"My . . . I . . ."

"Come on. We'll drink up all the beer on Mars."

—for Mark Martin

THE CATHARINE WHEEL

WHEEL

Ian McDonald

"The Catharine Wheel" was purchased by Shawna McCarthy and was published in the January, 1984, issue of IAsfm, *with an atmospheric illustration by Broeck Steadman. This was McDonald's first sale, and its evocative, dream-vivid portrait of everyday life on a future Mars was strange and yet achingly familiar, like a phantasm that fades with the morning light. McDonald continued to grow throughout the decade, contributing a number of other stories to* IAsfm, *as well as to* Interzone *and various other British markets, and by the beginning of the 1990s it was clear that the genre had gained an ambitious and daring prose stylist, and a major—and highly individual—new voice.*

Ian McDonald's books include the well-received novels Desolation Road *and* Out on Blue Six, *and the critically acclaimed collection* Empire Dreams. *He lives in Belfast.*

"Come on, lad, come . . ." you hear a voice call, and, peering through the crowd for its source (so familiar, so familiar) you see him. There: past the sherbet sellers and the raucous pastry hawkers; past the crowds of hopeful Penitential Mendicants and Poor Sisters of Tharsis who press close to the dignitaries' rostrum; past the psalm-singing Cathars and the vendors of religious curios; there, he is coming for you, Naon Asiim, with hand outstretched. Through steam and smoke and constables wielding shockstaves who try to keep the crowd away from the man of the moment: here he comes, just for you, your Grandfather, Taam Engineer. You look at your mother and father, who swell with pride and say "Yes, Naon, go on, go with him." So he takes your hand and leads you up through the pressing, pressing crowd and the people cheer and wave at you but you have no time to wave back or even make out their faces because your head is whirling with the shouts and the music and the cries of the vendors.

The people part before Taam Engineer like grass before the scythe. Now you are on the rostrum beside him and everyone of those thousands of thousands of people crushing into the station falls silent as the old man holds up the Summoner for all to see. There is a wonderful quiet for a moment, then a hiss of steam and the chunt-chunt of rumbling wheels and like every last one of those thousands of thousands of people, you let your breath out in a great sigh because out from the pressure-shed doors comes the Greatest of the Great; the fabulous "Catharine of Tharsis" at the head of the last Aries Express.

Do you see pride in Taam Engineer's eye, or is that merely the light catching it as he winks to you and quick as a flash throws you into the control cab? He whispers something to you which is lost beneath the cheering and the music, but you hear the note of pride in it, and you think that is just right, for the Class 88 "Catharine of Tharsis" has never looked as well as she does on this, her final run. The black and gold livery of Bethlehem-Ares glows with love and sacred cherry-branches are crossed on the nose above the sun-bright polished relief of the Blessed Lady herself. Well-wishers have stuck holy medals and ikons all over the inside of the cab, too. Looking at them all leads you to realize that the cab is much smaller than you had ever imagined. Then you see the scars where the computer modules have been torn out to make room for a human driver and you remember that all those nights when you lay awake in bed pretending that the thunder of wheels was the Night Mail, the Lady was far away, hauling hundred-car ore trains on the automated run from Iron Hills to Bessemer. Since before you were born, ''Catharine of Tharsis'' has been making that slow pull up the kilometer-high Illawarra Bank. You have never seen her as she is today, the pride of Bethlehem-Ares, but your imagination has.

Now the people are boarding; the dignitaries and the faithful and the train enthusiasts and the folk who just want to be there at the end of a little piece of history: there they are, filing into the 20 cars and taking their seats for the eight-hour journey.

''Hurry up, hurry up,'' Taam Engineer says, anxious to be off. He pours you a sherbet from the small coldchest and you sip it, feeling the cool grittiness of it on your tongue, counting the passengers eighty, ninety, a hundred, still a bit dazed that you are one of them yourself. Then the doors seal, hsssss. Steam billows; the crowd stands back, excited and expectant, but not as excited or expectant as you. Down the line a red light turns green. The old man grins and taps instructions into the computer.

Behind you, the drowsy djinn wakes and roars in fury, but it is tightly held in its magnetic bottle. Just as well, you think, because your grandfather has told you that it is as hot as the center of the sun back there.

The crowds are really cheering now and the bands are playing for all they are worth and every loco in the yard, even the dirty old locals, are sounding their horns in salute as ''Catharine of Tharsis'' gathers speed. The constables are trying to keep back the crazy wheel-symboled Cathars who are throwing flower petals onto the track in front of you. Grandfather Taam is grinning from ear to ear and sounding the triple steam-horns like the trumpets of Judgment Day, as if to say, ''Make way, make way, this is a `real` train!''

The train picks up speed slowly, accelerating up the long upgrade called Jahar Incline under full throttle, up through the shanty towns and their thrown-together ramshackle depots whose names you have memorized like a mantra: Jashna, Purwani, Wagga-Wagga, Ben's Town, Park-and-Bank, Llandyff, Acheson, Salt Beds, Mananga Loop.

Now you are away from the stink and the press of the shanties, out into the open fields and you cheer as Grandfather Taam opens up the engines and lets the Lady run. "Catharine of Tharsis" throws herself at the magical 300 km/hr speed barrier and in the walled fields by the side of the track, men with oxen and autoplanters stop and look up from the soil to wave at the black-gold streak.

"Faster, Grandfather, faster!" you shriek and Grandfather Taam smiles and orders, "More speed, more speed!" The fusion engines reply with a howl of power. "Catharine of Tharsis" finds that time barrier effortlessly and shatters it and at 355 km/hr the last ever Aries Express heads out into the Grand Valley.

For a long time I moved without style or feeling, wearing simple homespun frocks and open sandals in cold weather. My hair I let grow into thick staring mats, my nails began to curl at the ends. When I washed (only when people complained of the smell), I did so in cold water, even though some mornings I would shiver uncontrollably and catch sight in the mirror of my hollow blue face. I permitted myself that one vanity, the mirror, as a record of my progress toward spirituality. When I saw those dull eyes following me I would hold their gaze and whisper, "The mortification of the flesh, the denial of the body," until they looked away with an expression other than disgust.

I allowed myself only the simplest foods; uncooked, unprocessed and as close to natural as I could take it—for the most part vegetable. Two meals a day, a breakfast and in the evening a dinner, with a glass of water at midday. Cold, of course, but with the taste of Commissary chemicals to it.

Patrick fears that I am wasting to a ghost before his eyes. I reassure him that I am merely abolishing the excess and taking on a newer, purer, form. "Purity," I whisper, "spirituality."

"Purity!" he says, "spirituality! I'll show you purity, I'll show you spirituality! It's us, Kathy; we are purity, we are spirituality because of the life we share together. It's the love that's pure, the love that's spiritual."

Poor Patrick. He cannot understand.

I've seen the needle and they said,—*This is purity*. Some showed me the secret spaces of their bodies and said,—*Here is spirituality*. Others held up the bottles for me to see:—*Look, purity: escape*; and I've seen the books, the red books, the blue books, the great brown ones dusty with age which say,—*Come inside, many have gone this way to wisdom before you*. What a pity that the blue books contradict the red books and the brown books cannot be read because they are so old. And you, Patrick, you are the slave of the book. You call it freedom: I have another name for what you give the name of Political Expression.

I've seen a thousand altars and breathed a thousand incenses, sung a thousand hymns, chanted a thousand canticles to gods a thousand years dead and been told,—*This is the way, the only way to spirituality*. Dancing-dervish under the love-lasers till dawn with men so beautiful they can only be artificial, I've been to the heart of the music where they say purity lies. Lies lies lies lies. The paintings, the altered states, the loves, the hates, the relationships: lies of the degenerates we have become.

Some day I will have to make Patrick leave. For his own sake as much as for the sake of my path to purity.

But he is my conscience. He makes me constantly ask, "Am I right, am I wrong?" and he must be a strong man indeed to be able to sleep night after night with the stinking animal into which I am changing. But I will cast him off, on that day when I achieve purity, because then I won't have any further need of my conscience.

In an age of decadence, I alone strive for purity. I saw it once, I looked spirituality in the face, and since that day I have sought in my own human way to embody it. But give Patrick his due: I am learning that perhaps my daily denials and asceticisms are not the best way to attain my goal. Perhaps the human way is not the way at all.

For the greatest spiritual experience (I would almost call it "Holy," but I don't believe in God) comes when I taphead into the ROTECH computers, in that instant when they cleave my personality away from my brain and spin it off through space.

To Mars.

I can't explain to Patrick how it feels, like I couldn't explain it to my colleagues on the terraform team how it felt that first time when I tapheaded into the orbital mirrors we were maneuvering into position to thaw the polar ice-caps.

I've tried to tell him (as I tried to tell them, hands dancing, eyes wide and bright) of the beauty of the freedom I felt; from the strangling stench of our decaying culture, from the vice of material things, from my body and the arbitrary dictates of its biology: eating, drinking, pissing, crapping, sleeping, screwing. He doesn't understand.

"Kathy, don't deny your body," he says, touching it. "Yours is a beautiful body."

No, Patrick, only spirit is beautiful, and the machine is beautiful, and only what is beautiful is real.

"But was she real?" you ask, and your grandfather replies, "Oh, certainly. I tell you, she was as real as you or me, as real as any of us. What use is a saint who isn't real?" So you look out through the screen at the blurred steel rail that stretches straight ahead as far as you can see, right over the rusty horizon, and you think, "Real, real, real as steel, real as a rail, rail made from steel." It is easy to make up rhymes to the beat of the wheels: diddley-dum, diddley-dum, real, real, real as steel.

An hour-and-a-half out. Back down the train the passengers are having lunch; the dignitaries in the first-class restaurant, everyone else from packages and parcels on their laps. Taam Engineer is sharing his lunch with you, savory pancakes and tea, because you did not bring any lunch with you as you never expected to be riding high at the head of the Aries Express deep in the magic Forest of Chryse.

You have heard a lot about the Forest of Chryse, that it is under the special protection of the Lady herself, that travelers come back from it with tales of wonders and marvels, with unusual gifts and miraculous powers, that some come back with only half a mind and some do not come back at all. Look at the trees, giant redwoods older than man reaching up three hundred, four hundred, five hundred meters tall; it is easy to believe that the machines that built the world are still working under the shadow of the branches and that Catharine of Tharsis walks with them in the forest she planted a thousand years ago. Aboard her namesake, you hurtle past at three hundred kilometers per hour and wonder how Saint Catharine could possibly have built an entire world.

"Look, son." Grandfather Taam nudges you and points to a place far up the valley where a great patch of brightness is sweeping across the Forest of Chryse towards you. You hold your breath as the huge disc of light passes slowly over you on its way to the distant rim walls. If you squint up through your fingers you can just about see the intensely bright dot of the sky-mirror way up there in orbit behind all the glare. Then you feel a blow to the back of your head . . . you see hundreds of intensely bright dots.

"How many times have you been told boy, don't stare at the sky-mirrors!" your grandfather bellows. "You can look at the light, but not at the mirror!"

But you treat yourself to one small extra peep anyway and you think of the men from ROTECH who are focusing all that light down on you, Naon Asiim.

"Remote Orbital Terraform and Environmental Control Headquarters." You whisper the name like a charm to keep the wind and the storm at bay and you remember what your friends told you: that the men up there who move the sky-mirrors have grown so different from ordinary people that they can never ever come down. That makes you shiver. Then you pass out from under the light, but out of the rear screens you can see its progress over the valley to the plateau lands beyond. In its wake you see a tiny silver bauble bowling across the sky.

"Look, Grandfather! A dronelighter!"

He gives it the barest glance, spits and touches one of the tiny ikons of Our Lady fastened above the driving desk. Then you realize what a mistake you have made, that it is the drone-lighters and the 'rigibles of the world that have made your grandfather the last to bear the proud name of "Engineer," they are the reason why the museum sidings are waiting for the Lady just beyond the crowds at Pulaski Station.

"I'm sorry, Grandfather." A hand ruffles your hair.

"Never mind, son, never worry. Look: see how that thing runs . . . It's getting out from under the skirts of the storm, running as fast as it can. They can't take the weather, they're flimsy, plasticy things, like glorified Festival kites."

"But *we* can take the weather."

"Go through it like a fist through wet rice-paper, my boy! I tell you, Bethlehem-Ares never lost a day, not even one single hour, to the weather: rain, hail, blizzard, monsoon, none of it stops the Lady!" He reaches out to touch the metal window-frame and you feel like shouting "hooray!" Taam Engineer (what, you wonder, will he call himself when the Lady is gone?) stabs a finger at the skyscreen.

"See that? Because of those things cluttering up the sky they have to move the weather about to suit them. That's what the mirror's for; those ROTECH boys are moving the storm up onto the plateau where it can blow itself to glory and not harm one single, delicate, dirigible. Puh!" He spits again. "I tell you, those things have no soul. Not like the Lady here, she's got a soul you can hear and feel when you open those throttles up, she's got a soul you can touch and smell like hot oil and steam. You don't drive her, she lets you become a little part of her and then she drives you. Like all ladies. Soul, I tell you." He hunts around for words but they evade him like butterflies. He waves his hands, trying to shape the ideas that mean so much to him, but the words will not come to him. "I tell you, how can you feel part of anything when you're flying way up there above everything? You're not part of anything up there like you're a bit of the landscape down here. I tell you, they've no soul. You know, soon it will be just them and the robots on the freight runs and then one day even they'll be gone, it'll be just the lighter-than-airs. The only engines you'll see'll be in the museums and God forbid that I should ever come to see that day." He looks at you like he wants you to back him up in what he has said, but you didn't really understand what he said because the rumble of the engines and the sway of the cab as it leans into the curves and drumming of the wheels saying "real, real, real as steel" is sending you off to sleep.

When I wake the sight disgusts me. Gap-toothed, crack-skinned, filthy-haired hag holding splintered nails up to the mirror whining, *The mortification of the flesh, the denial of the body.* Hideous. Futile.

Sleep came hard to me last night. Lying beside Patrick, staring at the ceiling, I had time and plenty to think. Letting the pieces tumble through my head, I saw how I was wrong, so wrong, so magnificently wrong. The mortification of the flesh is empty. It only serves to focus the mind more closely on the body it seeks to deny. Disciplining the body does not discipline the mind, for the greater the denial the greater the attention the body must be given. This is not the way to spirituality.

So before Patrick wakes I shower. I wash my hair, I trim my nails, I depilate, I deodorize, I even repaint the tekmark on my forehead and dress in the most nearly fashionable outfit I own. On the train downtown I just sit and watch the people. They do not know that I was the girl with the sunken eyes and the stinking hair they were so careful not to be seen staring at. Now I am just another face on a train. By denying the body I only drew more attention to it. The only way to achieve purity is to escape totally from the body. But that is impossible while we are on this earth. Not so on Mars.

Tapheading, for me, is like waking from a dream into a new morning. Eyes click open to the vast redscapes of Mars. You can hear it shouting, Real, real! with the voice of the polar wind. Let me tell you about the polar wind. For a hundred thousand years it blew cold and dry from the ice itself, but we have moved our orbital mirrors in over the pole and are thawing the cap. So now the winds have reversed direction and great thunderheads of cloud are piling up layer upon layer in the north. Some day it will rain, the first rain on Mars for fifty thousand years. I will rejoice at the feel of it on my plastic skin, I will laugh as it fills the ditches and dikes of our irrigation systems and I shall doubtless cry on the day when it touches the seeds of the Black Tulips I have planted and quickens them to life. But that is in the future. Maybe this year, maybe next year, maybe five years from now.

For the present I take joy in lifting my head from the planting and seeing the rows of Johnny Appleseeds digging and dropping and filling and moving on. They are mine. No. They are *me*. I can be any one of them I choose to be, from Number 11 busily spraying organic mulch over the seedbeds to Number 35 trundling back to base with a damaged tread.

But I can be much more than that. If I blink back through the ROTECH computer network I can be a dronelighter blowing tailored bacteria into the air, or a flock of orbital mirrors bending light from round the far side of the sky, or an automated hatchery growing millions of heat-producing, oxygen-generating Black Tulip seeds for the Johnny Appleseeds, or a channel-cutter building the fabulous Martian canals after all these millennia, or a Seeker searching deep beneath the volcanic shield of Tharsis for a magma core to tap for geothermal energy, or an aveopter flying condor patrol high over the Mare Boreum, which will one day indeed be a Sea of Trees. . . .

I can be whatever I want to be. I am free. I am pure spirit, unbound to any body. And this is my vision of purity, of spirituality: to be forever free from this body, from earth and its decadence, to fly on into a pure future and build a new world as it ought to be built; as a thing of spirit, pure and untainted by human lusts and ambitions. This is a future that stretches far beyond my human lifespan. They say it will be eight hundred years before a man can walk naked in the forests we are growing in Chryse. Two hundred years will pass after that before the first settlers arrive on the plains of Deuteronomy. A thousand years, then, to build a whole world in. That will give me enough time to make it a proper world.

This is my vision, this is my dream. I am only now beginning to realize how I may achieve it.

But first I must dream again. . . .

It is not the rattle of the rain that has woken you, nor the slam of a passing ore-train on the slow up-line; it is something far less tangible than that, it is something you feel like the crick in your neck and the dryness in your mouth and the gumminess around your eyes that you get from having fallen asleep against the side window. So knuckle your eyes open, sniff the air. You can smell the rain, but you can smell something else too, like electricity, like excitement, like something waiting to happen.

Look at the screen, what do you see? Wind blowing billows across endless kilometers of wet yellow grass that roll away to the horizon. Low rings of hills like the ancient burial mounds of Deuteronomy lie across the plain: eroded impact craters, Taam Engineer tells you. This is Xanthe, a land as different as different can be from the forests of Chryse or the paddy-fields of the Great Oxus. A high, dry plainland where the Grand Valley begins to slope up to the High Country of Tharsis. But today the rains have come out of season to the stony plain, carried on an unnatural wind, for the ROTECH engineers and their sky-mirrors are driving the storm away from the peopled lowlands to the Sinn Highlands where it can blow and rain and rage and trouble no one. The sky is hidden by a layer of low, black, curdled cloud and the wind from the Sea of Trees blows curtains of rain across the grassland. Miserable.

You ask your grandfather how much longer and he says, "Not long, son, the storm will blow out within the hour and Xanthe's a poor land anyway, fit only for grazers and goatherds and getting through as quickly as possible." Grandfather Taam smiles his special secret smile and then you realize that, according to the story, this is where it all happened, where Taam Engineer—your own grandfather!—met the saint and so averted a dreadful accident. Now you know where the feeling of excitement has come from. Now you know why Grandfather Taam has brought you on the great Lady's last haul.

So you tell the old man, this is where it all happened and he smiles that secret smile again and says, "Yes, this is where it all happened all those years ago, long before you were even thought of; it was here the Lady worked a miracle and saved five hundred lives, yes, we'll be there soon, and look, even the weather is deciding to improve, look."

Out across the hills the sky is clearing from the North West. Light is pouring through the dirty clouds and the rain has blown away leaving the air jewel-bright and clear. "Catharine of Tharsis" explodes out into the sunlight, a shout of black and gold and the plains about her steam gently in the afternoon sun.

Lights flash on the control desk. Even though you do not understand what they mean, they look important. You direct Taam Engineer's attention to them, but he just nods and then ignores them. He even sits back and lights a cheroot. You thought he had given up those dirty things years ago, but when you ask him if there is anything wrong, he says,

"Nothing, boy, nothing," and tells you she's only doing what her high station expects of her, but you haven't time to think about that because the train is slowing down. Definitely, unmistakably. Her speed is now well under 100. You look to Taam Engineer, but he grins roguishly and does not even touch the keypad to demand more speed. He just sits there, arms folded, puffing on his cheroot as the speed drops and drops and it becomes obvious that the train is not just slowing, but stopping.

The nonstop Rejoice-to-Llangonnedd Aries Express grinds past a stationary chemical train down-bound from the sulphur beds of Pavo. The engines whine as they deliver power to the squealing brakes and the 700-ton train comes to a stand right out there in the middle of the pampas with not even a station or even a signal pylon to mark it as special and worthy of the attention of "Catharine of Tharsis."

A hiss of steam startles you, it is that quiet. Cooling metal clicks. Even the hum of the engines is gone, the fusion generators are shut right down. The rust-red chemical train looks almost sinister in its stillness.

"What now?" you whisper, painfully aware of how loud your voice sounds. Grandfather Taam nods at the door.

"We get out."

The door hisses open and he jumps out, then lifts you down to the ground. You can see the staring faces pressed to the windows all the way down the train.

"Come on," says Grandfather Taam and he takes you by the hand and leads over the slow down-line (you glance nervously at the waiting chemical train, half-expecting the automated locomotive to suddenly blare into life), down the low embankment and into the tall grass. He grinds his filthy cheroot out on the ground, says, "It should be around here somewhere," and starts thrashing about, whish whish swush, in the wet grass. You can hear him muttering.

"Aha! Got it! A bit overgrown, but that just goes to show how long it is since a human engineer ran this line. I tell you, in my day we kept the weeds down and polished the silverwork so bright you could see it shining from ten kilometers down the track. Come and look at this, son . . ."

He has cleared the grass away from a small stone pedestal. Inlaid in tarnished metal is the nine-spiked wheel-symbol of Saint Catharine. You can feel the devotion as your grandfather bends to rub the dirt of the years from the small memorial. When it is clean and silver-bright again he bids you sit with him on the damp crushed grass and listen as he tells you his tale.

I have told Patrick what I am going to do. I used the simplest words, the most restrained gestures, the shortest sentences, for I know how incoherent I become when I am excited. I did my best to explain, but all I did was scare him. Seeing me transformed, my body clean, my face pretty, again the Kathy Haan he had once loved, and then to hear me tell him of how I am going to cast this world away and live forever on Mars is too great a shock for him. He does not have to tell me. I know he thinks I am mad. More than just "mad." Insane. My explanations will do no good, he can't understand and I'm not going to force him to.

"One favor, Patrick. You know people who can get these things, could you get me two lengths of twistlock monofiber?"

"What for?"

"I need it."

". . . for your mad 'escape,' don't tell me. Forget it. No, Kathy."

"But listen, Patrick . . ."

"No, no, no, I've listened enough to you already. You're a persistent bitch; if I listen to your voice long enough I'll find myself agreeing with whatever insane notion you suggest."

"But it's not insanity. It's survival, it's the only way for me to go."

"Oh, yes, the only way you can be pure, the only way you can achieve spirituality. . . . What is it that's driven you to this, Kathy? It's suicide, that's exactly what it is!"

"The Crazy Angel, Patrick. At some time or another the Crazy Angel touches us all and we just have to go with the flow."

But he doesn't see the joke: if there is no God, how can there be any angel at all, Crazy or otherwise, unless it is me?

"Are we not enough? There was a time when it was enough for us to have each other. What more do you want, what more is there?"

"Do you really want me to answer that, Patrick?" I give him one of my fascinating half-smiles that used to excite him so much. Now it only angers him.

"Then what does Mars offer that I don't?"

Same question. This time I choose to answer it.

"Sanity."

"Sanity! Hah! You talk to me about sanity? That's rich, Kathy Haan, that is rich."

I remain patient. I will not allow Patrick to disturb me. I will not lose my head or shout at him. To do so would only be to play the game according to his rules, and his sick society's rules.

"Sanity," I say, "in a world where words like hunger and fear and disease and war and decadence and degeneration don't have any meaning, in a world that one day will be so much more than your earth could ever be. Freedom from a world that registers its terrorists, Patrick Byrne, and lets them kill who they will for their high and lofty registered ideals!"

That stings him, but I am relentless, I am the voice of final authority: the angel is speaking through me and won't be silent.

"And you will let me go, Patrick, you will get me those lengths of monofiber from your Corps friends, because either I go or your sick, sick society will have me off the top of a building in a week, and that is a promise, Patrick Byrne, a Kathy Haan promise: either way I go; either way you lose."

"Bitch!" he roars and spins round, hand raised to strike, but no one may lay hands on the Crazy Angel and live, and the look in my eyes stops him cold. Serenity.

"Bitch. God, maybe you are an angel after all, maybe you are a saint."

"Not a saint, Patrick, never a saint. A saint who doesn't believe in God? Not Saint Kathy, just a woman out of time who wanted something more than her world had to offer. Now, will you get me those bits of twistlock fiber?"

"All right. I can't fight the Crazy Angel. How long?"

I hold my hands about half a meter apart. "Two of them, with grips at both ends and a trigger-release twistlock set to fifth-second decay so they won't ever find out how I did it."

"I'll get them. It'll take some time."

"I can wait."

Expressions flow as words across his face. Then he turns away from me.

"Kathy, this is suicide!"

"So what? It's legal, like everything else from political murder to public buggery."

"It's suicide."

"No. Not this. To stay behind, to try and live one more year on this rotting world, that's suicide. More than that, it's the end of everything, because then I'll have even thrown all my hope away."

It is a story old and stale with telling and retelling, but here, sitting on the damp grass under the enormous sky, it feels as if it is happening to you for the first time. Taam Engineer's eyes are vacant, gazing into years ago; he does not even notice how his stained fingers trace the starburst shape of the Catharine Wheel on the pedestal.

"I tell you, I thought we were done then. I'd given up all hope when that pump blew, with us so far out into the wilderness (and it was wilderness then, this was years back before ROTECH had completed manforming the Grand Valley . . . we were so far out that no help could ever reach us in time, not even if they sent the fastest flyer down from their skystations, and there were five hundred souls aboard, man, woman and child. . . .

"So I ordered them to evacuate the train, even though I knew right well that they could never get far enough away to outrun the blast when the fusion engines exploded. . . . But I had them run all the same, run to those hills over there . . . you know, to this day I don't know if they have a name, those hills . . . but I thought that if they could reach the far side then they might be safe, knowing full well that they never would. . . .

"All the time I was counting off the seconds until the pressure vessel would crack and all that superheated steam would blow my beauty to glory and us with her. I can remember that I had one thought in my head that kept running round and round and round: 'God, save the train, please, save the train God . . .' That was when the miracle happened."

An afterbreath of wind stirs the grass around you. It feels deliciously creepy.

"I don't know if it was my calling or the train's agony that brought her, and I don't think it matters much; but on the horizon I saw a black dot, way out there . . ." He points out across the waving grass and if you squint along the line of his finger into the sun you too can see that black dot rushing towards you. "An aveopter, black as sin and big as a barn, bigger even; circling over the line, and I tell you, it was looking for me, for the one who called it. . . ." Taam Engineer's hands fly like aveopters, but he is too busy watching the great black metal hawk coming lower and lower and lower to notice them. "And I swear she took the loco in her claws, boy, in her metal claws, and every bit of bright-work on her ran with blue fire. Then I heard it. The most terrible sound in the world, the scream of the steam release valve overloading and I knew that was it and

I scrambled down this bank as fast as I could and threw myself onto the ground because death was only a second behind me, and do you know what I saw?''

Though you have heard the story a hundred tellings before, this time it takes your breath away. So you shake your head, because for once you do not know.

''I tell you, every one of those five hundred souls, just standing there in the long grass and staring for all they were worth. Not one of them trying to run, I say, so I turned myself belly-up and stared too, and I tell you, it was a thing so worth the staring that I couldn't have run, though my life depended on it.

''They'd stripped her down and laid her bare and unplugged the fusion generators and, by the Mother-of-Us-All, they were fusing up the cracks in the containment vessel and running the pumps from zero up to red and down again, and those pumps, those God-blind-'em pumps, they were singing so sweetly that day it was like the Larks of the Argyres themselves.''

''Who, Grandfather?'' you say, swept away by the story. ''Who were they?''

''The Angels of Saint Catharine herself, I tell you. They had the look of great metal insects, like the crickets you keep in a cage at home, but as big as lurchers and silver all over. They came out of the belly of the aveopter and a-swarmed all over my locomotive.''

He slaps his thighs.

''Well, I knew she was saved then, and I was whooping and cheering for all I was worth and so was every man-jack of those five hundred souls by the time those silver crickets had finished their work and put her back together again. Then they all just packed back into the belly of that big black aveopter and she flew off over the horizon and we never saw her again, none of us.

''So, I got up into the cab and everything was all quiet and everything smelt right and every readout was normal and every light green, and I put the power on as gentle as gentle and those engines just roared up and sang, and those pumps, those pumps that so near killed us all, they were humming and trilling like they were fresh from the shop. Then I knew I'd seen a miracle happen, that the Blessed Lady, Saint Catharine herself, had intervened and saved us all. And I tell you this, I would still never have believed it had it not been for those five hundred souls who witnessed every little thing she did and some of them even had it recorded and you can see those pictures to this day.''

Up on the track the chemical train fires up. The shocking explosion of sound makes you both jump. Then you laugh and up on the embankment the robot train moves off: cunk, cunk, cunk, cunk. Taam Engineer rises to watch it. When it is gone he pats the small stone pedestal.

"So of course we named the engine after her and put this here to commemorate the miracle. I tell you, all the engineers (in the days when we used to have human engineers) on the Grand Valley run would sound their horns when they went by as a mark of respect, and also in the hope that if they gave the Lady her due, one day she might pull them out of trouble. You see, we know that the Lady's on our side.''

He offers you a hand and drags you up damp-assed from the ground. As you climb the embankment you see all the faces at the windows and the hands waving ikons and charms and medallions and holy things. It makes you look at "Catharine of Tharsis" again, as something not quite believable, half locomotive and half miracle.

Grandfather Taam lifts you up the cab steps. Suddenly a question demands to be asked.

"Grandfather, then why do the trains stop now if they only used to whistle?''

He reaches for the flask of tea and pours you a scalding cup. Behind you the djinn rumbles into life again.

"I'll tell you for why. Because she is not a saint of people, but a saint of machines. Remember that, because the day came when the last engineer was paid off this line and they turned it over to the machines and then they felt that they could honor their Lady as best they knew.''

Lights blink red white green yellow blue all over the cab. The light glints off the holy medals and ikons but somehow it is not as pretty as it once was.

As if it were aware of my imminent escape into spirituality, the ugliness is drawing closer to me. Yesterday in the train I saw a licensed beggar kicked to death by three masked men. No one raised voice nor hand in protest. For one of the masks held out a Political Activist Registry card for us all to see while the other two beat the old man to death in accordance with their political ideals. Everyone looked out of the windows or at the floor or at the advertisements for sunny holidays and personal credit extensions. Anywhere but at the beggar or at each other.

I am ashamed. I too looked away and did nothing.

We left him on the floor of the car for others to take care of when we stepped off at our stop. A smart man I vaguely know with a highcaste tekmark glanced at me and whispered, "We certainly must remember to respect peoples' right to political expression; goodness knows what terrible things might happen if we don't."

Oh, Patrick, how many beggars have you killed in the name of political expression? Damn you, Patrick Byrne, for all the love I've wasted on a man who a hundred years ago would have been hunted down and torn apart for the common murderer he was. Dear God, though I know you aren't there, what sort of a people are we when we call terrorists "heroes" and murder "political expression"? What sort of a person is it who would dare to say she loved one? A Kathy Haan, that's what. But I will be rid of him.

Escape is two lengths of twistlocked monofiber wrapped up in my pouch, but have I the courage to use it? Cowardice is a virtue now, everyone has their Political Activist card to wave as justification for their fear. Be brave, Kathy.

I like to think of myself as the first Martian at these times.

It's not the loneliness that scares me. I have been alone for twenty-four years now and there is no lonelier place than the inside of your skull. What terrifies me is the fear of gods.

Deiophobia.

"Maybe you are an angel after all, maybe you are a saint," Patrick had said. What I fear most is that I may become more than just a saint, that the ultimate blasphemy to all that the sacrifice of Kathy Haan stood for will be for me to become the Creator God of the world I am building: the Earth Mother, the Blessed Virgin Kathy, the Cherished and Adored Womb of the humanity I despise.

I do not want to be God, I don't even particularly want to be human. I only want to be free from the wheel.

Smiles and leers greet me from friend and satyr alike.

"Morning, Kathy (thighs, Kathy) 'day, Kathy, (breasts Kathy) . . ." I take my chair, still warm from the flesh of its previous occupant whom I have never known and probably never will, now. Warm up drill: codes, ciphers, and calibrations. The sensor helmet meshes with my neural implants and nobody sees me slip the coils of monofiber from my pouch and throw a couple of loops around the armrests.

Lightspeed will be the death of me. The monofiber is merely the charm I chose to invoke it.

"O.K., Kathy, taphead monitoring on . . ."

Needles slip into my brain and I slip my wrists through the loops, concealing the twistlock control studs in my palms. I had not thought death would be so easy.

Brainscans worm across the ceiling.

Listen: I have not much time to tell you this, so listen well. It takes six minutes for the oxygen level in the brain to fall to the critical point after which damage is irreversible. It is easy to do this. Damage to two major arteries will do very nicely, provided there is no rapid medical attention.

But: it takes four minutes for the coded tadon pulse containing the soul of Kathy Haan to reach Mars. You can add. You know that if you add another four minutes return time from ROTECH to Earth that leaves you with a brain so like shredded cabbage that there's no way they'll ever be able to pour poor Kathy back into it again. I shall be free and I shall live forever as a creature of pure spirit.

I have invented a totally new sin. Is it fitting then that I should become a saint?

All I need do is press the buttons. The molecular kink in the monofiber will contract, neatly severing my wrists. A fifth of a second later they will dissolve completely. Lightspeed will do the rest. All I need do is press the buttons. They are hidden in my palms, slick with sweat.

"O.K., Kathy, counting down to persona transfer. Preliminary tadon scan on, transfer pulse on in five seconds . . . four . . ."

The mortification of the flesh, I whisper. Behind me someone shouts. Too late.

" . . . one."

I press the buttons.

• • •

Green lights all the way down the line on the final run into Llangonnedd. Clear road: dirty freighters pulled into sidings blare their horns and the ugly, ugly robot locals squawk their nasty Klaxons as the Lady races by. Suburban passengers blink as she streaks past; by the time the shout reaches their lips she is around the next bend and leaning into the one after that like a pacehound.

And all the lights are green. More magic. Grandfather Taam tells you that you never get a full run of greens coming into Llangonnedd, no, not even for the Aries Express. Never ever. It must be more magic, of the same kind that let the Lady reach the incredible 450 kilometers per hour out there on the flats beyond Hundred Lakes. Grandfather Taam tells you she never touched 450 before, never ever, not even 400. Why, the people who built her had told him themselves that she would blow apart if she went over 390.

You reckon that engineers know nothing about engines and their special magic. After all, they are just engineers, but Grandfather Taam is an Engineer. Looking out of the side windows even a leisurely 250 seems frighteningly fast in these crowded suburbs. Canal flash houses flash fields flash park flash factories flash: you can feel your eyes widening in apprehension as the stations and the signals hurl themselves out of the distance at you. And all the lights are green.

That can only mean one thing.

"She's doing this, isn't she, Grandfather?"

A station packed with round-mouthed commuters zips by. Taam Engineer lights a cheroot.

"Must be. I've hardly had to lay a finger on those buttons for the past hour or so."

Beneath you the brakes start to take hold, slowing you down from your mad rampage through outer Llangonnedd to a more civilized pace. You say, "She really must love this train very much."

Grandfather Taam looks straight ahead of him down the silver track.

"After all, she did save it."

"But it wasn't the people, was it, Grandfather? It was nothing to do with the five hundred souls; she saved the train because it was the train she wanted to save. All those people were extra, weren't they?"

"They didn't matter to her one bit, boy."

"And you said she's a saint of machines, didn't you? Not a saint of people? That's why she loves the train, why she loved it enough not to let it die, isn't it? If there hadn't been a single person there, she would still have saved the train, wouldn't she? But, if that's true, why do people love her?"

"Love her? Who said anything about loving her? I tell you, boy, I have little love for Catharine of Tharsis. Respect yes, love no. And I'll tell you why. Because if she hadn't thought the train was worth saving, if she hadn't loved the train, she would just have let it blow those five hundred people to hell without a single thought. That's the kind of God those crazy Cathars are worshipping, but as to why they love her, I don't know. Do you have any idea why people would love someone like that?"

He looks straight at you. You have been expecting this question. You know that he has never been able to answer it himself, and that it is the reason why he brought you along on this ride.

"I don't know what I think . . . If she's really like that, then I think that most people must be very foolish most of the time, especially when they have to look for someone to help them when things go wrong and then put the blame on when things don't happen like they want. People are like that. I think if I were a saint like Saint Catharine I would be a saint of machines, too. Then I wouldn't care what people said about me or thought of me because I wouldn't be doing anything for them and they could cry away and pray away all day like those silly Cathars and the Poor Sisters of Tharsis and I wouldn't care one bit, because machines are never foolish."

"Catharine of Tharsis" has slowed right down. The end of the journey is near now. Tomorrow Taam Engineer and you will be flying home on one of those dreadful 'rigibles and "Catharine of Tharsis" will be taken away to the museum for foolish people to stare at and marvel over her record-breaking final run. And now you understand.

"Grandfather, of course I'd be a saint of machines! Because I could fly with the aveopters and the sky-mirrors and even the great Sky Wheel herself and I could burrow with the Seekers and swim with the 'Mersibles, but most of all I could run with the Lady of Tharsis faster than she ever ran before and show off to everyone what a wonderful engine she is before they put her away for good in a museum. People are always moaning and complaining about their troubles and their problems; they won't let you run and be free from them, people won't let you do things like that!''

''Ah, the ways of saints and children,'' Taam Engineer says as the Lady rumbles over the Raj-Canal into the glassite dome of Pulaski station. Already you can hear the roars and the cheers of the crowds and every loco in the yards is sounding its horn in salute.

''Here, button three,'' Grandfather Taam says and you reply to the people with the wonderful blare of the steam horns. You press and press and press that button and the trumpets sound and sound and sound until the notes shatter against the glass roof of the station. And how the crowds cheer! Taam Engineer is hanging out of the window waving to the mobs of petal-throwing Cathars as the ''Catharine of Tharsis'' glides in to Platform Three as smooth as smooth. You are sliding the other side window open ready to cheer out when something stops you. An odd feeling like a persistent itch in the nose that suddenly stops or a noise in your ears that you never hear until it goes away. A kind of click. You shake your head but it is gone and you shout and wave for all you are worth to the excited people. They wave and call back to you, but you do not see them because you are really thinking about the click. For a second or so it puzzles you. Then you realize that it is nothing very important, it is only the empty space filling in where once there might have been a saint.

MARS NEEDS BEATNIKS

George Alec Effinger

"Mars Needs Beatniks" was purchased by Shawna McCarthy and appeared in the January, 1984, issue of IAsfm, *with an illustration by Arthur George. Over the years, Effinger has provided a good number of stories to the magazine, some somber, some . . . not. When he sets himself to it, Effinger can produce some of the funniest short science fiction ever written, putting him in the select company of people like R. A. Lafferty, Robert Sheckley, Howard Waldrop, John Sladek, and Avram Davidson. In the remarkably silly story that follows—one of his not-somber ones—he takes some of the Beat Generation On the Road to a brand-new destination. Would you believe . . . Mars?*

Perhaps the *hot young writer of the 1970s, George Alec Effinger has subsequently maintained a reputation as one of the most creative innovators in SF, and one of the genre's finest short-story writers. His first novel,* What Entropy Means to Me *(recently re-released), is considered a cult classic in some circles, and his most recent, and most popular, novel—the gritty and fascinating* When Gravity Fails—*was a prime contender for the 1987 Hugo Award. His short story "Schrodinger's Kitten," set in the same milieu, went on to win him a Hugo Award in 1988, and his new novel,* A Fire in the Sun, *the sequel to* When Gravity Fails, *was a top contender for the 1989 Hugo, as well. His many other books include the novels* The Wolves of Memory, The Bird of Time, Those Gentle Voices, *and* Utopia 3, *and the collections* Mixed Feelings, Irrational Numbers, *and* Idle Pleasures. *Effinger lives in New Orleans.*

Here is the story as promised and like virtually on time, I expect my check immediately or I will have my mother call you EVERY HOUR ON THE HOUR until you capitulate. I will accept no repeat *no* editing as my writing is diamond-pure heartbeat true inner beatific vision stuff. If you mess with it you mess with the pulse of the universe and like the Lords of Karma will see to it that your old lady catches something in the back seat of a new Edsel and not only that but when you get home from work tonight all your Lester Lanin records will have scratches like right in the most fabulous places. It has been a pleasure doing business with you.

MARS: THE SQUARE PLANET

(And don't put some new headline on this like "Little Green Men Dig That Earth Jive." We—Norman and me—won't stand for it, and we'll make you look like nowhere the next time those people from *Life* interview us.)

(And I want my by-line at least as big as whoever does those very not-with-it predictions for you. Speaking of which, the Martians gave us a few and you can use them if you want. Like in the next five years there will be over a *hundred square feet* [italics mine] of knotty pine rec room paneling for every man, woman, and child in the country. Weird, no? You wouldn't dare print that. Nobody will pay attention. Rumors about movie stars they believe no matter how crazy, but a genuine Martian prophet earns nothing but scorn and derision. How typical. How square. I ask myself why I'm doing this and it isn't just the princely sum of money you will be sending IMMEDIATELY because, you dig, the diamond-pure prose is reward enough. It makes the *Saturday Review* squirm in print and like it's good for them.)

The visions began sometime in June, 1959.

We were called to New Orleans. They call that city The Big Easy, and it is. We came because New Orleans, like St. Louis and Chicago, is the birthplace of jazz, and jazz is the birthplace of us. Yet somehow there was something weird happening. We arrived at different times, not knowing the others were coming too, but we joined together in a magical congregation of far-out hipness.

I have wept for two days. I have worked to tell this story, and for two entire days it has beaten me. It is a big story, a fearless and holy story, and a story about the cool Zen American dream in its absolute most pure and incandescent state. The story is about jazz, poetry, Mars, dreams, freight cars, air that smells like spice, and the best minds of our generation. When I begin the story with the jazz, I'm afraid you'll like give up before the rainbow portals come into it. When I begin with the ancient dead sea bottoms, I know you'll get wigged by the great tenor saxophone of Sonny Rollins. It has been a problem of organization, you dig, a matter of putting all the seemingly unrelated pieces together. I can do that easy, no sweat; just tell me, where do I start?

I came to New Orleans first, and I took a place on the patio of the Café du Monde, where you eat hot beignets covered with powdered sugar and drink coffee with chicory and stare across the square at the old cathedral. You like pretend you're not in America at all, but in some quaint European cathedral town where they like imported palm trees and banana plants during the night when you weren't looking. The breeze is warm and humid, and the coffee-brown river is only a short distance on the other side of the railroad tracks, and you can hear the calliope music from the steamboats. That was my place.

It wasn't until Allen arrived that the visions began. He had the first one, and he told me about it. He had come down from New York, from the sanctified ruins near Tompkins Square and he wandered around New Orleans looking for his place, delighted by the groovy street names which hold so much magic: Bourbon Street, Basin Street, Rampart Street. He ran into a jazz funeral for some old Negro, some ancient worshipful trumpet player who was being put to rest by his brothers— "sending him off," they call it—and Allen joined the procession, thinking "Yes! Yes!" that he was accepted and no one told him to split that Negro funeral scene. The musicians were mournfully swinging through the hot brick streets, sliding out some scat version of "Just a Closer Walk with Thee," but on the way back Allen flipped when the band broke into a frantic and happy "Rampart Street Parade" and followed that with "When the Saints." It was like a moving street party with laughing and dancing and people waving umbrellas and just purely swinging. No grief here, man, we done send him off. The funeral worked its way back to the starting place and then, like a New Orleans summer shower, evaporated, fell apart and disappeared, and all the Negro musicians and the Negro preacher and the Negro family members and the Negro second-liners following and dancing and clapping, they all went away somewhere, leaving Allen alone and lost on some narrow street of beat cottages and shuttered doors. Allen grinned; this was his place.

His vision came after dark, in a small, dim, smoky spot on Toulouse around the corner from Bourbon Street. Paintings like cool jazz hung on the walls in the red light, and bullfight posters, and scenes of exotic places like Frisco, and pictures of kids with big sad eyes and puppies, and notices for poetry readings and rallies. Candles burned on chianti bottles. Chicks in black toreador pants, black turtleneck sweaters, their hair cut short or pulled back in ponytails, eyes closed, listened to the cat on stage blow. Allen grabbed a chair and leaned back against the grimy wall and closed his eyes. No one bugged him. No one demanded that he order something or get out. Relaxed, at peace, centered, Allen had the first vision.

He was somewhere else. He was like *somewhere else*. The sun was too small in the sky and the sky was too blue. Red sand whispered over the barren ground toward the hills as dark as twilight. The air smelled sharp and peppery; he could almost taste it. There was a light sound, music maybe or just his soul singing. He was lost but like it didn't make any difference because he was with-it. He tried to pick up on where he was but there weren't any roads or signs or anything. He started walking toward the hills and after a while he came to a canal. He knelt and drank because he was thirsty, and the water fizzed and tasted sweet and like cool. A gentle wind soothed him. He saw a strange boat far away on the canal, a boat with a sail made of spiderwebs, a delicate green fluted boat that glided nearer, and as it came nearer it like whispered real gone poetry to him, blowing so true that Allen dug it: this was no place on Earth. This was that weird planet so many flipped-out chicks claim they come from.

When the slight ghost of a boat came to where Allen was standing, a cooled-out voice spoke to him. Allen woke up startled, in this jazz joint. On the narrow stage some square creep was pretending he knew one end of his sax from the other. He was playing the kind of stuff you'd expect from some guy working a gig at Nathan's Coney Island, you dig? Allen was completely drugg but he remembered the vision.

Jack and Neal arrived the same day, touched base at the corner of St. Claude and Elysian Fields like kids in a playground game, and then immediately split town again in a freight car that was taking them to someplace like Memphis or Port Arthur. When they got there they jumped out and found a ride and came back to New Orleans again. They had their vision huddled in the back of the watermelon shed in the French Market, with the old Negro men sitting around them talking softly and laughing. Jack and Neal saw the twin moons rising over the dusky hills, and a brittle white city of fragile towers and rainbow portals where the canal turned westward toward the weary sun. Urgent voices husky with love led them across the warm sand, and they stopped to eat fruit the color of copper pennies and sweet as morning. The voices murmured and Jack and Neal said like nothing, there was nothing to say and nothing to do but follow. They came to the hills but they did not know how to go on. They awoke, and the old men were still telling stories as ancient as themselves, and the watermelons were piled higher than a man's head, and Jack and Neal shivered when they remembered what they had lost.

Lawrence split his bookstore in San Francisco and came to New Orleans and had his vision leaning against a whitewashed tomb in St. Louis Cemetery #2. He awoke cold and frightened and like desperate for what he had glimpsed.

Denise arrived in New Orleans and sat at the foot of the levee and watched the pushboats shoving barges against the Mississippi, and dreamed of great sandships crossing the rust deserts of another world. She dug the voices and the music bit, she tasted the wind and the sweet fruit, and she awoke to find a cat blowing a Dixieland horn and a kid tap-dancing for nickels.

William knew New Orleans and had been in New Orleans and had lived there, so when he arrived like he wasn't too surprised until he had a vision of golden roses and silver tears, of stones that murmured and clouds that brought sadness instead of rain. He awoke to find a New Orleans that swung different than it ever had before.

And Norman came to New Orleans too, because everybody else was cutting out for there and because he was frantic to be part of this scene, and he felt that if he told everybody he was hip loud enough and often enough somebody would believe him. He never had a vision, though.

Jack and Neal's story:

Later much later than five o'clock in the morning Neal and I are falling out by the river flowing from all the great states up north that like spill and vomit themselves body and soul into the water and I'm digging it slip by in the dawn with the sun coming up as I'm telling myself in the southwest—we all learned as bright and eager kids that the sun around which we whirl in our beat eternal dance stands in the middle and the Earth itself comes up in the morning—I come up in the morning and I've never known a chick yet who didn't like mutter something and roll over and leave me wondering why the sun is coming up in the southwest which it looks like it's doing because upriver is north and downriver is south and I forgot that the goddamn river curves around this crazy city like crazy first one way then the other so you never know which direction you're facing and upriver and downriver don't mean a goddamn thing—America is having this problem every morning and like nobody in California cares all they care about is their surf which comes in straight and true and full of girls and in New York they don't care that the sun is coming up in the southwest because behind all the nowhere skyscrapers they don't know that the sun is even up yet until two in the afternoon and by that time it doesn't make a hell of a lot of difference where it came from—Denise is with us since we met last night under the sprawling live oaks of New Orleans all live oaks sprawl just like chestnut trees spread as in "Under the spreading chestnut tree" thus also the like sprawling live oaks of Audubon Park someday we'll teach the oaks to spread too and then the park will be more intimate—squirrels hopped across the grass like stones skipping across this river except like they don't have stones here all they have are little white shells which are useless for skipping I know I've tried—Lawrence is sitting behind us reciting his goddamn poem again I wish he'd write another one we're all bored as hell with it but it made him famous and he figures how many poems did Homer write—two, right and Lawrence has like no pretensions to being as famous as Homer so he'll stop with one—William is getting high on the simple natural things the sun the river the floating logs the graceful ferryboats the cries of the gulls the tea he scored from some motorcycle brute—Allen walks up and sounds us what we're doing, man, what we're doing is digging the goddamn Mississippi River reflecting the goddamn sun rising in the southwest goddamn it—Allen thinks he's goddamn Walt Whitman and he wants to know what we're doing he's munching a goddamn doughnut and he's got powdered sugar all over his beard and his pants and Walt Whitman would never bug us what we're doing we're cheering the birds Allen we're digging the bugs sucking blood out of our arms what the hell does it look like— Neal comes over carrying a watermelon and nothing to cut it up with—What do the Negro kids do with them Allen asks and Denise sighs and says like They cut them up—by now the sun is high and it's daytime and we want to start getting with what we're supposed to be doing here but the river just keeps rolling like in the funky old song it really does and Neal says he's going to sit there until he sees the whole show so we cut out and leave him but then we run into Norman and that like kisses off the morning—Neal comes after us and sees Norman and says he wishes he'd stayed by the river where there were only rats but I say like we're all here for some reason—this goes down cool and there is general agreement.

Norman's story:

It was while I was listening to the radio, some station playing a recording of Sonny Rollins. I was eating oysters in a place on Iberville Street with white tiles on the floor and a long wooden counter. I was standing against the counter eating big, salty oysters. The radio was playing and I recognized that tenor sax. Then suddenly I wasn't leaning against the counter any longer. I was kneeling on a rocky hillside, and the wind was cold and the sun pale above me. I stood up and looked around. I didn't know where I was or how I had come there.

I saw a chick walking along a path not far away. I called to her. "Hello," I said.

The chick stopped and looked at me. She didn't say anything. She was tall and slender, dressed in a kind of free and unself-conscious way. She had huge, beautiful eyes and a wide mouth. It was a sensuous mouth, but I knew that it could also be cruel as well as afraid. She looked depressed. Her hair was pale gold and long, her skin as pale as the blossom of a magnolia, her eyes—they were green, not hazel eyes but the green of summer grass. "Hello," she said at last. Then she looked away from me.

"Hello," I said when I had walked nearer. "My name is Norman. Where am I?"

She made an odd little gesture. "This is . . . here," she said. "Mars."

"Oh," I said, "that explains it. I'm from Earth. The third planet. My name is Norman and I've written a very successful novel and many of the leading pseudo-intellectuals seem to believe that single-handedly I will lead American fiction out of the sterility and emptiness of the postwar period. I was eating oysters in a place in New Orleans and now I'm on Mars. I have my failings, I suppose, and my successes, but none of that explains why I've made this journey or how. None of that matters. The how and the why don't matter. All that matters is that I'm here. With you, on Mars."

She looked up at me. "I know all of this," she said. "I knew you would say just those words."

"How? How did you know?"

She gave me a crooked smile. "Aren't you ever lonely, Norman?" she asked. Suddenly she seemed cheap and gaudy.

"It would be better if I were a movie producer, wouldn't it?" I asked. I wanted to wound her, to see her flinch. "Or a well-known musician."

"It really doesn't make any difference," she said. She tossed her blonde hair over her shoulder and looked away, toward the empty red dust horizon.

"Isn't it enough that I've come? Isn't it enough that I'm the greatest novelist of my generation?"

She turned toward me again. Her green eyes were filled with intense pain. "We had novelists here too, once."

"What happened to them?"

She shrugged. "They all died," she said. I wanted a cigarette.

That was Norman's story. It wasn't until we all got to Mars that we found out that it wasn't true, that he'd been like faking it. That didn't wig me out; I've had my suspicions about Norman ever since I dug that like he couldn't tell the difference between Gerry Mulligan and Paul Desmond, and they don't even blow the same horn. Sometimes Norman's like nowhere, man.

The visions ended. Nobody had another vision, although Norman claimed that he had like dreamed about this groovy place where academic honors grew on trees and the reviewers who said they hated your stuff were hunted down like dogs. Norman followed us around New Orleans but nobody paid any more attention to him; that would have been like encouraging him and it was too hot for that. We had sausage gumbo for lunch except for me, I had a cheeseburger on French bread and a cold bottle of Dixie, and that may have been one of the reasons I could not make the Martian scene with the others. Maybe I was not with-it. Maybe I was not real solid. I should have had the gumbo instead of something as hopelessly square as a cheeseburger. Maybe now I'd be roaming the brittle cities of Mars, clothed in white samite the way all alien geniuses are supposed to be. Look at me, I'm wearing these beat jeans and a shirt from Penney's and holed up in a glacial pad three blocks off Myrtle Avenue. For the want of a bowl of gumbo immortality was lost.

So instead of visions we soon cut out for the real thing, the true Mars of our dreams, through this frantic pink doorway in the air. It appeared out of like nowhere, on a streetcar about two o'clock in the morning. We were the only passengers and the conductor and the motorman never dug it. Denise saw it first and she nudged me and I nudged Jack and pretty soon like everybody had been nudged, even Norman. I picked up on what it was right off and so did everybody else except Norman, but Allen grabbed him by the arm and kicked his butt through the pretty pink cloud. Says Norman, as he landed on his face in the red sand, Dig it, Arizona.

We all looked up toward heaven, needing like strength to deal with this nebbish, and Lawrence said Man, we're here for sure this time and Norman just stared at him, still thinking he was like in the Painted Desert or something and flipping over *that* miracle.

Neal informed him that there were like two moons in the sky and Norman said I can dig that. Refraction.

Nobody ever again tried to explain a thing to him.

We had split the world of our birth and now we dug that Mars had welcomed us in all her dry and red and sandy splendor. I took a deep breath and the air was just as crazy as in the vision. We looked around, expecting that somebody would be like waiting to lay his bit on us, we were there for some reason. We waited for a long time and the moons just slid across the sky like some gone cat and his old lady on their way to meet the man. It got cold. This is Mars? I thought, like if it was, where was the music and the poetry? What was the point, man? So far this interplanetary scene was nowhere, and I hoped each minute that I'd wake up in some far far better place, like the Hotsy Totsy on Bourbon Street which wasn't nearly so ethereal but a lot warmer and they had naked women on stage too.

"Peace, brothers," said a booming voice all around us.

William like wigged out, too frantic already without his tea to hide behind. The rest of us kind of flipped too.

And then this far-out couple of Martians appeared, out of a cloud or something. They were tall and thin and dressed in white with big golden eyes and no hair and ears like the curled leaves of a plastic philodendron, shiny and covered with dust. "I bring you glad tidings," said the second Martian.

Denise thought that was funny and when Allen asked her what she was laughing at she said the Martian sounded like an angel of the Lord and we all thought that was like pretty funny too except Norman who for a minute thought it might be true. The Martians waited until we got over our laughing.

"Like you are the real soul of Earth," said the first one. "Like you embrace the truth and heart and sinews of your people." We couldn't argue with that.

"Lay some truth on us," said the second Martian.

So Allen, high on the two moons or the golden eyes or pills, came out with this:

> Naked souls, sensitive as clams from their shells untimely
>   ripp'd,
> dragged through caressing mists of wonder and out-
>   rage to some empty giant vacant lot of the gods
> questioning their sanity and their visions, violated fu-
>   rious willing to understand willing to get with-it
> not loving not caring not hating but sharing only the holy
>   urge to report, having found the human condition in
>   the bus station
> in a locker in a zipper bag in a cellophane bag filled
>   with some anonymous substance, and slammed the
>   locker door shut again
> desperate not for knowledge but for feelings, and denied
>   forever the blessing they seek by their own turbulent
>   brains
> who bore the burden of their dreams until their dreams
>   could bear them
> who stepped lightly over the threshold of promises and
>   found, instead of demons, angels with golden eyes and
>   empty hearts
> asking nothing of the universe except its answers its
>   secrets and every one of its treasures, sure that there
>   must be new kicks somewhere
> alone except for each other, with no sure idea of what
>   good each other might be except for company, and in
>   no need of company
> except for the company of each other

> *forsaking Paterson Tangier Frisco New York for a whole*
> *world reminding them of a mighty Asbury Park without*
> *the boardwalk*
> *without the arcades and without the ocean, an Asbury*
> *Park of the mind*
> *forsaking Buddha Christ Jehovah for God knows what*
> *new gods and what new temples and what new pro-*
> *hibitions—*

The first Martian raised his hand and said, "Wow, man, we're impressed, but we'll dig the rest of it some other time. Later."

Allen tried to tell him that he wasn't finished yet, that the groovy ad lib poem had at least another hundred lines to go, he could feel it, he knew he could blow like that for a couple of hours but the Martians looked drugg by the whole idea.

Denise gave them a swinging poem about suicide and advertising and Lawrence copped out with a rhymed couplet and I couldn't think of anything and they didn't even bother to ask Norman. They had the same opinion of Norman that we did. Jack and Neal put their heads together and spun this far-out narrative that none of us could figure, about steam locomotives and crumbling cathedrals in the sky and shock therapy and the clean cool sun of Mars as bright as brass. The Martians seemed to dig it, but I couldn't make sense out of any three words in a row. And William added a long and rambling history of the use of paregoric in treating loneliness boredom and perversion.

"Listen up," said the first Martian. "We have like brought you here because we are a bugged race."

"We are wasted and strung out," said the second Martian, "and there's no hope of getting straight."

Denise sounded them about the poetry and music and singing and unearthly beauty, man, and they told us that all of that was in the past, long dead, a memory scene and nothing more. It brought us down to hear them talking like that. Jack said he didn't know we were getting an unfurnished planet.

"We're hip," said the first Martian. He let go a silvery tear from his golden eye. "All we got left here are a few funky pillars and the dry ditches where the fizzy water used to be."

"We thought your energy and creative spirit would like turn on this dying place," said the second Martian. "We brought you here to save the gig."

William didn't dig the idea at all. He said it was a shuck, and that we'd been busted for some eternal stretch in the interplanetary slammer.

The first Martian smiled. "Cool yourselves out," he said, "and dig our bit. Fall in with us for a few years and we can turn this place into a swinging spot again. We can make like these funky copies of you so your landlords and old ladies and your various other connections won't miss you. The copies won't be able to blow a lick, not the way you can, because like that's something we can't lay on them. That's why you're here in the first place. They'll just hold your place in line at the Unemployment Office. Then in twenty-five years we'll send you back to Earth, and you won't be a day older and you'll have such far-out wisdom that every hipster and square in the world will dig what you're sending."

William wanted to know if he could keep his copy of himself when he came home, but the second Martian said, "No, like we may be pretty with-it, but we're not *that* weird." William shrugged like he wasn't too disappointed.

"So," said the first Martian, "what's the word, hummingbird?"

Lawrence said Crazy, because not many people dig us now. We could get with these cats, and swing with them until we put the color back in their pillars and the fluted boats and whispering stones.

Neal was the next to agree and Jack agreed and Denise and Allen and William and Lawrence and Norman and me. Groovy, we said, let's go blow some jazzy verse.

The first Martian looked sad, you dig, and held up his hands. "All but those two," he said, and he pointed at Norman and me.

"They are not hip, they are not cool," said the second Martian.

"They do not share the real existential malaise," said the first.

"They do not feel the crazy pulse of life, they do not dig the goneness of the void."

"They do not relate to the oneness of the worlds."

"They are into the whole ego bit, man."

"They are trying to hustle us for fame. They are squares wearing beards and talking hip, but they are a drag, man."

I thought Norman was going to flip his wig but I could handle it. Doing the Mars bit wasn't such a turn-on for me, and these Martian cats had me bugged from in front. I figured we could go back and do our writing thing for the folks at home for twenty-five years, and with Allen and Jack and Neal and Denise and Lawrence and William like out of the way we could become the boss hipsters, the voices of our generation. I laid that on Norman but he could never get with being left out of anything. The Martians escorted us back through the pink cloud without another word, and we were back on Earth just like that, back in New York in the middle of winter. Where was New Orleans, where was June? I don't know. We were standing on the corner of MacDougal and W. 3rd, and Norman's running after the fading cloud like Dorothy yelling at the Wizard in the balloon Take me with you! and I'm like wigging out at the poor bastard. Shane, I yelled, Come back Shane! It was just too weird.

Norman was sure that it was all because of the filthy word he introduced into modern literature and he promised he'd never do it again but the Martians were gone and we never heard from them again. So here we are, like stuck here on Earth while the rest of those cats are blowing sweetly among the sapphire spires and spider ships of Mars, beneath those two gone moons, grooving on ancient jazz and forgetting all about Eisenhower and Nkrumah and Sick Humor and the Champagne Lady and Brigitte Bardot and *Peyton Place*. Norman can like cool out and become the savior of the American novel in the latter half of the twentieth century, and I will end up the gonest poet and music critic of the *Village Voice* or something, and who needs Mars? In twenty-five years—1984, crazy, no?— Jack and Neal and those other cats are going to show up in their white robes and lyres and want their old jobs back, like swinging with the Martians made them farther out than anybody else and groovier and too with-it for words. We got twenty-five years to get ready for them and if they want to make the big scene then they're going to have to climb over Norman and me first. We'll see who's beat and who's hip and who's not.

As for the copies of Jack and Neal and Denise and William and Lawrence and Allen, the Martian cats were right about them: like they can't make a single line of poetry or one with-it image. So if you don't hear much from Jack and Neal and the rest between now and 1984, you know why. But like the fake Denise and the fake Lawrence are crazy canasta sharks, and sometimes Norman and I will invite them over for a night at a quarter of a cent a point. And the fake William turns out this wild avocado dip. So Norman and I got a lock on the prose and poetry industry at the moment, and we aim to keep it like that. If you want to know what happens, you just fall in come 1984. It's going to be War of the Worlds time. You dig?

GREEN MARS

Kim Stanley Robinson

"Green Mars" was purchased by Shawna McCarthy and appeared in the September, 1985, issue of IAsfm, with a cover and illustration by J. K. Potter. One of the classic Mars stories of the eighties—perhaps the classic Mars story—it was the first story I thought of when I began to assemble this anthology, and clearly the one story that had to be in the book. You'll soon see why, as Robinson sweeps us along with him to a vividly realized future Mars, for an exciting and evocative story about a band of men and women determined to climb the tallest mountain in the Solar System—Olympus Mons.

Kim Stanley Robinson sold his first story in 1976, and he quickly established himself as one of the most respected and critically acclaimed writers of his generation. His story "Black Air" won the World Fantasy Award in 1984, and his novella "The Blind Geometer," an IAsfm story, won the Nebula Award in 1987. His excellent novel The Wild Shore *was published in 1984 as the first title in the resurrected Ace Special line, and was one of the most critically acclaimed novels of the year. Other Robinson books include the novels* Icehenge, The Memory of Whiteness, *and* The Gold Coast, *and the landmark collec-*

tion, The Planet on the Table. *His most recent books are* Escape from Kathmandu, *a new collection, and a new novel,* The Pacific Shore. *Upcoming is a trilogy of novels set on a future Mars. Many Robinson stories have appeared in* IAsfm *over the last few years, and we're pleased to be able to say that we have several more in inventory. Robinson and his wife, Lisa, are back in the United States again after several years in Switzerland, and have just added a new baby son to their family.*

Olympus Mons is the tallest mountain in the solar system. It is a broad shield volcano, six hundred kilometers in diameter and twenty-seven kilometers high. Its average slope angles only five degrees above the horizontal, but the circumference of the lava shield is a nearly continuous escarpment, a roughly circular cliff that drops six kilometers to the surrounding forests. The tallest and steepest sections of this encircling escarpment stand near South Buttress, a massive prominence which juts out and divides the south and south-east curves of the cliff (on the map, it's at 15 degrees North, 132 degrees West). There, under the east flank of South Buttress, one can stand in the rocky upper edge of the Tharsis forest, and look up at a cliff that is twenty-two thousand feet tall.

Seven times taller than El Capitan, three times as tall as Everest's south-west face, twice as tall as Dhaulagiri wall: four miles of cliff, blocking out the western sky. Can you imagine it? (It's hard.)

"I can't get a sense of the scale!" the Terran, Arthur Sternbach, shouts, hopping up and down.

Dougal Burke, looking up through binoculars, says, "There's quite a bit of foreshortening from here."

"No, no. That's not it."

• • •

The climbing party has arrived in a caravan of seven field-cars. Big green bodies, clear bubbles covering the passenger compartments, fat field tires with their exaggerated treads, chewing dust into the wind: the cars' drivers have parked the cars in a rough circle, and they sit in the middle of a rocky meadow like a big necklace of paste emeralds.

This battered meadow, with its little stands of bristlecone pine and noctis juniper, is the traditional base camp for South Buttress climbs. Around the cars are treadmarks, wind-walls made of stacked rock, half-filled latrine trenches, cairn-covered trash dumps, and discarded equipment. As the members of the expedition wander around the camp, stretching and talking, they inspect some of these artifacts. Marie Whillans picks up two Ultralite oxygen cylinders stamped with letters that identify them as part of an expedition she climbed with more than a century ago. Grinning, she holds them overhead and shakes them at the cliff, beats them together. "Home again!" *Ping! Ping! Ping!*

One last field-car trundles into the meadow, and the expedition members already in the camp gather around it as it rolls to a halt. Two men get out of the car. They are greeted enthusiastically: "Stephan's here! Roger's here!"

But Roger Clayborne is in a bad mood. It has been a long trip for him. It began in Burroughs six days ago, when he left his offices at the Government House for the last time. Twenty-seven years of work as Minister of the Interior came to an end as he walked out the tall doors of Government House, down the broad marble steps and onto the trolley that would take him to his flat. Riding along with his face in the warm wind, Roger looked out at the tree-filled capital city he had rarely left during his stint in the government, and it struck him that it had been twenty-seven years of continuous defeat. Too many opponents, too many compromises, until the last unacceptable compromise arrived, and he found himself riding out of the city with Stephan, into the countryside he had avoided for twenty-seven years, over rolling hills covered by grasses and studded by stands of walnut, aspen, oak, maple, eucalyptus, pine: every leaf and every blade of grass a sign of his defeat. And Stephan wasn't much help; though a conservationist like Roger, he had been a member of the Greens for years. "That's where the real work can be done," he insisted as he lectured Roger and neglected his driving. Roger, who liked Stephan well enough, pretended his agreement and stared out his window. He would have preferred Stephan's company in smaller doses—say a lunch, or a game of batball. But on they drove along the wide gravel highway, over the windblown steppes of the Tharsis bulge, past the farms and towns in Noctis Labyrinthus, down into the forests of east Tharsis, until Roger fell prey to that feeling one gets near the end of a long journey, that all his life had been part of this trip, that the traveling would never end this side of the grave, that he was doomed to wander over the scenes of all his defeats and failures endlessly, and never come to any place that did not include them all, right in the rearview mirror. It was a long drive.

For—and this was the worst of it—he remembered everything.

Now he steps from the car door to the rocky soil of base camp. A late addition to the climb (Stephan invited him along when he learned of the resignation), he is introduced to the other climbers, and he musters the cordial persona built over many years in office. "Hans!" he says as he sees the familiar smiling face of the areologist Hans Boethe. "Good to see you. I didn't know you were a climber."

"Not one like you, Roger, but I've done my share in Marineris."

"So"—Roger gestures west—"are you going to find the explanation for the escarpment?"

"I already know it," Hans declares, and the others laugh. "But if we find any contributing evidence . . ."

A tall rangy woman with leathery cheeks and light brown eyes appears at the edge of the group. Stephan quickly introduces her. "Roger, this is our expedition leader, Eileen Monday."

"We've met before," she says quickly as she shakes his hand. She looks down and smiles an embarrassed smile. "A long time ago, when you were a canyon guide."

The name, the voice; the past stirs, quick images appear in his mind's eye, and Roger's uncanny memory calls back a hike—(he once guided treks through the fossae canyon to the north)—a *romance*, yes, with a leggy girl: Eileen Monday, standing now before him. They were lovers for quite some time, he recalls; she a student in Burroughs, a city girl, and he—off in the back country. It hadn't lasted. But that was over two hundred years ago! A spark of hope strikes in him—"You *remember*?" he says.

"I'm afraid not." Wrinkles fan away under her eyes as she squints, smiles the embarrassed smile. "But when Stephan told me you'd be joining us—well—you're known to have a complete memory, and I felt I should check. Maybe that means I did remember something. Because I went through my old journals and found references to you. I only started writing the journals in my eighties, so the references aren't very clear. But I know we met, even if I can't say I remember it." She looks up, shrugs.

It is a common enough situation for Roger. His "total recall" (it is nothing of the sort, of course) encompasses most of his three hundred years, and he is constantly meeting and remembering people who do not recall him. Most find it interesting, some unnerving; this Eileen's sunchapped cheeks are a bit flushed; she seems both embarrassed and perhaps a bit amused. "You'll have to tell me about it," she says with a laugh.

Roger isn't in the mood to amuse people. "We were about twenty-five."

Her mouth forms a whistle. "You really do remember everything."

Roger shakes his head; the chill in the shadowed air fills him, the momentary thrill of recognition and recall dissipates. It's been a very long trip.

"And we were . . . ?" she prods.

"We were friends," Roger says, with just the twist on *friends* to leave her wondering. It is disheartening, this tendency of people to forget; his unusual facility makes him a bit of a freak, a voice from another time. Perhaps his conservation efforts grow out of this retention of the past; he still knows what the planet was like, back there in the beginning. When he's feeling low he tends to blame his generation's forgetfulness on their lack of vigilance, and he is often, as he is now, a bit lonely.

Eileen has her head crooked, wondering what he means.

"Come on, Mr. Memory," Stephan cries to him. "Let's

eat! I'm starving, and it's freezing out here.''

"It'll get colder," Roger says. He shrugs at Eileen, follows Stephan.

In the bright lamplight of the largest base camp tent the chattering faces gleam. Roger sips at a bowl of hot stew. Quickly the remaining introductions are made. Stephan, Hans, and Eileen are familiar to him, as is Dr. Frances Fitzhugh. The lead climbers are Dougal Burke and Marie Whillans, current stars of New Scotland's climbing school; he's heard of both of them. They are surrounded in their corner by four younger colleagues of Eileen's, climbing guides hired by Stephan to be their porters: "We're the Sherpas," Ivan Vivanov says to Roger cheerfully, and introduces Ginger, Sheila, and Hannah. The young guides appear not to mind their supporting role in the expedition; in a party of this size there will be plenty of climbing for all. The group is rounded off by Arthur Sternbach, an American climber visiting Hans Boethe. When the introductions are done they all circle the room like people at any cocktail party anywhere. Roger works on his stew and regrets his decision to join the climb. He forgot (sort of) how intensely social big climbs must be. Too many years of solo bouldering, in the rock valleys north of Burroughs. That was what he had been looking for, he realizes; an endless solo rockclimb, up and out of the world.

Stephan asks Eileen about the climb and she carefully includes Roger in her audience. "We're going to start up the Great Gully, which is the standard route for the first thousand meters of the face. Then, where the first ascent followed the Nansen Ridge up to the left of the gully, we're planning to go right. Dougal and Marie have seen a line in the aerial photos that they think will go, and that will give us something new to try. So we'll have a new route most of the way. And we'll be the smallest party ever to climb the scarp in the South Buttress area.''

"You're kidding!" Arthur Sternbach cries.

Eileen smiles briefly. "Because of the party size, we'll be carrying as little oxygen as possible, for use in the last few thousand meters.''

"And if we climb it?" Roger asks.

"There's a cache for us when we top out—we'll change

equipment there, and stroll on up to the caldera rim. That part will be easy.''

"I don't see why we even bother with that part," Marie interjects.

"It's the easiest way down. Besides, some of us want to see the top of Olympus Mons," Eileen replies mildly.

"It's just a big hill," says Marie.

Later Roger leaves the tent with Arthur and Hans, Dougal and Marie. Everyone will spend one last night of comfort in the cars. Roger trails the others, staring up at the escarpment. The sky above it is still a rich twilight purple. The huge bulk of the wall is scarred by the black line of the Great Gully, a deep vertical crack just visible in the gloomy air. Above it, a blank face. Trees rustle in the wind; the dark meadow looks wild.

"I can't believe how tall it is!" Arthur is exclaiming for the third time. He laughs out loud. "It's just unbelievable!"

"From this vantage," Hans says, "the top is over seventy degrees above our real horizon."

"You're kidding! I can't believe it!" And Arthur falls into a fit of helpless giggling. The Martians following Hans and his friend watch with amused reserve. Arthur is quite a bit shorter than the rest of them, and suddenly to Roger he seems like a child caught after breaking into the liquor cabinet. Roger pauses to allow the others to walk on.

The big tent glows like a dim lamp, luminous yellow in the dark. The cliff-face is black and still. From the forest comes a weird yipping yodel. Some sort of mutant wolves, no doubt. Roger shakes his head. Long ago any landscape exhilarated him; he was in love with the planet. Now the immense cliff seems to hang over him like his life, his past, obliterating the sky, blocking off any progress westward. The depression he feels is so crushing that he almost sits on the meadow grass, to plunge his face in his hands; but others will be leaving the tent. Again, that mournful yowling: the planet, crying out, Mars is gone! Mars is gone! Ow-ooooooooo! Homeless, the old man goes to sleep in a car.

But as always, insomnia takes its share of the night. Roger lies in the narrow bed, his body relaxed, his consciousness bouncing helplessly through scenes from his life. Insomnia, memory:

some of his doctors have told him there is a correlation between the two. Certainly for him the hours of insomniac awareness and half-sleep are memory's playground, and no matter what he does to fill the time between lying down and falling asleep (like reading to exhaustion, or scratching notes), tyrannical memory will have its hour.

This night he remembers all the nights in Burroughs. All the opponents, all the compromises. The Chairman handing him the order to dam and flood Coprates Chasma, with his little smile and flourish, the touch of hidden sadism. The open dislike from Noyova, that evening years before, after the Chairman's appointments: "The Reds are finished, Clayborne. You shouldn't be holding office—you are the leader of a dead party." Looking at the Chairman's dam construction bill and thinking of Coprates the way it had been in the previous century, when he had explored it, it occurred to him that ninety percent of what he had done in office, he did to stay in a position to be able to do anything. That was what it meant to work in government. Or was it a higher percentage? What had he really done to preserve the planet? Certain bills balked before they began, certain development projects delayed; all he had done was resist the doings of others. Without much success. And it could even be said that walking out on the Chairman and his "coalition" cabinet was only another gesture, another defeat.

He recalls his first day in office. A morning on the polar plains. A day in Burroughs, in the park. In the Cabinet office, arguing with Novoyov. And on it will go, for another hour or more, scene after scene until the memories become fragmented and dreamlike, spliced together surrealistically, stepping outside the realm of memory into sleep.

There are topographies of the spirit, and this is one of them.

Dawn on Mars. First the plum sky, punctuated by a diamond pattern of four dawn mirrors that orbit overhead and direct a little more of Sol's light to the planet. Flocks of black choughs caw sleepily as they flap and glide out over the talus slope to begin the day's hunt for food. Snow pigeons coo in the branches of a grove of tawny birch. Up in the talus, a clatter of rocks; three Dall sheep are looking surprised to see the base camp meadow occupied. Sparrows flit overhead.

Roger, up early with a headache, observes all the stirring wildlife indifferently. He hikes up into the broken rock of the talus to get clear of it. The upper rim of the escarpment is struck by the light of the rising sun, and now there is a strip of ruddy gold overhead, bathing all the shadowed slope below with reflected sunlight. The dawn mirrors look dim in the clear violet sky. Colors appear in the tufts of flowers scattered through the rock, and the green juniper needles glow. The band of lit cliff quickly grows; even in full light the upper slopes look sheer and blank. But that is the effect of distance and foreshortening. Lower on the face, crack systems look like brown rain stains, and the wall is rough-looking, a good sign. The upper slopes, when they get high enough, will reveal their own irregularities.

Dougal hikes out of the rock field, ending some dawn trek of his own. He nods to Roger. "Not started yet, are we?" His English is accented with a distinctly Scottish intonation.

In fact they are. Eileen and Marie and Ivan have gotten the first packs out of the cars, and when Roger and Dougal return they are distributing them. The meadow becomes noisier as the long equipment sorting ends and they get ready to take off. The packs are heavy, and the Sherpas groan and joke when they lift theirs. Arthur can't help laughing at the sight of them. "On Earth you couldn't even *move* a pack that size," he exclaims, nudging one of the oversized bags with a foot. "How do you balance with one of these on?"

"You'll find out," Hans tells him cheerfully.

Arthur finds that balancing the mass of his pack in Martian gravity is difficult. The pack is almost perfectly cylindrical, a big green tube that extends from the bottom of his butt to just over his head; with it on his back he looks like a tall green snail. He exclaims at its lightness relative to its size, but as they hike through the talus its mass swings him around much more than he is prepared for. "Whoah! Look out there! Sorry!" Roger nods and wipes sweat from his eye. He sees that the first day is one long lesson in balance for Arthur, as they wind their way up the irregular slope through the forest of house-sized boulders.

Previous parties have left a trail with rock ducks and blazes chopped onto boulder faces, and they follow it wherever they can find it. The ascent is tedious; although this is one of the smaller fans of broken rock at the bottom of the escarpment (in some areas mass wasting has collapsed the entire cliff into talus), it will still take them all of a very long day to wind their way through the giant rockpile to the bottom of the wall proper, some seven hundred meters above base camp.

At first Roger approves of the hike through the jumbled field of house-sized boulders. "The Khumbu Rockfall," Ivan calls out, getting into his Sherpa persona as they pass under a big stone serrac. But unlike the Khumbu Icefall below the fabled Everest, this chaotic terrain is relatively stable; the overhangs won't fall on them, and there are few hidden crevasses to fall into. No, it is just a rockfield, and Roger likes it. Still, on the way they pass little pockets of chir pine and juniper, and ahead of Roger, Hans apparently feels obliged to identify every flower to Arthur. "There's aconite, and those are anemones, and that's a kind of iris, and those are gentians, and those are primulas. . . ." Arthur stops to point. "What the hell is that!"

Staring down at them from a flat-topped boulder is a small furry mammal. "It's a dune dog," Hans says proudly. "They've clipped some marmot and Weddell seal genes onto what is basically a wolverine."

"You're kidding! It looks like a miniature polar bear."

Behind them Roger shakes his head, kicks idly at a stand of tundra cactus. It is flowering; the six-month Martian spring is beginning. Syrtis grass tufting in every wet sandy flat. Little biology experiments, everywhere you look; the whole planet one big laboratory. Roger sighs. Arthur tries to pick one of each variety of flower, making a bouquet suitable for a state funeral, but after too many falls he gives up, and lets the colorful bundle hang from his hand. Late in the day they reach the bottom of the wall. The whole world is in shadow, while the clear sky overhead is still a bright lavender. Looking up they cannot see the top of the escarpment any more; they will not see it again unless their climb succeeds.

Camp One is a broad, flat circle of sand, surrounded by boulders that were once part of the face, and set under a slight overhang formed by the sheer rampart of basalt that stands to the right side of the Great Gully. Protected from rockfall, roomy and comfortable to lie on, Camp One is perfect for a big lower camp, and it has been used before; between the rocks they find pitons, oxygen cylinders, buried latrines overgrown with bright green moss.

The next day they wind their way back down through the talus to Base Camp—all but Dougal and Marie, who take the day to look at the routes leading out of Camp One. For the rest of them, it's off before dawn, and down through the talus at nearly a running pace; a quick reloading; and back up in a race to reach Camp One again before nightfall. Every one of the next four days will be spent in the same way, and the Sherpas will continue for three more days after that, threading the same trail through the boulders, until all the equipment has been lugged up to Camp One.

In the same way that a tongue will go to a sore tooth over and over, Roger finds himself following Hans and Arthur to hear the areologist's explanations. He has realized, to his chagrin, that he is nearly as ignorant about what lives on Mars as Arthur is.

"See the blood pheasant?"

"No."

"Over there. The head tuft is black. Pretty well camouflaged."

"You're kidding. Why, there it is!"

"They like these rocks. Blood pheasants, redstarts, accentors—more of them here than we ever see."

Later: "Look there!"

"Where?"

Roger finds himself peering in the direction Hans has pointed.

"On the tall rock, see? The killer rabbit, they call it. A joke."

"Oh, a joke," Arthur says carefully. Roger makes a revision in his estimation of the Terran's subtlety. "A rabbit with fangs?"

"Not exactly. Actually there's very little hare in it—more lemming and pika, but with some important traits of the lynx added. A very successful creature. Some of Harry Whitebook's work. He's *very* good."

"So some of your biological designers become famous?"

"Oh yes. Very much so. Whitebook is one of the best of the mammal designers. And we seem to have a special love for mammals, don't we?"

"I know I do." Several puffing steps up waist-high blocks. "I just don't understand how they can survive the cold!"

"Well, it's not that cold down here, of course. This is the top of the alpine zone, in effect. The adaptations for cold are usually taken directly from arctic and antarctic creatures. Many seals can cut the circulation to their extremities when necessary to preserve heat. And they have a sort of anti-freeze in their blood—a glycoprotein that binds to the surface of ice crystals and stops their growth—stops the accumulation of salts. Wonderful stuff. Some of these mammals can freeze limbs and thaw them without damage to the flesh."

"You're kidding," Roger whispers as he hikes.

"You're kidding!"

"And these adaptations are part of most Martian mammals. Look! There's a little foxbear! That's Whitebook again."

Roger stops following them. No more Mars.

Black night. The six big box tents of Camp One glow like a string of lamps at the foot of the cliff. Roger, out in the rubble relieving himself, looks back at them curiously. It is, he thinks, an odd group. People from all over Mars (and a Terran). Only climbing in common. The lead climbers are funny. Dougal sometimes seems a mute, always watching from a corner, never speaking. A self-enclosed system. Marie speaks for both of them, perhaps. Roger can hear her broad Midlands voice now, hoarse with drink, telling someone how to climb the face. She's happy to be here. Roger? He shakes his head, returns to the tents.

Inside Eileen's tent he finds a heated discussion in progress. Marie Whillans says, "Look, Dougal and I have already gone nearly a thousand meters up these so-called blank slabs. There are cracks all over the place."

"As far as you've gone there are," Eileen says. "But the true slabs are supposed to be above those first cracks. Four hundred meters of smooth rock. We could be stopped outright."

"So we could, but there's got to be *some* cracks. And we

can bolt our way up any really blank sections if we have to. That way we'd have a completely new route.''

Hans Boethe shakes his head. ''Putting bolts in some of this basalt won't be any fun.''

''I hate bolts anyway,'' Eileen says. ''The point is, if we take the Gully up to the first amphitheater, we know we've got a good route to the top, and all the upper pitches will be new.''

Stephan nods, Hans nods, Frances nods. Roger sips a cup of tea and watches with interest. Marie says, ''The *point* is, what kind of climb do we want to have?''

''We want to get to the top,'' Eileen says, glancing at Stephan, who nods. Stephan has paid for most of this expedition, and so in a sense it's his choice.

''Wait a second,'' Marie says sharply, eyeing each of them in turn. ''That's not what it's about. We're not here just to repeat the Gully route, are we?'' Her voice is accusing and no one meets her eye. ''That wasn't what I was told, anyway. I was told we were taking a new route, and that's why I'm here.''

''It will inevitably be a new route,'' Eileen says. ''You know that, Marie. We trend right at the top of the Gully and we're on new ground. We only avoid the blank slabs that flank the Gully to the right!''

''I think we should try those slabs,'' Marie says, ''because Dougal and I have found they'll go.'' She argues for this route, and Eileen listens patiently. Stephan looks worried; Marie is persuasive, and it seems possible that her forceful personality will overwhelm Eileen's, leading them onto a route rumored to be impossible.

But Eileen says, ''Climbing *any* route on this wall with only eleven people will be doing something. Look, we're only talking about the first 1200 meters of the climb. Above that we'll tend to the right whenever possible, and be on new ground above these slabs.''

''I don't believe in the slabs,'' Marie says. And after a few more exchanges: ''Well, that being the case, I don't see why you sent Dougal and me up the slabs these last few days.''

''I didn't send you up,'' Eileen says, a bit exasperated. ''You two choose the leads, you know that. But this is a fundamental choice, and I think the Gully is the opening pitch we came to make. We do want to make the top, you know. Not just of the wall, but the whole mountain.''

After more discussion Marie shrugs. "Okay. You're the boss. But it makes me wonder. Why are we making this climb?"

On the way to his tent Roger remembers the question. Breathing the cold air, he looks around. In Camp One the world seems a place creased and folded: horizontal half stretching away into darkness—back down into the dead past; vertical half stretching up to the stars—into the unknown. Only two tents lit from within now, two soft blobs of yellow in the gloom. Roger stops outside his darkened tent to look at them, feeling they say something to him; the eyes of the mountain, looking. . . . Why is he making this climb?

Up the Great Gully they go. Dougal and Marie lead pitch after pitch up the rough, unstable rock, hammering in pitons and leaving fixed ropes behind. The ropes tend to stay in close to the right wall of the gully, to avoid the falling rock that shoots down it all too frequently. The other climbers follow from pitch to pitch in teams of two and three. As they ascend they can see the four Sherpas, tiny animals winding their way down the talus again.

Roger has been teamed with Hans for the day. They clip themselves onto the fixed rope with jumars, metal clasps that will slide up the rope but not down. They are carrying heavy packs up to Camp 2, and even though the slope of the Gully is only fifty degrees here, and its dark rock knobby and easy to climb, they both find the work hard. The sun is hot and their faces are quickly bathed with sweat.

"I'm not in the best of shape for this," Hans puffs. "It may take me a few days to get my rhythm."

"Don't worry about me," Roger says. "We're going about as fast as I like."

"I wonder how far above Camp 2 is?"

"Not too far. Too many carries to make, without the power reels."

"I look forward to the vertical pitches. If we're going to climb we might as well climb, eh?"

"Especially since the power reels will pull our stuff up."

"Yes." Breathless laugh.

• • •

Steep, deep ravine. Medium gray andesite, an igneous volcanic rock, speckled with crystals of dark minerals, knobbed with hard protrusions. Pitons hammered into small vertical cracks.

Midday they meet with Eileen, Arthur, and Frances, the team above, who are sitting on a narrow ledge in the wall of the Gully, jamming down a quick lunch. The sun is nearly overhead; in an hour they will lose it. Roger and Hans are happy to sit on the ledge. Lunch is lemonade and several handfuls of the trail mix Frances has made. The others discuss the gully and the day's climb, and Roger eats and listens. He becomes aware of Eileen sitting on the ledge beside him. Her feet kick the wall casually, and the quadriceps on the tops of her thighs, big exaggerated muscles, bunch and relax, bunch and relax, stretching the fabric of her climbing pants. She is following Hans's description of the rock and appears not to notice Roger's discreet observation. Could she really *not remember* him? Roger breathes a soundless sigh. It's been a long life. And all his effort—

"Let's get up to Camp 2," Eileen says, looking at him curiously.

Early in the afternoon they find Marie and Dougal on a broad shelf sticking out of the steep slabs to the right of the Great Gully. Here they make Camp 2: four large box tents, made to withstand rockfalls of some severity.

Now the verticality of the escarpment becomes something immediate and tangible. They can only see the wall for a few hundred meters above them; beyond that it is hidden, except up the steep trough in the wall that is the Great Gully, etching the vertical face just next to their shelf. Looking up this giant couloir they can see more of the endless cliff above them, dark and foreboding against the pink sky.

Roger spends an hour of the cold afternoon sitting at the Gully edge of their shelf, looking up. They have a long way to go; his hands in their thick pile mittens are sore, his shoulders and legs tired, his feet cold. He wishes more than anything that he could shake the depression that fills him; but thinking that only makes it worse.

Eileen Monday sits beside him. "So we were friends once, you say."

"Yeah." Roger looks her in the eye. "You don't remember at all?"

"It was a long time ago."

"Yes. I was twenty-six, you were about twenty-three."

"You really remember that long ago?"

"Some of it, yes."

Eileen shakes her head. She has good features, Roger thinks. Fine eyes. "I wish I did. But as I get older my memory gets even worse. Now I think for every year I live I lose at least that much in memories. It's sad. My whole life before I was seventy or eighty—all gone." She sighs. "I know most people are like that, though. You're an exception."

"Some things seem to be stuck in my mind for good," says Roger. He can't believe it isn't true of everyone! But that's what they all say. It makes him melancholy. Why live at all? What's the point? "Have you hit your three hundredth yet?"

"In a few months. But—come on. Tell me about it."

"Well . . . you were a student. Or just finishing school, I can't remember." She smiles. "Anyway, I was guiding groups in hikes through the little canyons north of here, and you were part of a group. We started up a—a little affair, as I recall. And saw each other for a while after we got back. But you were in Burroughs, and I kept guiding tours, and—well, you know. It didn't last."

Eileen smiles again. "So I went on to become a mountain guide—which I've been for as long as I can remember—while you moved to the city and got into politics!" She laughs and Roger smiles wryly. "Obviously we must have impressed each other!"

"Oh yes, yes." Roger laughs shortly. "Searching for each other." He grins lopsidedly, feeling bitter. "Actually, I only got into government about forty years ago. Too late, as it turned out."

Silence for a while. "So that's what's got you down," Eileen says.

"What?"

"The Red Mars party—out of favor."

"Out of existence, you mean."

She considers it. "I never could understand the Red point of view—"

"Few could, apparently."

"—Until I read something in Heidegger, where he makes a distinction between *earth* and *world*. Do you know it?"

"No."

"*Earth* is that blank materiality of nature that exists before us and more or less sets the parameters on what we can do. Sartre called it facticity. *World* then is the human realm, the social and historical dimension that gives earth its meaning."

Roger nods his understanding.

"So—the Reds, as I understood it, were defending earth. Or planet, in this case. Trying to protect the primacy of planet over world—or at least to hold a balance between them."

"Yes," Roger said. "But the world inundated the planet."

"True. But when you look at it that way, you can see what you were trying to do was hopeless. A political party is inevitably part of the world, and everything it does will be worldly. And we only know the materiality of nature through our human senses—so really it is only world that we know directly."

"I'm not sure about that," Roger protested. "I mean, it's logical, and usually I'm sure it's true—but sometimes"—He smacks the rock of their shelf with his mittened hand. "You know?"

Eileen touches the mitten. "World."

Roger lifts his lip, irritated. He pulls the mitten off and hits the cold rock again. "Planet."

Eileen frowns thoughtfully. "Maybe."

And there *was* hope, Roger thought fiercely. We could have lived on the planet the way we found it, and confronted the materiality of Earth every day of our lives. We could have.

Eileen is called away to help with the arrangement of the next day's loads. "We'll continue this later," she says, touching Roger lightly on the shoulder.

He is left alone over the Gully. Moss discolors the stone under him, and grows in cracks in the couloir. Swallows shoot down the Gully like falling stones, hunting for cliff mice or warm-blooded lizards. To the east, beyond the great shadow of the volcano, dark forests mark the sunlit Tharsis bulge like blobs of lichen. Nowhere can one see Mars, just Mars, the primal Mars. Clenching a cold, rope-sore fist, Roger thinks, *They forgot*. They forgot what it was like to walk out onto the empty face of old Mars.

Once he walked out onto the Great Northern Desert. All of Mars's geographical features are immense by Terran scales, and just as the southern hemisphere is marked by huge canyons, basins, volcanoes, and craters, the northern hemisphere is strangely, hugely smooth; in fact it had, in its highest latitudes, surrounding what at that time was the polar ice cap (it is now a small sea), a planet-ringing expanse of empty, layered sand. Endless desert. And one morning before dawn Roger walked out of his campsite and hiked a few kilometers over the broad wave-like humps of the windswept sand, and sat down on the crest of one of the highest waves. There was no sound but his breath, his blood pounding in his ears, and the slight hiss of the oxygen regulator in his helmet. Light leaked over the horizon to the southeast and began to bring out the sand's dull ochre, flecked with dark red. When the sun cracked the horizon the light bounced off the short steep faces of the dunes and filled everything. He breathed the gold air, and something in him bloomed, he became a flower in a garden of rock, the sole consciousness of the desert, its focus, its soul. Nothing he had ever felt before came close to matching this exaltation, this awareness of brilliant light, of illimitable expanse, of the glossy, intense *presence* of material things. He returned to his camp late in the day, feeling that a moment had passed—or an age. He was nineteen years old, and his life was changed.

Just being able to remember that incident, after two hundred and eighty-odd years have passed, makes Roger a freak. Less than one percent of the population share this gift (or curse) of powerful, long-term recollection. These days Roger feels the ability like a weight—as if each year were a stone, so that now he carries the crushing burden of three hundred red stones everywhere he goes. He feels angry that others forget. Perhaps it is envious anger.

Thinking of that walk when he was nineteen reminds Roger of a time years later, when he read Herman Melville's novel *Moby Dick*. The little black cabin boy Pip (and Roger had always identified himself with Pip in *Great Expectations*), "the most insignificant of the *Pequod's* crew," fell overboard while his whaleboat was being pulled by a harpooned whale. The boat flew onward, leaving Pip alone. "The intense concentration of self in the middle of such a heartless immensity, my God! who can tell it?" Abandoned on the ocean surface alone, Pip grew more and more terrified, until "By the merest chance the ship itself at last rescued him; but from that hour the little Negro went about the deck an idiot. . . . The sea had jeeringly kept his finite body up, but drowned the infinite of his soul."

Reading that made Roger feel strange. Someone had lived an hour very like his day on the polar desert, out in the infinite void of nature. And what had seemed to Roger rapture, had driven Pip insane.

It occurred to him, as he stared at the thick book, that perhaps he had gone mad as well. Terror, rapture—these extremities of emotion circumnavigate the spirit and approach each other again, though departing from the origin of perception in opposite directions. Mad with solitude, ecstatic with Being—the two parts of the recognition of self sit oddly together. But Pip's insanity only shocked Roger into a sharper love for his own experience of the "heartless immensity." He *wanted* it; and suddenly all the farthest, most desolate reaches of Mars became his special joy. He woke at night and sat up to watch dawns, the flower in the garden of rock. And wandered days like John in the desert, seeing God in stones and frost and skies that arched like sheets of fire.

Now he sits on a ledge on a cliff on a planet no longer his, looking down on plains and canyons peppered with life, life *created by the human mind*. It is as if the mind has extruded itself into the landscape: each flower an idea, each lizard a thought. . . . There is no heartless immensity left, no mirror of the void for the self to see itself in. Only the self, everywhere, in everything, suffocating the planet, cloying all sensation, imprisoning every being.

Perhaps this perception itself was a sort of madness.

The sky itself, after all (he thought), provides a heartless immensity beyond the imagination's ability to comprehend, night after night.

Perhaps he needed an immensity he could imagine the extent of, to feel the perception of it as ecstasy rather than terror.

• • •

Roger sits remembering his life and thinking over these matters, as he tosses granules of rock—little pips—over the ledge into space.

To his surprise, Eileen rejoins him. She sits on her heels, recites quietly,

> "I love all waste
> And solitary places, where we taste
> The pleasure of believing what we see
> Is boundless, as we wish our souls to be."

"Who said that?" Roger asks, startled by the lines.

"Shelley," Eileen replies. "In 'Julian and Maddalo.'"

"I like it."

"Me too." She tosses a pip over herself. "Come join us for dinner?"

"What? Oh, sure, sure. I didn't know it was time."

That night, the sound of the tent scraping stone, as the wind shifts it and shifts it. The scritching of thought as world scrapes against planet.

Next day they start spreading out. Marie, Dougal, Hannah, and Ginger take off early up the Gully, around a rib and out of sight, leaving behind a trail of fixed rope. Occasionally those left below can hear their voices, or the ringing of a piton being hammered into the hard rock. Another party descends to Camp 1, to begin dismantling it. When they have got everything up to Camp 2, the last group up will bring the fixed ropes up with them. Thus they will set rope above them and pull it out below them, all the way up the wall.

Late the next day Roger climbs up to carry more rope to Marie and Dougal and Hannah and Ginger. Frances comes with him.

The Great Gully is steeper above Camp 2, and after a few hours of slow progress Roger finds his pack growing very heavy. His hands hurt, the footholds grow smaller and smaller, and he finds he must stop after every five or ten steps. "I just don't have it today," he says as Frances takes over the lead.

"Me neither," she says, wheezing for air. "I think we'll have to start using oxygen during the climbing pretty soon."

But the lead climbers do not agree. Dougal is working his way up a constriction in the Gully, knocking ice out of a crack with his ice axe, then using his fists for chocks and his twisted shoe soles for a staircase, and stepping up the crack as fast as he can clear it. Marie is belaying him and it is left to Hannah and Ginger to greet Roger and Frances. "Great, we were just about to run out of rope."

Dougal stops and Marie takes the opportunity to point to the left wall of the Gully. "Look," she says, disgusted. Roger and Frances see a streak of light blue—a length of xylar climbing rope, hanging free from a rust-pitted piton. "That Terran expedition, I bet," Marie says. "They left ropes the entire way, I hear."

From above Dougal laughs.

Marie shakes her head. "I hate seeing stuff like that."

Frances says, "I think we'd better go onto oxygen pretty soon."

She gets some surprised stares. "Why?" asks Marie. "We've barely started."

"Well, we're at about four kilometers above the datum—"

"Exactly," Marie says. "I *live* higher than that."

"Yes, but we're working pretty hard here, and going up pretty fast. I don't want anyone to get edema."

"I don't feel a thing," Marie says, and Hannah and Ginger nod.

"I could use a bit of oxygen," Dougal says from above, grinning down at them briefly.

"You don't feel edema till you have it," Frances says stiffly.

"Edema," says Marie, as if she doesn't believe in it.

"Marie's immune," Dougal calls down. "Her head can't get more swollen than it already is."

Hannah and Ginger giggle at Marie's mock glare, her tug on the rope to Dougal.

"Down you come, boy."

"On your head."

"We'll see how the weather goes," Frances says. "But either way, if we make normal progress we'll be needing oxygen soon."

This is apparently too obvious to require comment. Dougal reaches the top of the crack, and hammers in a piton; the ringing strikes grow higher and higher in pitch as the piton sets home.

• • •

That afternoon Roger helps the leads set up a small wall tent. The wall tents are very narrow and have a stiff inflatable floor; they can be hung from three pitons if necessary, so that the inhabitants rest on an air-filled cushion hanging in space, like window-washers. But more often they are placed on ledges or indentations in the cliff-face, to give the floor some support. Today they have found that above the narrowing of the Great Gully is a flattish indentation protected by an overhang. The cracks above the indentation are poor, but with the addition of a couple of rock bolts the climbers look satisfied. They will be protected from rockfall, and tomorrow they can venture up to find a better spot for Camp 3 without delay. As there is just barely room (and food) for two, Roger and Frances begin the descent to Camp 2.

During the descent Roger imagines the cliff face as flat ground, entertained by the new perspective this gives. Ravines cut into that flat land: vertically these are called gulleys, or couloirs, or chimneys, depending on their shape and tilt. Climbing in these gives the climber an easier slope and more protection. Flat land has hills, and ranges of hills: these vertically are knobs, or ridges, or shelfs, or buttresses. Depending on their shape and tilt these can either be obstacles, or in the case of some ridges, easy routes up. Then walls become ledges, and creeks become cracks—although cracking takes its own path of least resistance, and seldom resembles water-carved paths.

As Roger belays Frances down one difficult pitch (they can see more clearly why their climb up was so tiring), he looks around at what little he can see: the gray and black walls of the gully, some distance above and below him; the steep wall of the rampart to the left of the gully. And that's all. A curious duality; because this topography stands near the vertical, in many ways he will never see it as well as he would an everyday horizontal hillside. But in other ways (looking right into the grain of the rock to see if one nearly detached knob will hold the weight of his entire body for a long step down, for instance) he sees it much more clearly, more *intensely* than he will ever ever see the safe world of flatness. This intensity of vision is something the climber treasures.

• • •

The next day Roger and Eileen team up, and as they ascend the gully with another load of rope, a rock the size of a large person falls next to them, chattering over an outcropping and knocking smaller rocks down after it. Roger stops to watch it disappear below. The helmets they are wearing would have been no protection against a rock that size.

"Let's hope no one is following us up," Roger says.

"Not supposed to be."

"I guess getting out of this gully won't be such a bad idea, eh?"

"Rockfall is almost as bad on the face. Last year Marie had a party on the face when a rock fell on a traverse rope and cut it. Client making the traverse was killed."

"A cheerful business."

"Rockfall is bad. I hate it."

Surprising emotion in her voice; perhaps some accident has occurred under her leadership as well? Roger looks at her curiously. Odd to be a climbing guide and not be more stoic about such dangers.

Then again, rockfall is the danger beyond expertise.

She looks up: distress. "You know."

He nods. "No precautions to take."

"Exactly. Well, there are some. But they aren't really sufficient."

The lead climbers' camp is gone without a trace, and a new rope leads up the left wall of the gully, through a groove in the overhang and out of sight above. They stop to eat and drink, then continue up. The difficulty of the next pitch impresses them; even with the rope it is hard going. They wedge into the moat between a column of ice and the left wall, and inch up painfully. "I wonder how long this lasts," Roger says, wishing they had their crampons with them. Above him, Eileen doesn't reply for over a minute. Then she says, "Three hundred more meters," as if out of the blue. Roger groans theatrically, client to guide.

Actually he is enjoying following Eileen up the difficult pitch. She has a quick rhythm of observation and movement that reminds him of Dougal, but her choice of holds is all her own—and closer to what Roger would choose. Her calm tone as they discuss the belays, her smooth pulls up the rock, the fine proportions of her long legs, reaching for the awkward foothold: a beautiful climber. And every once in a while there is a little jog at Roger's memory.

Three hundred meters above they find the lead climbers, out of the gully and on a flat ledge that covers nearly a hectare, on the left side this time. From this vantage they can see parts of the cliff face to the right of the gully, above them. "Nice campsite," Eileen remarks. Marie, Dougal, Hannah, and Ginger are sitting about, resting in the middle of setting up their little wall tents. "Looked like you had a hard day of it down there."

"Invigorating," Dougal says, eyebrows raised.

Eileen surveys them. "Looks like a little oxygen might be in order." The lead group protests. "I know, I know. Just a little. A cocktail."

"It only makes you crave it," Marie says.

"Maybe so. We can't use much down here, anyway."

In the midday radio call to the camps below, Eileen tells the others to pack up the tents from Camp 1. "Bring those and the power reels up first. We should be able to use the reels between these camps."

They all give a small cheer. The sun disappears behind the cliff above, and they all groan. The leads stir themselves and continue setting up the tents. The air chills quickly.

Roger and Eileen descend through the afternoon shadows to Camp 2, as there is not enough equipment to accommodate more than the lead group at Camp 3. Descending is easy on the muscles compared to the ascent, but it requires just as much concentration as going up. By the time they reach Camp 2 Roger is very tired, and the cold sunless face has left him depressed again. Up and down, up and down.

That night during the sunset radio conversation Eileen and Marie get into an argument when Eileen orders the leads down to do some portering. "Look, Marie, the rest of us haven't led a single pitch, have we? And we didn't come on this climb to ferry up goods for you, did we?" Eileen's voice has a very sharp, cutting edge to it when she is annoyed. Marie insists the first team is making good time, and is not tired yet. "That's not the point. Get back down to Camp 1 tomorrow, and finish bringing it up. The bottom team will move up and reel Camp 2 up to 3, and those of us here at 2 will carry one load up to 3 and have a bash at the lead after that. That's the way it is, Marie—we leapfrog in my climbs, you know that.''

Sounds behind the static from the radio, of Dougal talking to Marie. Finally Marie says, ''Aye, well you'll need us more when the climbing gets harder anyway. But we can't afford to slow down much.''

After the radio call Roger leaves the tents and sits on his ledge bench to watch the twilight. Far to the east the land is still sunlit, but as he watches the landscape darkens, turns dim purple under the blackberry sky. Mirror dusk. A few stars sprinkle the high dome above him. The air is cold but still, and he can hear Hans and Frances inside their tent, arguing about glacial polish. Frances is an areologist of some note, and apparently she disagrees with Hans about the origins of the escarpment; she spends some of her climbing time looking for evidence in the rock.

Eileen sits down beside him. ''Mind?''

''No,'' he says.

She says nothing, and it occurs to him she may be upset. He says, ''I'm sorry Marie is being so hard to get along with.''

She waves a mittened hand to dismiss it. ''Marie is always like that. It doesn't mean anything. She just wants to climb.'' She laughs. ''We go on like this every time we climb together, but I still like her.''

''Hmph.'' Roger raises his eyebrows. ''I wouldn't have guessed.''

She does not reply. For a long time they sit there. Roger's thoughts return to the past, and helplessly his spirits plummet again.

''You seem . . . disturbed about something,'' Eileen ventures.

''Ehh,'' Roger says. ''About everything, I suppose.'' And winces to be making such a confessional. But she appears to understand; she says,

''So you fought all the terraforming?''

''Most of it, yeah. First as head of a lobbying group. You must be part of it now—Martian Wilderness Explorers.''

''I pay the dues.''

''Then in the Red government. And in the Interior Ministry,

after the Greens took over. But none of it did any good.''

"And why, again?''

"Because," he bursts out—stops—starts again: "Because I liked the planet the way it was when we found it! A lot of us did, back then. It was so beautiful . . . or not just that. It was more overwhelming than beautiful. The size of things, their shapes—the whole planet had been evolving, the land-forms themselves I mean, for five billion years, and traces of *all* that time were still on the surface to be seen and read, if you knew how to look. It was so wonderful to be out there. . . .''

"The sublime isn't always beautiful.''

"True. It transcended beauty, it really did. One time I walked out onto the polar desert, you know. . . .'' But he doesn't know how to tell it. "And so, and so it seemed to me that we already had an Earth, you know? That we didn't need a Terra up here. And everything they did eroded the planet that we came to. They destroyed it! And now we've got—whatever. Some kind of park. A laboratory to test out new plants and animals and all. And everything I loved so much about those early years is gone. You can't find it anywhere anymore.''

In the dark he can just see her nodding. "And so your life's work . . .''

"Wasted!'' He can't keep the frustration out of his voice. Suddenly he doesn't want to, he wants her to understand what he feels, he looks at her in the dark, "A three-hundred-year life, entirely wasted! I mean I might as well have just . . .'' He doesn't know what.

Long pause.

"At least you can remember it,'' she says quietly.

"What good is that? I'd rather forget, I tell you.''

"Ah. You don't know what that's like.''

"Oh, the past. The God-damned past. It isn't so great. Just a dead thing.''

She shakes her head. "Our past is never dead. Do you know Sartre's work?''

"No.''

"A shame. He can be a big help to we who live so long. For instance, in several places he suggests that there are two ways of looking at the past. You can think of it as something dead and fixed forever; it's part of you, but you can't change it, and you can't change what it means. In that case your past limits or even controls what you can be. But Sartre doesn't agree with that way of looking at it. He says that the past is constantly altered by what we do in the present moment. The *meaning* of the past is as fluid as our freedom in the present, because every new act that we commit can revalue the entire thing!"

Roger humphs. "Existentialism."

"Well, whatever you want to call it. It's part of Sartre's philosophy of freedom, for sure. He says that the only way we can possess our past—whether we can remember it or not, I say—is to add new acts to it, which then give it a new value. He calls this 'assuming' our past."

"But sometimes that may not be possible."

"Not for Sartre. The past is always assumed, because we are *not* free to stop creating new values for it. It's just a question of what those values will be. For Sartre it's a question of *how* you will assume your past, not whether you will."

"And for you?"

"I'm with him on that. That's why I've been reading him these last several years. It helps me to understand things."

"Hmph." He thinks about it. "You were an English major in college, did you know that?"

But she ignores the comment. "So—" She nudges him lightly, shoulder to shoulder. "You have to decide how you will assume this past of yours. Now that your Mars is gone."

He considers it.

She stands. "I have to plunge into the logistics for tomorrow."

"Okay. See you inside."

A bit disconcerted, he watches her leave. Dark tall shape against the sky. The woman he remembers was not like this. In the context of what she has just said, the thought almost makes him laugh.

For the next few days all the members of the team are hard at work ferrying equipment up to Camp 3, except for two a day who are sent above to find a route to the next camp. It turns out there is a feasible reeling route directly up the gully, and most of the gear is reeled up to Camp 3 once it is carried to Camp 2. Every evening there is a radio conversation, in which Eileen takes stock and juggles the logistics of the climb, and gives the next day's orders. From other camps Roger listens to her voice over the radio, interested in the relaxed tone, the method she has of making her decisions right in front of them all, and the easy way she shifts her manner to accommodate whoever she is speaking with. He decides she is very good at her job, and wonders if their conversations are simply a part of that. Somehow he thinks not.

Roger and Stephan are given the lead, and early one mirror dawn they hurry up the fixed ropes above Camp 3, turning on their helmet lamps to aid the mirrors. Roger feels strong in the early going. At the top of the pitch the fixed ropes are attached to a nest of pitons in a large, crumbling crack. The sun rises and suddenly bright light glares onto the face. Roger ropes up, confirms the signals for the belay, starts up the gully.

The lead at last. Now there is no fixed rope above him determining his way; only the broad flat back and rough walls of the gully, looking much more vertical than they have up to this point. Roger chooses the right wall and steps up onto a rounded knob. The wall is a crumbling, knobby andesite surface, black and a reddish gray in the harsh morning blast of light; the back wall of the gully is smoother, layered like a very thick-grained slate, and broken occasionally by horizontal cracks. Where the back wall meets the side wall the cracks widen a bit, sometimes offering perfect footholds. Using them and the many knobs of the wall Roger is able to make his way upward. He pauses several meters above Stephan at a good-looking vertical crack to hammer in a piton. Getting a piton off the belt sling is awkward. When it is hammered in he pulls a rope through and jerks on it. It seems solid. He climbs above it. Now his feet are spread, one in a crack, one on a knob, as his fingers test the rock in a crack above his head; then up, and his feet are both on a knob in the intersection of the walls, his left hand far out on the back wall of the gully to hold onto a little indentation. Breath rasps in his throat. His fingers get tired and cold. The gully widens out and grows shallower, and the intersection of back and side wall becomes a steep narrow ramp of its own. Fourth piton in, the ringing hammer strikes filling the morning air. New problems: the degraded rock of this ramp offers no good cracks, and Roger has to do a tension traverse over to the middle of the gully to find a better way up. Now if he falls he will swing back into the side wall like a pendulum. And he's in the rockfall zone. Over to the left side wall, quickly a piton in. Problem solved. He loves the immediacy of problem solving in climbing, though at this moment he is not aware of his pleasure. Quick look down: Stephan a good distance away, and below him! Back to concentrating on the task at hand. A good ledge, wide as his boot, offers a resting place. He stands, catches his breath. A tug on the line from Stephan; he has run out the rope. Good lead, he thinks, looking down the steep gully at the trail left by the green rope, looping from piton to piton. Perhaps a better way to cross the gully from right to left? Stephan's helmeted face calls something up. Roger hammers in three pitons and secures the line. "Come on up!" he cries. His fingers and calves are tired. There is just room to sit on his bootledge: immense world, out there under the bright pink morning sky! He sucks down the air and belays Stephan's ascent, pulling up the rope and looping it carefully. The next pitch will be Stephan's; Roger will have quite a bit of time to sit on this ledge and feel the intense solitude of his position in this vertical desolation. "Ah!" he says. Climbing up and out of the world. . . .

It is the strongest sort of duality: facing the rock and climbing, his attention is tightly focused on the rock within a meter or two of his eyes, inspecting its every flaw and irregularity. It is not particularly good climbing rock, but the gully slopes at about seventy degrees in this section, so the actual technical difficulty is not that great. The important thing is to *understand* the rock fully enough to find only good holds and good cracks— to recognize suspect holds and avoid them. A lot of weight will follow them up these fixed ropes, and although the ropes will probably be renailed, his piton placements will likely stand. One has to see the rock and the world beneath the rock.

And then he finds a ledge to sit and rest on, and turns around, and there is the great rising expanse of the Tharsis Bulge. Tharsis is a continent-sized bulge in the Martian surface; at its center it is eleven kilometers above the Martian datum, and the three prince volcanoes lie in a line, northeast to southwest on the bulge's highest plateau. Olympus Mons is at the far northwestern edge of the bulge, almost on the great expanse of Amazonis Planitia. Now, not even halfway up the great

volcano's escarpment, Roger can just see the three prince volcanoes poking over the horizon to the southeast, demonstrating
perfectly the size of the planet itself. He looks around one-
eighteenth of Mars.

By midafternoon Roger and Stephan have run out their 300
meters of rope, and they return to Camp 3 pleased with themselves. The next morning they hurry up the fixed ropes in the
mirror dawn, and begin again. At the end of Roger's third pitch
in the lead he comes upon a good site for a camp: a sort of
pillar bordering the Great Gully on its right side ends abruptly
in a flat top that looks very promising. After negotiating a
difficult short traverse to get onto the pillar top, they wait for
the midday radio conference. Consultation with Eileen confirms
that the pillar is about the right distance from Camp 3, and
suddenly they are standing in Camp 4.

"The Gully ends pretty near to you anyway," Eileen says.

So Roger and Stephan have the day free to set up a wall tent
and then explore. The climb is going well, Roger thinks: no
major technical difficulties, a group that gets along fairly well
together . . . perhaps the great South Buttress will not prove to
be that difficult after all.

Stephan gets out a little sketchbook. Roger glances at the
filled pages as Stephan flips through them. "What's that?"

"Chir pine, they call it. I saw some growing out of the rocks
above Camp 1. It's amazing what you find living on the side
of this cliff!"

"Yes," Roger says.

"Oh, I know, I know. You don't like it. But I'm sure I don't
know why." He has a blank sheet of the sketchbook up now.
"Look in the cracks across the gully. Lot of ice there, and
then patches of moss. That's moss champion, with the lavender
flowers on top of the moss cushion, see?"

He begins sketching and Roger watches, fascinated. "That's
a wonderful talent to have, drawing."

"Skill. Look, there's edelweiss and asters, growing almost
together." He jerks, puts fingers to lips, points. "Pika," he
whispers.

Roger looks at the broken niches in the moat of the gully
opposite them. There is a movement and suddenly he sees
them—two little gray furballs with bright black eyes—three—

the last scampering up the rock fearlessly. They have a hole at the back of one niche for a home. Stephan sketches rapidly, getting the outline of the three creatures, then filling them in. Bright Martian eyes.

And once, in the Martian autumn in Burroughs, when the leaves covered the ground and fell through the air, leaves the color of sand, or the tan of antelopes, or the green of green apples, or the white of cream, or the yellow of butter—he walked through the park. The wind blew stiffly from the southwest out of the big funnel of the delta, bringing clouds flying overhead swiftly, scattered and white and sunbroken to the west, bunched up and dark dusky blue to the east; and the evergreens waved their arms in every shade of dark green, before which the turning leaves of the hardwoods flared; and above the trees to the east a white walled church, with reddish arched roof tiles and a white bell tower, glowed under the dark clouds. Kids playing on the swings across the park, yellow-red aspens waving over the brick city hall beyond them to the north—and Roger felt—wandering among widely-spaced white-trunked trees that thrust their white limbs in every upward direction—he felt—feeling the wind loft the gliding leaves over him—he felt what all the others must have felt when they walked around, that Mars had become a place of exquisite beauty. In such lit air he could see every branch, leaf and needle waving under the tide of wind, crows flying home, lower clouds lofting puffy and white under the taller black ones, and it all struck him all at once: freshly colored, fully lit, spacious and alive in the wind—what a world! What a world.

And then, back in his offices, he hadn't been able to tell anyone about it. It wouldn't have been like him.

Remembering that, and remembering his recent talk with Eileen, Roger feels uncomfortable. His past overpowered that day's walk through the park: what kind of assumption was that?

Roger spends his afternoon free climbing above Camp 4, looking around a bit and enjoying the exercise of his climbing skills. They're coming back very quickly. But the rock is nearly crack-free once out of the Gully, and he decides free climbing is not a good idea. Besides, he's noticed a curious thing: about fifty meters above Camp 4, the Great Central Gully is gone. It ends in a set of overhangs like the ribs under the protruding wall of a building. Definitely not the way up. And yet the face to the right of the overhangs is not much better; it too tilts out and out, until it is almost sheer. The few cracks breaking this mass will not be easy to climb. In fact, Roger doubts he *could* climb them, and wonders if the leads are up to it. Well, sure, he thinks. They can climb anything. But it looks awful. Hans has talked about the volcano's "hard eon," when the lava pouring from the caldera was denser and more consistent than in the volcano's earlier years. The escarpment, being a sort of giant boring of the volcano's flow history, naturally reflects the changes in lava consistency in its many horizontal bands. So far they have been climbing on softer rock—now they have reached the bottom of a harder band. Back in Camp 4 Roger looks up at what he can see of the cliff above, and wonders where they will go.

Another duality: the two halves of the day, forenoon and afternoon. Forenoon is sunny and therefore hot: a morning ice and rock shower in the Gully, and time to dry out sleeping bags and socks. Then noon passes and the sun disappears behind the cliff above. For an hour or so they have the weird half-light of the dusk mirrors, then they too disappear, and suddenly the air is biting, bare hands risk frostnip, and the lighting is indirect and eerie: a world in shadow. Water on the cliff-face ices up, and rocks are pushed out—there is another period when rocks fall and go whizzing by. People bless their helmets and hunch their shoulders in, and discuss again the possibility of shoulder pads. In the cold the cheery morning is forgotten, and it seems the whole climb takes place in shadow.

When Camp 4 is established they try several reconnaissance climbs through what Hans calls the Jasper Band. "It looks like orbicular jasper, see?" He shows them a dull rock and after cutting away at it with a laser saw shows them a smooth brown surface, speckled with little circles of yellow, green, red, white. "Looks like lichen," Roger says. "Fossilized lichen."

"Yes. This is orbicular jasper. For it to be trapped in this basalt implies a metamorphic slush—lava partially melting rock in the throat above the magma chamber, and then throwing it all up. . . ."

So it was the Jasper Band, and it was trouble. Too sheer—close to vertical, really, and without an obvious way up. "At least it's good hard rock," Dougal says cheerfully.

Then one day Arthur and Marie return from a long traverse out to the right, and then up. They hurry into camp grinning ear to ear.

"It's a ledge," Arthur says. "A perfect ledge. I can't believe it. It's about half a meter wide, and extends around this rampart for a couple hundred meters, just like a damn sidewalk! We just walked right around that corner! Completely vertical above and below—talk about a view!"

For once Roger finds Arthur's enthusiasm fully appropriate. The Thank God Ledge, as Arthur has named it ("There's one like this in Yosemite"), is a horizontal break in the cliff-face, and a flat slab just wide enough to walk on is the result. Roger stops in the middle of the ledge to look around. Straight up: rock and sky. Straight down: the tiny tumble of the talus, appearing directly below them, as Roger is not inclined to lean out too far to see the rock in between. The exposure is astonishing. "You and Marie walked along this ledge without ropes?" Roger says.

"Oh, it's fairly wide," Arthur replies. "Don't you think? I ended up crawling there where it narrows just a bit. But mostly it was fine. Marie walked the whole way."

"I'm sure she did." Roger shakes his head, happy to be clipped onto the rope that has been fixed about chest high above the ledge. With its aid he can appreciate this strange ledge—perfect sidewalk in a completely vertical world: the wall hard, knobby, right next to his head—under him the smooth surface of the ledge, and then empty space.

Verticality. Consider it. A balcony high on a tall building will give a meager analogy: experience it. On the side of this cliff, unlike the side of any building, there is no ground below. The world below is the world of belowness, the rush of air under your feet. The forbidding smooth wall of the cliff, black and upright beside you, halves the sky. Earth, air; the solid here and now, the air infinite; the wall of basalt, the sea of gases. Another duality: to climb is to live on the most symbolic plane of existence and the most physical plane of existence *at the same time*. This too the climber treasures.

At the far end of the Thank God Ledge there is a crack system that breaks through the Jasper Band—it is like a narrow, miniature version of the Great Gully, filled with ice. Progress upward is renewed, and the cracks lead up to the base of an ice-filled half-funnel, that divides the Jasper Band even further. The bottom of the funnel is sloped just enough for Camp 5, which becomes by far the most cramped of the campsites. That Thank God Ledge traverse means that using the power reels is impossible between Camps 4 and 5, however. Everyone makes ten or twelve carries between the two camps. Each time Roger walks the sidewalk through space, his amazement at it returns.

While the carries across the ledge are being made, and Camps 2 and 3 are being dismantled, Arthur and Marie have begun finding the route above. Roger goes up with Hans to supply them with rope and oxygen. The climbing is "mixed," half on rock, half on black ice rimed with dirty hard snow. Awkward stuff. There are some pitches that make Roger and Hans gasp with effort, look at each other round-eyed. "Must have been Marie leading." "I don't know, that Arthur is pretty damn good." The rock is covered in many places by layers of black ice, hard and brittle—years of summer rain followed by frost have caked the exposed surfaces at this height. Roger's boots slip over the slick ice repeatedly. "Need crampons up here."

"Except the ice is so thin, you'd be kicking rock."

"Mixed climbing."

"Fun, eh?"

Breath rasps over knocking heartbeats. Holes in the ice have been broken with ice-axes; the rock below is good rock, lined with vertical fissures. A chunk of ice whizzes by, clatters on the face below.

"I wonder if that's Arthur and Marie's work."

Only the fixed rope makes it possible for Roger to ascend this pitch, it is so hard. Another chunk of ice flies by, and both of them curse.

Feet appear in the top of the open-book crack they are ascending.

"Hey! Watch out up there! You're dropping ice chunks on us!"

"Oh! Sorry, didn't know you were there." Arthur and Marie jumar down the rope to them. "Sorry," Marie says again. "Didn't know you'd come up so late. Have you got more rope?"

"Yeah."

The sun disappears behind the cliff, leaving only the street-lamp light of the dusk mirrors. Arthur peers up at them as Marie stuffs their packs with the new rope. "Beautiful," he exclaims. "They have parhelia on Earth, too, you know—a natural effect of the light when there's ice crystals in the atmosphere. It's usually seen in Antarctica—big halos around the sun, and at two points of the halo these mock suns. But I don't think we ever had four mock suns per side. Beautiful!"

"Let's go," Marie says without looking up. "We'll see you two down at Camp 5 tonight." And off they go, using the rope and both sides of the open-book crack to quickly lever their way up.

"Strange pair," Stephan says as they descend to Camp 5.

The next day they take more rope up. In the late afternoon, after a very long climb, they find Arthur and Marie, sitting in a cave in the side of the cliff that is big enough to hold their entire base camp. "Can you believe this?" Arthur cries. "It's a damn hotel!"

The cave's entrance is a horizontal break in the cliff face, about four meters high and over fifteen from side to side. The floor of the cave is relatively flat, covered near the entrance with a thin sheet of ice, and littered with chunks of the roof, which is bumpy but solid. Roger picks up one of the rocks from the floor and moves it to the side of the cave, where floor and roof come together to form a narrow crack. Marie is trying to get somebody below on the radio, to tell them about the find. Roger goes to the back of the cave, some twenty meters in from the face, and ducks down to inspect the jumble of rocks in the long crack where floor and roof meet. "It's going to be nice to lay out flat for once," Stephan says. Looking out the cave's mouth Roger sees a wide smile of lavender sky.

• • •

When Hans arrives he gets very excited. He bangs about in the gloom hitting things with his ice axe, pointing his flashlight into various nooks and crannies. "It's tuff, do you see?" he says, holding up a chunk for their inspection. "This is a shield volcano, meaning it ejected very little ash over the years, which is what gave it its flattened shape. But there must have been a few ash eruptions, and when the ash is compressed it becomes tuff—this rock here. Tuff is much softer than basalt and andesite, and over the years this exposed layer has eroded away, leaving us with our wonderful hotel."

"I love it," says Arthur.

The rest of the team joins them in the mirror dusk, but the cave is still uncrowded. Although they set up tents to sleep in, they place the lamps on the cave floor, and eat dinner in a large circle, around a collection of glowing little stoves. Eyes gleam with laughter as the climbers consume bowls of stew. There is something marvelous about this secure home, tucked in the face of the escarpment three thousand meters above the plain. It is an unexpected joy to loll about on flat ground, unharnessed. Hans has not stopped prowling the cave with his flashlight. Occasionally he whistles.

"Hans!" Arthur calls when the meal is over and the bowls and pots have been scraped clean. "Get over here, Hans. Have a seat. There you go. Sit down." Marie is passing around her flask of brandy. "All right, Hans, tell me something. Why is this cave here? And why, for that matter, is this escarpment here? Why is Olympus Mons the only volcano anywhere to have this encircling cliff?"

Frances says, "It's not the *only* volcano to have such a feature."

"Now, Frances," Hans says. "You know it's the only big shield volcano with a surrounding escarpment. The analogies from Iceland that you're referring to are just little vents of larger volcanoes."

Frances nods. "That's true. But the analogy may still hold."

"Perhaps." Hans explains to Arthur: "You see, there is still not a perfect agreement as to the cause of the scarp. But I think I can say that my theory is generally accepted—wouldn't you agree, Frances?"

"Yes . . ."

Hans smiles genially, and looks around at the group. "You

see, Frances is one of those who believe that the volcano originally grew up through a glacial cap, and that the glacier made
in effect a retaining wall, holding in the lava and creating this
drop-off after the glacial cap disappeared.''

''There are good analogies in Iceland for this particular shape
for a volcano,'' Frances says. ''And it's eruption under and
through ice that explains it.''

''Be that as it may,'' Hans says, ''I am among those who
feel that the *weight* of Olympus Mons is the cause of the scarp.''

''You mentioned that once before,'' Arthur says, ''but I
don't understand how that would work.''

Stephan voices his agreement with this, and Hans sips from
the flask with a happy look. He says,

''The volcano is extremely old, you understand. Three or
four billion years, on this same site, or close to it—very little
tectonic drift, unlike on Earth. So, magma upwells, lava spills
out, over and over and over, and it is deposited over softer
material—probably the gardened regolith that resulted from the
intensive meteor bombardments of the planet's earliest years.
A tremendous weight is deposited on the surface of the planet,
you see, and this weight increases as the volcano grows. As
we all know now, it is a very, very big volcano. And eventually
the weight is so great that it squishes out the softer material
beneath it. We find this material to the northeast, which is the
downhill side of the Tharsis bulge, and is naturally the side
that the pressured rock would be pushed out to. Have any of
you visited the Olympus Mons aureole?'' Several of the climbers nod. ''Fascinating region.''

''Okay,'' Arthur says, ''but why wouldn't that just sink the
whole area? I would think that there would be a depression
circling the edge of the volcano, rather than this cliff.''

''Exactly!'' Stephan cries.

But Hans is shaking his head, a smile on his face. He gestures
for the brandy flask again. ''The point is, the lava shield of
Olympus Mons is a single unit of rock—layered, admittedly,
but essentially one big cap of basalt, placed on a slightly soft
surface. Now by far the greatest part of the weight of this cap
is near the center—the volcano's peak, you know, still so far
above us. So—the cap is a unit, a single piece of rock—and
basalt has a certain flexibility to it, as all rock does. So the
cap itself is somewhat flexible. Now, the center of the cap sinks

the farthest, being heaviest—and the outside edge of the shield, being part of a single flexible cap, *bends upward.*"

"Up twenty thousand feet?" Arthur demands, incredulous. "You're kidding!"

Hans shrugs. "You must remember that the volcano stands twenty-five kilometers above the surrounding plains. The volume of the volcano is one hundred times the volume of Earth's largest volcano, Mauna Loa, and for three billion years at least it has been pressing down on this spot."

"But it doesn't make sense that the scarp would be so symmetrical if that was what happened," Frances objected.

"On the contrary. In fact that is the really wonderful aspect of it. The outer edge of the lava shield is lifted up, okay? Higher and higher, until the flexibility of the basalt is *exceeded.* In other words, the shield is just so flexible and no more. At the point where the stress becomes too much, the rock sheers off, and the inner side of the break continues to rise, while what is beyond the break point subsides. So, the plains down below us are still part of the lava aureole of Olympus Mons, but they are beyond the break point. And as the lava was everywhere approximately the same thickness, it gave away everywhere at about the same distance from the peak, giving us the roughly circular escarpment, which we now climb!"

Hans waves a hand with an architect's pride. Frances sniffs. Arthur says, "It's hard to believe." He taps the floor. "So the other half of this cave is underneath the talus wash down there?"

"Exactly!" Hans beams. "Though the other half was never a cave. This was probably a small, roughly circular layer of tuff, trapped in much harder basaltic lava. But when the shield broke and the escarpment was formed, the tuff deposit was cut in half, exposing its side to erosion. And a few eons later we have our cozy cave."

"Hard to believe," Arthur says again.

Roger sips from the flask and silently agrees with Arthur. It's remarkable how difficult it is to transfer the areologist's theories, in which mountains act like plastic or toothpaste, to the vast hard basalt reality underneath and above them. "It's the amount of time necessary for these transformations that's difficult to imagine," he says aloud. "It must take . . ." he waves a hand.

"Billions of years," Hans says. "We cannot properly imagine that amount of time. But we can see the sure signs of its passing."

And in three centuries we can destroy those signs, Roger says silently. Or most of them. And make a park instead.

Above the cave the cliff face lays back a bit, and the smoothness of the Jasper Band is replaced by a jumbled, complicated slope of ice gullies, buttresses, and shallow horizontal slits that mimic their cave below. These steps, as they call them, are to be avoided like crevasses on level ground, as the overhanging roof of each is a serious obstacle. the ice gullies provide the best routes up, and it becomes a matter of navigating up what appears to be a vertical delta, like the tracing of a lightning bolt burned into the face and then frozen. Every morning as the sun hits the face there is an hour or so of severe ice and rock fall, and in the afternoons in the hour after the sun leaves the face there is another period of rockfall. There are some close calls and one morning Hannah is hit by a chunk of ice in the chest, bruising her badly. "The trick is to stay in the moat between the ice in the gully and the rock wall," Marie says to Roger as they retreat down a dead-end couloir.

"Or to be where you want to be by the time the sun comes up," Dougal adds. And on his advice to Eileen, they begin rising long before dawn to make the exposed parts of the climb. In the frigid dark a wristwatch alarm beeps. Roger twists in his bag, trying to turn it off; but it is his tent mate's. With a groan he sits up, reaches over and switches on his stove. Soon the metal rings in the top of the cubical stove are glowing a friendly warm orange, heating the tent's air and giving a little bit of light to see by. Eileen and Stephan are sitting in their bags, beating sleep away. Their hair is tousled, their faces lined, puffy, tired. It is three A.M. Eileen puts a pot of ice on the stove, dimming their light. She turns on a lamp to its lowest illumination, which is still enough to make Stephan groan. Roger digs in a food pouch for tea and dried milk. Breakfast is wonderfully warming, but suddenly he has to visit the cave's convenient yet cold latrine. Boots on—the worst part of dressing. Like sticking one's feet into iceblocks. Then out of the warm tent into the intense cold of the cave's air. Through the dark to the latrine. The other tents glow dimly; time for another dawn assault on the upper slopes.

By the time Archimedes, the first dawn mirror, appears, they have been on the slopes above the cave for nearly an hour, climbing by the light of their helmet lamps. The mirror dawn is better; there is enough light to see well, and yet the rock and ice have not yet been warmed enough to start falls. Roger climbs the ice gullies using crampons; he enjoys using them, kicking into the plastic ice with the front points of the crampons, and adhering to the slopes as if glued to them. Below him Arthur keeps singing a song in tribute to his crampons: "Spiderman, Spiderman, Spiderman, Spidermannnnn. . . ." But once above the fixed ropes, there is no extra breath for singing; the lead climbing is extremely difficult. Roger finds himself spread-eagled on one pitch, right foot spiked into the icefall, left foot digging into a niche the size of his toenail; left hand holding the shaft of the ice axe, which is firmly planted in the icefall above, and right hand laboriously turning the handle of an ice screw, which will serve as piton in this little couloir: and for a moment he realizes he is ten meters above the nearest belay, *hanging there by three tiny points*. And gasping for breath.

At the top of that pitch there is a small outcropping to rest on, and when Eileen pulls herself up the fixed rope she finds Roger and Arthur laid out over the rock in the morning sunlight like fish set out to dry. She surveys them as she catches her wind, gasping herself. "Time for oxygen," she declares. In the midday radio call she tells the next teams up to bring oxygen bottles along with the tents and other equipment for the next camp.

With three camps established above the cave, which serves as a sort of base camp to return to from time to time, they are making fair progress. Each night only a few of them are in any given camp. They are forced to use oxygen for almost all of the climbing, and most of them sleep with a mask on, the regulator turned to its lowest setting. The work of setting up the high camps, which they try to do without oxygen, becomes exhausting and cold. When the camps are set and the day's climbing is done, they spend the shadowed afternoons wheezing around the camps, drinking hot fluids and stamping their feet to keep them warm, waiting for the sunset radio call and the next day's orders. At this point it's a pleasure to leave the thinking to Eileen.

One afternoon climbing above the highest camp with Eileen, Roger stands facing out as he belays Eileen's lead up a difficult pitch. Thunderheads like long-stemmed mushrooms march in lines blown to the northeast. Only the tops of the clouds are higher than they. It is late afternoon and the cliff-face is a shadow. The cottony trunks of the thunderheads are dark, shadowed gray—then the thunderheads themselves bulge white and gleaming into the sunny sky above, actually casting some light back onto the cliff. Roger pulls the belay rope taut, looks up at Eileen. She is staring up her line of attack, which has become a crack in two walls meeting at ninety degrees. Her oxygen mask covers her mouth and nose. Roger tugs once—she looks down—he points out at the immense array of clouds. She nods, pulls the mask to one side. "Like ships!" she calls down. "Ships of the line!"

Roger pulls his mask over a cheek. "Do you think a storm might come?"

"I wouldn't be surprised. We've been lucky so far." She replaces her mask and begins a layback, shoving the fingers of both hands in the crack, putting the soles of both boots against the wall just below her hands, and pulling herself out to the side so that she can walk sideways up one of the walls. Roger keeps the belay taut.

Mars's prevailing westerlies strike Olympus Mons, and the air rises, but does not flow over the peak; the mountain is so tall it protrudes out of much of the atmosphere, and the winds are therefore pushed around each side. Compressed in that way, the air comes swirling off the eastern flank cold and dry, having dumped its moisture on the western flank, where glaciers form. This is the usual pattern, anyway; but when a cyclonic system sweeps out of the southwest, it strikes the volcano a glancing blow from the south, compresses, lashes the southeast quadrant of the shield, and rebounds to the east intensified.

"What's the barometer say, Hans?"

"Six hundred millibars."

"You're kidding!"

"That's not too far below normal, actually."

"You're kidding."

"It is low, however. I believe we are being overtaken by a low-pressure system."

The storm begins as katabatic winds: cold air falling over the edge of the escarpment and dropping toward the plain. Sometimes the force of the west wind over the plateau of the shield blows the gusts out beyond the actual cliff face, which will then stand in perfect stillness. But the slight vacuum fills again with a quick downward blast, that makes the tents boom and stretch their frames. Roger grunts as one almost squashes the tent, shakes his head at Eileen. She says, "Get used to it— there are downdrafts hitting the upper face more often than not." WHAM! "Although this one does seem to be a bit stronger than usual. But it's not snowing, is it?"

Roger looks out the little tent door window. "Nope."

"Good."

"Awful cold, though." He turns in his sleeping bag.

"That's okay. Snow would be a really bad sign." She gets on the radio and starts calling around. She and Roger are in Camp 8 (the cave is now called Camp 6); Dougal and Frances are in Camp 9, the highest and most exposed of the new camps; Arthur, Hans, Hannah, and Ivan are in Camp 7; and the rest are down in the cave. They are a little overextended, as Eileen has been loath to pull the last tents out of the cave. Now Roger begins to see why. "Everyone stay inside tomorrow morning until they hear from me at mirror dawn. We'll have another conference then."

The wind rises through the night, and Roger is awakened at three A.M. by a particularly hard blast to the tent. There is very little sound of the wind against the rock—then a BANG and suddenly the tent is whistling and straining like a tortured thing. It lets off and the rocks hoot softly. Settle down and listen to the airy breathing WHAM, the squealing tent is driven down into the niche they have set it in—then sucked back up. The comforting hiss of the oxygen mask, keeping his nose warm for once—WHAM. Eileen is apparently sleeping, her head buried in her sleeping bag; only her bunting cap and the oxygen hose emerge from the drawn-up opening at the top. Roger can't believe the gunshot slaps of the wind don't wake her. He checks his watch, decides it is futile to try falling back asleep. New frost condensation on the inside of the tent falls on his face like snow, scaring him for a moment. But a flashlight gleam directed out the small clear panel in the tent door reveals there is no snow. By the dimmest light of the lamp Roger sets their pot of ice on the square bulk of the stove and turns it on. He puts his chilled hands back in the sleeping bag to watch the stove heat up. Quickly the rings under the pot are a bright orange, palpably radiating heat.

An hour later it is considerably warmer in the tent. Roger sips hot tea, tries to predict the wind's hammering. The melted water from the cave's ice apparently has some silt in it; Roger, along with three or four of the others, has had his digestion upset by the silt, and now he feels a touch of the glacial dysentery coming on. Uncomfortably he quells the urge. Some particularly sharp blows to the tent wake Eileen; she sticks her head out of her bag, looking befuddled.

"Wind's up," Roger says. "Want some tea?"

"Mmmph." She pulls away her oxygen mask. "Yeah." She takes a full cup and drinks. "Thirsty."

"Yeah. The masks seem to do that."

"What time is it?"

"About four."

"Ah. My alarm must have woken me. Almost time for the call."

Although it is cloudy to the east, they still get a distinct increase of light when Archimedes rises. Roger pulls on his cold boots and groans. "Gotta go," he says to Eileen, and unzips the tent just far enough to get out.

"Stay harnessed up!"

Outside, one of the katabatic blasts shoves him hard. It's very cold, perhaps 20 degrees Celsius below, so that the wind chill factor when it is blowing hardest is extreme. Unfortunately, he does have a touch of the runs. Much relieved, and very chilled, he pulls his pants up and steps back into the tent. Eileen is on the radio. People are to stay inside until the winds abate a little, she says. Roger nods vigorously. When she is done she laughs at him. "You know what Dougal would say."

"Oh, it was very invigorating all right."

She laughs again.

Time passes. When he warms back up Roger dozes off. It's actually easier to sleep during the day, when the tent is warmer.

He is rudely awakened late in the morning by a shout from outside. Eileen jerks up in her bag and unzips the tent door. Dougal sticks his head in, pulls his oxygen mask onto his chest, frosts them with hard breathing. "Our tent has been smashed by a rock," he says, almost apologetically. "Frances has got her arm broke. I need some help getting her down."

"Down where?" Roger says involuntarily.

"Well, I thought to the cave, anyway. Or at least to here— our tent's crushed, she's pretty much out in the open right now—in her bag, you know, but the tent's not doing much."

Grimly Eileen and Roger begin to pull their climbing clothes on.

Outside the wind rips at them and Roger wonders if he can climb. They clip onto the rope and jumar up rapidly, moving at emergency speed. Sometimes the blasts of wind from above are so strong that they can only hang in against the rock and wait. During one blast Roger becomes frightened—it seems impossible that flesh and bone, harness, jumar, rope, piton, and rock will all hold under the immense pressure of the down-draft. But all he can do is huddle in the crack the fixed rope follows and hope, getting colder every second.

They enter a long snaking ice gully that protects them from the worst of the wind, and make better progress. Several times rocks or chunks of ice fall by them, dropping like bombs or giant hailstones. Dougal and Eileen are climbing so fast that it is difficult to keep up with them. Roger feels weak and cold; even though he is completely covered, his nose and fingers feel frozen. His intestines twist a little as he crawls over a boulder jammed in the gully, and he groans. Better to have stayed in the tent on this particular day.

Suddenly they are at Camp 9—one big box tent, flattened at one end. It is flapping like a big flag in a gale, cracking and snapping again and again, nearly drowning out their voices. Frances is glad to see them; under her goggles her eyes are red-rimmed. "I think I can sit up in a sling and rappel down if you can help me," she says over the tent noise.

"How are you?" asks Eileen.

"The left arm's broken just above the elbow. I've made a

bit of a splint for it. I'm awfully cold, but other than that I don't feel too bad. I've taken some painkillers, but not enough to make me sleepy.''

They all crowd in what's left of the tent and Eileen turns on a stove. Dougal dashes about outside, vainly trying to secure the open end of the tent and end the flapping. They brew tea and sit in sleeping bags to drink it. "What time is it?" "Two." "We'd better be off soon." "Yeah."

Getting Frances down to Camp 8 is slow, cold work. The exertion of climbing the fixed ropes at high speed was just enough to keep them warm on the climb up; now they have to hug the rock and hold on, or wait while Frances is belayed down one of the steeper sections. She uses her right arm and steps down everything she can, helping the process as much as possible.

She is stepping over the boulder that gave Roger such distress, when a blast of wind hits her like a punch, and over the rock she tumbles, face against it. Roger leaps up from below and grabs her just as she is about to roll helplessly onto her left side. For a moment all he can do is hang there, holding her steady. Dougal and Eileen shout down from above. No room for them. Roger double-sets the jumar on the fixed rope above him, pulls up with one arm, the other around Frances's back. They eye each other through the goggles—she scrambles for a foothold blindly—finds something and takes some of her weight herself. Still, they are stuck there. Roger shows Frances his hand and points at it, trying to convey his plan. She nods. He unclips from the fixed rope, sets the jumar once again right below Frances, descends to a good foothold and laces his hands together. He reaches up, guides Frances's free foot into his hands. She shifts her weight onto that foot and lowers herself until Roger keeps the hold in place. Then the other foot crosses to join Roger's two feet—a good bit of work by Frances, who must be hurting. Mid-move another gust almost wrecks their balance, but they lean into each other and hold. They are below the boulder, and Dougal and Eileen can now climb over it and belay Frances again.

They start down once more. But the exertion has triggered a reaction inside Roger, and suddenly he has to take a shit. He curses the cave silt and tries desperately to quell the urge, but it won't be denied. He signals his need to the others and jumars down the fixed rope away from them, to get out of the way of the descent and obtain a little privacy. Pulling his pants down while the winds drag him around the fixed rope is actually a technical problem, and he curses continuously as he relieves himself. It is without a doubt the coldest shit of his life. By the time the others get to him he is shivering so hard he can barely climb.

They barge into Camp 8 around sunset, and Eileen gets on the radio. The lower camps are informed of the situation and given their instructions. No one questions Eileen when her voice has that edge in it.

The problem is that their camp is low on food and oxygen. "I'll go down and get a load," Dougal says.

"But you've already been out a long time," Eileen says.

"No, no. A hot meal and I'll be off again. You should stay here with Frances, and Roger's chilled down."

"We can get Arthur or Hans to come up."

"We don't want movement up, do we? They'd have to stay up here, and we're out of room as it is. Besides, I'm the most used to climbing in this wind in the dark."

Eileen nods. "Okay."

"You warm enough?" Dougal asks Roger.

Roger can only shiver. They help him into his bag and dose him with tea, but it is hard to drink. Long after Dougal has left he is still shivering.

"Good sign he's shivering," Frances says to Eileen. "But he's awfully cold. Maybe too hypothermic to warm up. I'm cold myself."

Eileen keeps the stove on high till there is a fug of warm air in the tent. She gets into Frances's bag with her, carefully avoiding her injured side. In the ruddy stove light their faces are pinched with discomfort.

"I'm okay," Frances mutters after a while. "Good'n warm. Get him."

Roger is barely conscious as Eileen pushes into his bag with him. He is resentful that he must move. "Get your outers off," Eileen orders. They struggle around, half in the bag, to get Roger's climbing gear off. Lying together in their thermal underwear, Roger slowly warms up. "Man, you *are* cold," Eileen says.

" 'Preciate it," Roger mutters wearily. "Don't know what happened."

"We didn't work you hard enough on the descent. Plus you had to bare your butt to a wind chill factor I wouldn't want to guess."

Body warmth, seeping into him. Long hard body pressed against him. She won't let him sleep. "Not yet. Turn around. Here. Drink this." Frances holds his eyelids up to check him. "Drink this!" He drinks. Finally they let him sleep.

Dougal wakes them, barging in with a full pack. He and the pack are crusted with snow. "Pretty desperate," he says with a peculiar smile. He hurries into a sleeping bag and drinks tea. Roger checks his watch—midnight. Dougal has been at it for almost twenty-four hours, and after wolfing down a pot of stew he puts on his mask, rolls to a corner of the tent, and falls into a deep sleep.

Next morning the storm is still battering the tent. The four of them get ready awkwardly—the tent is better for three, and they must be careful of Frances's arm. Eileen gets on the radio and orders those below to clear Camp 7 and retreat to the cave. Once climbing they find that Frances's whole side has stiffened up. Getting her down means they have to hammer in new pitons, set up rappeling ropes for her, lower her with one of them jumaring down the fixed rope beside her, while occasionally hunkering down to avoid hard gusts of wind. They stop in Camp 7 for an hour to rest and eat, then drop to the cave. It is dusk by the time they enter the dark refuge.

So they are all back in the cave. The wind swirls in it, and the others have spent the previous day piling rocks into the south side of the cave mouth, to build a protective wall. This helps a bit.

As the fourth day of the storm passes in the whistle and flap of wind, and an occasional flurry of snow, all the members of the climb crowd into one of the large box tents, sitting upright and bumping arms so they will all fit.

"Look, I don't want to go down just because one of us has a busted arm," Marie says.

"I can't climb," says Frances. It seems to Roger that she is holding up very well; her face is white and her eyes look drugged, but she is quite coherent and very calm.

"I *know* that," Marie says. "But we could split up. It'll only take a few people to get you back down to the cars. The rest of us can take the rest of the gear and carry on. If we get to the cache at the top of the scarp, we won't have to worry about supplies. If we don't, we'll just follow you down. But I don't fancy us giving up now—that's not what we came for, eh? Going down when we don't have to?"

Eileen looks at Ivan. "It'd be up to you to get Frances down."

Ivan grimaces, nods. "That's what Sherpas are for," he says gamely.

"Do you think four will be enough for it?"

"More would probably just get in the way."

There is a quick discussion of their supply situation. Hans is of the opinion that they are short enough on supplies to make splitting up dangerous. "It seems to me that our primary responsibility is to get Frances to the ground safely. The climb can be finished another time."

Marie argues with this, but Hans is supported by Stephan, and it seems neither side will convince the other. After an apprehensive silence, Eileen clears her throat.

"Marie's plan sounds good to me," she says briefly. "We've got the supplies to go both ways, and the Sherpas can get Frances down by themselves."

"Neither group will have much margin for error," Hans says.

"We can leave the water for the group going down," Marie says. "There'll be ice and snow the rest of the way up."

"We'll have to be a bit more sparing with the oxygen," Hans says. "Frances should have enough to take her all the way down."

"Yes," Eileen says. "We'll have to get going again in the next day or two, no matter what the weather's like."

"Well?" says Marie. "We've proved we can get up and down the fixed ropes in any weather. We should get up and fix Camp 9 as soon as we can. Tomorrow, say."

"If there's a bit of a break."

"We've got to stock the higher camps—"

"Yeah. We'll do what we can, Marie. Don't fret."

While the storm continues they make preparations to split up. Roger, who wants to stay clear of all that, helps Arthur to build the wall at the cave's entrance. They have started at the southern end, filling up the initial crack of the cave completely. After that they must be satisfied with a two-meter-high wall, which they extend across the entrance until the boulders on the floor of the cave are used up. Then they sit against the wall and watch the division of the goods. Wind still whistles through the cave, but sitting at the bottom of the wall they can feel that they did some good.

The division of equipment is causing some problems. Marie is very possessive about the oxygen bottles: "Well, you'll be going down, right?" she demands of Ivan. "You don't need oxygen at all once you get a couple camps down."

"Frances will need it a lot longer than that," Ivan said. "And we can't be sure how long it'll take to get her down."

"Hell, you can *reel* her down once you get past the Thank God Ledge. Shouldn't take you any time at all—"

"Marie, get out of this," Eileen snaps. "We'll divide the supplies—there's no reason for you to bother with this."

Marie glares, stomps off to her tent.

Arthur and Roger give each other the eye. The division goes on. Rope will be the biggest problem, it appears. But everything will be tight.

At the first break in the winds the rescue party—Frances and the four Sherpas—take off. Roger descends with them to help them cross the Thank God Ledge, and to recover the fixed rope there. The wind still gusts, but with less violence. In the middle of the ledge crossing Frances loses her balance and swings around; Roger reaches her (not noticing he ran) and holds her in. "We have to stop meeting like this," Frances says, voice muffled by her mask.

When they reach the Great Gully, Roger says his good-byes. The Sherpas are cheery enough, but Frances is white-faced and quiet. She has said hardly a word in the last couple of days, and Roger cannot tell what she is thinking. "Bad luck," he tells her. "You'll get another chance, though."

"Thanks for grabbing me during the descent from Camp 9," she says just as he is about to leave. She looks upset. "You're awfully quick. That would have hurt like hell if I had rolled onto my left side."

"I'm glad I could help," Roger says. Then, as he leaves: "I like how tough you've been."

A grimace from Frances.

On the way back Roger must free the fixed rope to recover it for the climb above, and so on the Thank God Ledge he is always belayed only to the piton ahead. If he were to fall he would drop—sometimes up to twenty-five meters—and swing like a pendulum over the rough basalt. The ledge becomes new again; he finds that the smooth surface of the sidewalk is indeed wide enough to walk on, but still—the wind pushes at his back—he is alone—the sky is low and dark, and threatens to snow—and all of a sudden the hair on his neck rises, the oxygen whistles in his mask as he sucks it down, the pitted rock face seems to glow with an internal light of its own, and all the world expands, expands ever outward, growing more immense with every pulse of his blood; and his lungs fill, and fill, and fill. . . .

Back in the cave Roger says nothing about the eerie moment on the ledge. Only Eileen and Hans are still in the cave—the others have gone up to supply the higher camps, and Dougal and Marie have gone all the way up to Camp 9. Eileen, Hans and Roger load up their packs—very heavy loads, they find when they duck out the cave—and start up the fixed ropes. Jumaring up the somewhat icy rope is difficult, in places dangerous. The wind strikes from the left now rather than from above. By the time they reach Camp 7 it is nearly dark, and Stephan and Arthur already occupy the single tent. In the mirror dusk and the strong side wind, erecting another tent is no easy task. There is not another level spot to set it on, either—they must place it on a slope, and tie it to pitons hammered into the cliff. By the time Eileen and Roger and Hans get into the new tent, Roger is freezing and starving and intensely thirsty. "Pretty bloody desperate," he says wearily, mimicking Marie and the Sherpas. They melt snow and cook up a pot of stew from their sleeping bags, and when they are done eating, Roger puts on his oxygen mask, sets the flow for sleep, and slumps off.

The moment on the Thank God Ledge jumps to mind and wakes him momentarily. Wind whips the taut walls of the tent, and Eileen, penciling logistic notes for the next day, slides down the slope under the tent until their two sleeping bags are one clumped mass. Roger looks at her: brief smile from that tired, puffy, frost-burned face. Great deltas of wrinkles under her eyes. His feet begin to warm up and he falls asleep to the popping of the tent, the hiss of oxygen, the scratching of a pencil.

That night the storm picks up again.

The next morning they take down the tent in a strong wind—hard work—and start portering loads up to Camp 8. Halfway between camps it begins to snow. Roger watches his feet through swirls of hard dry granules. His gloved fingers twist around the frigid jumar, sliding it up the frosted rope, clicking it home, pulling himself up. It is a struggle to see footholds in the spindrift, which moves horizontally across the cliff face, from left to right as he looks at it. The whole face appears to be whitely streaming to the side, like a wave. He finds he must focus his attention entirely on his hands and feet. His fingers, nose and toes are very cold. He rubs his nose through the mask, feels nothing. The wind pushes him hard, like a giant trying to make him fall. In the narrow gullies the wind is less strong, but they find themselves climbing up through waves of avalanching snow, drift after drift of it piling up between their bodies and the slope, burying them, sliding between their legs and away. One gully seems to last forever. Intermittently Roger is concerned about his nose, but mostly he worries about the immediate situation: moving up the rope, keeping a foothold. Visibility is down to about fifty meters—they are in a little white bubble flying to the left through white snow, or so it appears.

At one point Roger must wait for Eileen and Hans to get over the boulder that Frances had such trouble with. His mind wanders and it occurs to him that their chances of success have shifted radically—and with them, the nature of the climb. Low on supplies, facing an unknown route in deteriorating weather—Roger wonders how Eileen will handle it. She has led expeditions before, but this kind only come about by accident.

She passes him going strong, beats ice from the rope, sweeps spindrift from the top of the boulder. Pulls up over it in one smooth motion. The wind cuts through Roger as he watches Hans repeat the operation: cuts through the laminated outer suit, the thick bunting inner suit, his skin. . . . He brushes spindrift from his goggles with a frigid hand and heaves up after them.

Though it is spring, the winter-like low-pressure system over Olympus Mons is in place, drawing the wet winds up from the south, creating stable storm conditions on the south and east arcs of the escarpment. The snow is irregular, the winds constant. For the better part of a week the seven climbers left on the face struggle in the miserable conditions. One night at sunset radio hour they hear from Frances and the Sherpas, down at base camp. There is a lot of sand in Martian snow, and their voices are garbled by static, but the message is clear: they are down, they are safe, they are leaving for Alexandria to get Frances's arm set. Roger catches on Eileen's averted face an expression of pure relief, and realizes that her silence in the past few days has been a manifestation of worry. Now, looking pleased, she gives the remaining climbers their instructions for the next day, in a fresh, determined tone.

Into camp at night, cold and almost too tired to walk. Big loaded packs onto the various ledges and niches that serve for this particular camp. Hands shaking with hunger. This camp—number 13, Roger believes—is on a saddle between two ridges overlooking a deep, twisted chimney. "Just like the Devil's Kitchen on Ben Nevis," Arthur remarks when they get inside the tent. He eats with gusto. Roger shivers and puts his hands two centimeters above the glowing stove ring. Transferring from climbing mode to tent mode is a tricky business, and tonight Roger hasn't done so well. At this altitude and in these winds, cold has become their most serious opponent. Overmitts off, and everything must be done immediately to get lightly gloved hands protected again as quickly as possible. Even if the rest of one's body is warmed by exertion, the fingertips will freeze within a few minutes. Yet so many camp operations can be done easier with hands out of mitts. Frostnip is the frequent result, leaving the fingers tender, so that pulling up a rockface, or even buttoning or zipping one's clothes, becomes a painful task. Frostnip blisters kill the skin, creating black patches that take a week or more to peel away. Now when they sit in the tents around the ruddy light of the stove, observing solemnly the progress of the cooking meal, they see across the pot faces blotched on cheek or nose: black skin peeling away to reveal bright new skin beneath. . . .

They climb onto a band of rotten rock, a tuff and lava composite that sometimes breaks right off in their hands. It takes Marie and Dougal two full days to find decent belay points for the hundred and fifty meters of the band, and every morning the rockfall is frequent and frightening. "It's a bit like swimming up the thing, isn't it?" Dougal comments. When they make it to the hard rock above, Eileen orders Dougal and Marie to the bottom of their "ladder," to get some rest. Marie makes no complaint now; each day in the lead is an exhausting exercise, and Marie and Dougal are beat.

Every night Eileen works out plans for the following day, revising them as conditions and the climbers' strength and health change. The logistics are complicated, and each day the seven climbers shift partners and positions in the climb. Eileen scribbles in her notebook and jabbers on the radio every dusk, altering the schedules and changing her orders with almost every new bit of information she receives from the higher camps. Her method appears chaotic. Marie dubs her the "Mad Mahdi," and scoffs at the constant change in plans; but she obeys them, and they work: every night they are scattered in two or three camps up and down the cliff, with everything that they need to survive the night, and get them higher the next day; and every new day they leap-frog up, pulling out the lowest camp, finding a place to establish a new high camp. The bitter winds continue. Everything is difficult. They lose track of camp numbers, and name them only high, middle, and low.

Naturally, three quarters of everyone's work is portering—carrying heavy loads up the fixed ropes of routes already established. Roger begins to feel that he is surviving the rigors of the weather and altitude better than most of the rest; he can carry more faster, and even though most days end in that state where each step up is ten breaths' agony, he finds he can take on more the next day. His digestion returns to normal, which is a blessing—a great physical pleasure, in fact. Perhaps improvement in this area masks the effects of altitude, or perhaps the altitude isn't bothering Roger yet; it is certainly true that high altitude affects people differently, for reasons unconnected with basic strength—in fact, for reasons not yet fully understood.

So Roger becomes the chief porter; Dougal calls him Roger Sherpa, and Arthur calls him Tenzing. The day's challenge becomes to do all the myriad activities of the day as efficiently as possible, without frostnip, without excessive discomfort, hunger, thirst, or exhaustion. He hums to himself little snatches of music. His favorite is the eight-note phrase repeated by the basses near the end of the first movement of Beethoven's Ninth: six notes down, two notes up, over and over and over. And each evening in the sleeping bag, warm, well-fed, and prone, is a little victory.

One night he wakes up to darkness and silence, fully awake in an instant, heart pounding. Confused, he thinks he may have dreamt of the Thank God Ledge. But then he notices the silence again and realizes his oxygen bottle has run out. It happens every week or so. He uncouples the bottle from the regulator, finds another bottle in the dark and clips it in place. When he tells Arthur about it next morning, Arthur laughs. "That happened to me a couple nights ago. I don't think anybody could sleep through their oxygen bottle running out—I mean you wake up *very* awake, don't you?"

In the hard rock band Roger porters up a pitch that leaves him whistling into his mask: the gullies have disappeared, above is a nearly vertical black wall, and breaking it is one lightning bolt crack, now marked by a fixed rope with slings attached, making it a sort of rope ladder. Fine for him, but the lead climb! "Must have been Dougal at it again."

And the next day he is out in the lead himself with Arthur, on a continuation of the same face. Leading is very unlike portering. Suddenly the dogged, repetitious, almost mindless work of carrying loads is replaced by the anxious attentiveness of the lead. Arthur takes the first pitch and finishes it bubbling over with enthusiasm. Only his oxygen mask keeps him from carrying on a long conversation as Roger takes over the lead. Then Roger is up there himself, above the last belay on empty rock, looking for the best way. The lure of the lead returns, the pleasure of the problem solved fills him with energy. Fully back in lead mode, he collaborates with Arthur—who turns out to be an ingenious and resourceful technical climber—on the best storm day yet: five hundred meters of fixed rope, their entire supply, nailed up in one day. They hurry back down to camp and find Eileen and Marie still there, dumping food for the next few days.

"By God are we a team!" Arthur cries as they describe the day's work. "Eileen, you should put us together more often. Don't you agree, Roger?"

Roger grins at Eileen, nods. "That was fun."

Marie and Eileen leave for the camp below, and Arthur and Roger cook a big pot of stew and trade climbing stories, scores of them: and every one ends, "but that was nothing compared to today."

Heavy snow returns and traps them in their tents, and it's all they can do to keep the high camp supplied. "Bloody desperate out!" Marie complains, as if she can't believe how bad it is. After one bad afternoon Stephan and Arthur are in the high camp, Eileen and Roger in the middle camp, and Hans, Marie, and Dougal in the low camp with all the supplies. The storm strikes Roger and Eileen's tent so hard that they are considering bringing in some rocks to weight it down more. A buzz sounds from their radio and Eileen picks it up.

"Eileen, this is Arthur. I'm afraid Stephan has come up too fast."

Eileen scowls fearfully, swears under her breath. Stephan has gone from low camp to the high one in two hard days' climbing.

"He's very short of breath, and he's spitting up bloody spit. And talking like a madman."

"I'm okay!" Stephan shouts through the static. "I'm fine!"

"Shut up! You're not fine! Eileen, did you hear that? I'm afraid he's got edema."

"Yeah," Eileen says. "Has he got a headache?"

"No. It's just his lungs right now, I think. Shut up! I can hear his chest bubbling, you know."

"Yeah. Pulse up?"

"Pulse weak and rapid, yeah."

"Damn." Eileen looks over at Roger. "Put him on maximum oxygen."

"I already have. Still . . ."

"I know. We've got to get him down."

"I'm okay!"

"Yeah," Arthur says. "He needs to come down, at least to your camp, maybe lower."

"Damn it," Eileen exclaims when off the radio. "I moved him up too fast."

An hour later—calls made below, the whole group in action—Roger and Eileen are out in the storm again, in the dark, their helmet headlights showing them only a portion of the snowfall. They cannot afford to wait until morning—pulmonary edema can be quickly fatal, and the best treatment by far is to get the victim lower, where his lungs can clear out the excess water. Even a small drop in altitude can make a dramatic difference. So off they go; Roger takes the lead and bashes ice from the rope, jumars up, scrabbles over the rock blindly with his crampon-tips to get a purchase in the snow and ice. It is bitterly cold, and his goggles allow the cold onto his eyes. They reach the bottom of the blank wall pitch that so impressed Roger, and the going is treacherous. He wonders how they will get Stephan down it. The fixed rope is the only thing making the ascent possible, but it does less and less to aid them as ice coats it and the rock face. Wind hammers them, and Roger has a sudden acute sensation of the empty space behind them. The headlight beams reveal only swirling snow. Fear adds its own kind of chill to the mix. . . .

By the time they reach high camp Stephan is quite ill. No more protests from him. "I don't know how we'll get him down," Arthur says anxiously. "I gave him a small shot of morphine to get the peripheral veins to start dilating."

"Good. We'll just have to truss him into a harness and lower him."

"Easier said than done, in this stuff."

Stephan is barely conscious, coughing and hacking with

every breath. Pulmonary edema fills the lungs with water; unless the process is reversed, he will drown. Just getting him
into the sling (another function of the little wall tents) is hard
work. Then outside again—struck by the wind—and to the
fixed ropes. Roger descends first, Eileen and Arthur lower
Stephan using a power reel, and Roger collects him like a large
bundle of laundry. After standing him upright and knocking
the frozen spittle from the bottom of his mask, Roger waits for
the other two, and when they arrive he starts down again. The
descent seems endless, and everyone gets dangerously cold.
Windblown snow, the rock face, omnipresent cold: nothing
else in the world. At the end of one drop Roger cannot undo
the knot at the end of his belay line, to send it back up for
Stephan. For fifteen minutes he struggles with the frozen knot,
which resembles a wet iron pretzel. Nothing to cut it off with,
either. For a while it seems they will all freeze because he
can't untie a knot. Finally he takes his climbing gloves off and
pulls at the thing with his bare fingers until it comes loose.

Eventually they arrive at the lower camp, where Hans and
Dougal are waiting with a medical kit. Stephan is zipped into
a sleeping bag, and given a diuretic and some more morphine.
Rest and the drop in altitude should see him back to health,
although at the moment his skin is blue and his breathing
ragged: no guarantees. He could die—a man who might live
a thousand years—and suddenly their whole enterprise seems
crazy. His coughs sound weak behind the oxygen mask, which
hisses madly on maximum flow.

"He should be okay," Hans pronounces. "Won't know for
sure for several hours."

But there they are—seven people in two wall tents. "We'll
go back up," Eileen says, looking to Roger. He nods.

And they go back out again. The swirl of white snow in their
headlights, the cold, the buffets of wind . . . they are tired, and
progress is slow. Roger slips once and the jumars don't catch
on the icy rope for about three meters, where they suddenly
catch and test his harness, and the piton above. A fall! The
spurt of fear gives him a second wind. Stubbornly he decides
that much of his difficulty is mental. It's dark and windy, but
really the only difference between this and his daytime climbs
during the last week is the cold, and the fact that he can't see

much. But the helmet lamps do allow him to see—he is at the center of a shifting white sphere, and the rock he must work on is revealed. It is covered with a sheet of ice and impacted snow, and where the ice is clear it gleams in the light like glass laid over the black rock beneath. Crampons are great in this— the sharp front points stick in the snow and ice firmly, and the only problem is the brittle black glass that will break away from the points in big jagged sheets. Even black ice can be distinguished in the bright bluish gleam of the lights, so the work is quite possible. Look at it as just another climb, he urges himself, meanwhile kicking like a maniac with his left foot to spike clear a crack where he can nail in another piton to replace a bad hold. The dizzying freeness of a pull over an outcropping; the long reach up for a solid knob: he becomes aware of the work as a sort of game, a set of problems to be solved despite cold or thirst or fatigue (his hands are beginning to tire from the long night's hauling, so that each hold hurts). Seen this way, it all changes. Now the wind is an opponent to be beaten, but also to be respected. The same of course is true of the rock, his principal opponent—and this a daunting one, an opponent to challenge him to his utmost performance. He kicks into a slope of hard snow and ascends rapidly.

He looks down as Eileen kicks up the slope: quick reminder of the stakes of this game. The light on the top of her helmet makes her look like a night insect, or a deep sea fish. She reaches him quickly; one long gloved hand over the wall's top, and she joins him with a smooth contraction of the bicep. Strong woman, Roger thinks, but decides to take another lead anyway. He is in a mood now where he doubts anyone but Dougal could lead as fast.

Up through the murk they climb.

An odd point is that the two climbers can scarcely communicate. Roger "hears" Eileen through varieties of tugging on the rope linking them. If he takes too long to study a difficult spot above, he feels a mild interrogatory tug on the rope. Two tugs when Roger is belaying means she's on her way up. Very taut belaying betrays her belief that he is in a difficult section. So communication by rope can be fairly complex and subtle. But aside from it, and the infrequent shout with the mask pulled up to one side (which includes the punishment of a face full of spindrift) they are isolated. Mute partners. The exchange of lead goes well—one passes the other with a wave—the belay is ready. Up Eileen goes. Roger watches and holds the belay taut. Little time for contemplating their situation, thankfully; but while taking a rest on crampon points in steps chopped out with his ice axe, Roger feels acutely the *thereness* of his position, cut off from past or future, irrevocably in this moment, on this cliff face that drops away bottomlessly, extends up forever. Unless he climbs well, there will never be any other reality.

Then they reach a pitch where the fixed rope has been cut in the middle. Falling rock or ice has shaved it off. A bad sign. Now Roger must climb a ropeless pitch, hammering in pitons on his way to protect himself. Every meter above the last belay is two meters fall. . . .

Roger never expected this hard a climb, and adrenaline banishes his exhaustion. He studies the first small section of a pitch that he knows is ten or twelve meters long, invisible in the dark snow flurries above. Probably Marie or Dougal climbed this crack the first time. He discovers that the crack just gives him room for his hands. Almost a vertical crack for a while, with steps cut into the ice. Up he creeps, crab-like and sure-footed. Now the crack widens and the ice is too far back in it to be of use—but the cramponed boots can be stuck in the crack and turned sideways, to stick tenuously into the thin ice coating the crack's interior. One creates one's own staircase, mostly using the tension of the twisted crampons. Now the crack abruptly closes and he has to look around, ah, there, a horizontal crack holding the empty piton. Very good—he hooks into it and is protected thus far. Perhaps the next piton is up this rampway to the right? Clawing to find the slight indentations that pass for handholds here, crouching to lean up the ramp in a tricky walk—he wonders about the crampons here . . . ah. The next piton, right at eye level. Perfect. And then an area lined with horizontal strata about a meter in thickness, making a steep—a very steep—ladder.

And at the top of that pitch they find the high camp tent, crushed under a load of snow. Avalanche. One corner of the tent flaps miserably.

Eileen comes up and surveys the damage in the double glare of their two headlamps. She points at the snow, makes a digging motion. The snow is so cold that it can't bind together—moving it is like kicking coarse sand. They get to work, having no other choice. Eventually the tent is free, and as an added benefit they are warmed as well, although Roger feels he can barely move. The tent's poles have been bent and some broken, and splints must be tied on before the tent can be redeployed. Roger kicks snow and ice chunks around the perimeter of the tent, until it is "certifiably bombproof," as the leads would say. Except if another avalanche hits it . . . something they can't afford to think about, as they can't move the camp anywhere else. They simply have to risk it. Inside, they drop their packs and start the stove and put a pot of ice on. Then crampons off, and into sleeping bags. With the bags around them up to the waist, they can start sorting out the mess. There is spindrift on everything, but unless it gets right next to the stove it will not melt. Digging in the jumbled piles of gear for a packet of stew, Roger feels again how tired his body is. Oxygen masks off, so they can drink. "That was quite an excursion." Raging thirst. They laugh with relief. He brushes an unused pot with his bare hand, guaranteeing a frostnip blister. Eileen calculates the chance of another avalanche without trepidation: ". . . so if the wind stays high enough we should be okay." They discuss Stephan, and sniff like hunting dogs at the first scent of the stew. Eileen digs out the radio and calls down to the low camp. Stephan is sleeping, apparently without discomfort. "Morphine will do that," Eileen says. They wolf down their meal in a few minutes.

The snow under the tent is torn up by boot prints, and Roger's sleeping surface is unbelievably lumpy. He rolls over until he is wedged against the length of Eileen's bag, coveting the warmth and hoping for a flatter surface. It is just as lumpy there. Eileen snuggles back into him and he can feel the potential for warmth; he can tell he will warm up. He wonders if getting into one bag would be worth the effort.

"Amazing what some people will do for fun," Eileen comments drowsily.

Short laugh. "This isn't the fun part."

"Isn't it? That climb . . ."

Big yawn. "That was some climb," he agrees. No denying it.

"That was a great climb."

"Especially since we didn't get killed."

"Yeah." She yawns too, and Roger can feel a big wave of sleep about to break over him and sweep him away. "I hope Stephan gets better. Otherwise we'll have to take him down."

In the next few days everyone has to go out several times in the storm, to keep the high camp supplied and to keep the fixed ropes free of ice. The work is miserable when they can do it, and sometimes they can't: the wind on some days shuts down everything, and they can only huddle inside and hope the tents hold to the face. One dim day Roger is sitting with Stephan and Arthur in low camp. Stephan has recovered from the edema, and is anxious to climb again. "No hurry," Roger says. "No one's going anywhere anyway, and water in the lungs is serious business. You'll have to take it slow—"

The tent door is unzipped and a plume of snow enters, followed by Dougal. He grins hello. The silence seems to call for some comment: "Pretty invigorating out there," he says to fill it, and looks after a pot of tea. The shy moment having passed he chats cheerfully with Arthur about the weather. Tea done, he is off again; he is in a hurry to get a load up to the high camp. A quick grin and he is out the tent and gone. And it occurs to Roger that there are two types of climber on their expedition (another duality): those who *endure* the bad weather and accidents and all the various difficulties of the face that are making this climb so uncomfortable; and those who, in some important, peculiar way, *enjoy* all the trouble. In the former group are Eileen, who has the overriding responsibility for the climb—Marie, who is in such a hurry for the top—and Hans and Stephan, who are less experienced and would be just as happy to climb under sunny skies and with few serious difficulties. Each of these is steady and resolute, without a doubt; but they endure.

Dougal, on the other hand, Dougal and Arthur: these two are quite clearly *enjoying* themselves, and the worse things get the more fun they seem to have. It is, Roger thinks, perverse. The reticent, solitary Dougal, seizing with quiet glee every possible chance to get out in the gale and climb. . . . "He certainly seems to be enjoying himself,'' Roger says out loud, and Arthur laughs.

"That Dougal!'' he cries. "What a Brit he is. You know climbers are the same everywhere. I come all the way to Mars and find just the people you'd expect to find on Ben Nevis. Course it stands to reason, doesn't it? That New Scotland school and all.''

It is true; from the very start of the colonization British climbers have been coming to Mars in search of new climbs, and many of them have stayed.

"And I'll tell you,'' Arthur continues, "those guys are never happier than when it's blowing force ten and dumping snow by the dumptruck. Or not snow, actually. More like sleet, that's what they want. One degree rain, or wet snow. Perfect. And you know why they want it? So they can come back in at the end of the day and say, 'Bloody desperate out today, eh mate?' They're all dying to be able to say that. 'Bluidy *das*perate, mite.' Ha! Do you know what I mean? It's like giving themselves a medal or something, I don't know.''

Roger and Stephan, smiling, nod. "Very macho,'' Stephan says.

"But Dougal!'' Arthur cries. "Dougal! He's too cool for that. He goes out there in the nastiest conditions he can possibly find—I mean look at him just now—he couldn't *wait* to get back out there! Didn't want to waste such a fine opportunity! And he climbs the hardest pitches he can find, too. Have you seen him? You've seen the routes he leaves behind. Man, that guy could climb buttered glass in a hurricane. And what does he say about it? Does he say that was pretty bloody desperate? No! He says,'' and Roger and Stephan join in, like a chorus: "How invigorating!''

"Yeah,'' Stephan says, laughing. "Pretty invigorating out there, all right.''

"The Scots,'' Arthur says, giggling away. "Martian Scots, no less. I can't believe it.''

"It's not just the Scots are strange,'' Roger points out. "What about you, Arthur? I notice you getting quite a giggle out of all this yourself, eh?''

"Oh, yeah, yeah,'' Arthur says. "I'm having a good time. Aren't you? I'll tell you, once we got on the oxygen I started feeling great. Before that it wasn't so easy. The air seemed really thin, I mean *really* thin. Elevations here don't mean anything to me, I mean you haven't got a sea level so what does elevation really mean, right? But your air is like nothing, man. So when we got on the bottle I could really feel the difference. A lifesaver. And then there's the gravity! Now that's wonderful. What is it, two fifths of a gee? Practically nothing! You might as well be on the moon! As soon as I learned to balance properly, I really started to have a good time. Felt like Superman. On this planet it just isn't that hard to go uphill, that's all.'' He laughs, toasts the other two with tea: ''On Mars, I'm Superman.''

High altitude pulmonary edema works fast, and one either succumbs or recovers very quickly. When Stephan's lungs are completely clear Hans orders him to keep on maximum oxygen intake, and he is given a light load and ordered to take it slow and only move up from one low camp to the next. At this point, Roger thinks, it would be more difficult to get him back down the cliff than keep on going to the top; a common enough climbing situation, but one that no one talks about. Stephan complains about his reduced role, but agrees to go along with it. For his first few days back out Roger teams with him and keeps a sharp eye on him. But Stephan climbs fairly rapidly, and only complains at Roger's solicitousness, and at the cold winds. Roger concludes he is all right.

Back to portering. Hans and Arthur are out in the lead, having a terrible time with a broad, steep rampart that they are trying to force directly. For a couple of days they are all stalled as the camps are stocked, and the lead party cannot make more than fifty or seventy-five meters a day. One evening on the radio while Hans describes a difficult overhang, Marie gets on the horn and starts in. ''Well, I don't know what's going on up there, but with Stephan sucking down the oxygen and you all making centimeters a day we're going to end up stuck on this damn cliff for good! What? I don't give a fuck *what* your troubles are, mate—if you can't make the lead you should bloody well get down and let somebody on there who can!''

''This is a big tuff band,'' Arthur says defensively. ''Once we get above this it's more or less a straight shot to the top—''

"*If* you've got any bloody oxygen it is! Look, what is this, a co-op? I didn't join a fucking co-op!"

Roger watches Eileen closely. She is listening carefully to the exchange, her finger on the intercom, a deep furrow between her eyes, as if she is concentrating. He is surprised she has not already intervened. But she lets Marie get off another couple of blasts, and only then does she cut in: "Marie! Marie! Eileen here—"

"I know that."

"Arthur and Hans are scheduled to come down soon. Meanwhile, shut up."

And the next day, Arthur and Hans put up three hundred meters of fixed rope, and top the tuff band. When Hans announces this on the sunset radio call (Roger can just hear Arthur in the background, saying in falsetto "So there! So there!"), a little smile twitches Eileen's mouth, before she congratulates them and gets on to the orders for the next day. Roger nods thoughtfully.

After they get above Hans and Arthur's band, the slope lays back a bit and progress is more rapid, even in the continuous winds. The cliff here is like a wall of immense irregular bricks which have been shoved back, so that each brick is set a bit behind the one below it. This great jumble of blocks and ledges and ramps makes for easy zig-zag climbing, and good campsites. One day, Roger stops for a break and looks around. He is portering a load from middle camp to high camp, and has gotten ahead of Eileen. No one in sight. There is a cloud layer far below them, a gray rumpled blanket covering the whole world. Then there is the vertical realm of the cliff-face, a crazed jumble of a block-wall, which extends up to a very smooth, almost featureless cloud layer above them. Only the finest ripples, like waves, mar this gray ceiling. Floor and ceiling of cloud, wall of rock: it seems for a moment that this climb will go on eternally, it is a whole world, an infinite wall that they will climb forever. When has it been any different? Sandwiched like this, between cloud and cloud, it is easy not to believe in the past; perhaps the planet is a cliff, endlessly varied, endlessly challenging.

Then in the corner of Roger's eye, a flash of color. He looks at the deep crack between the ledge he is standing on and the next vertical block. In the twisted ice nestles a patch of moss campion. Cushion of black-green moss, a circle of perhaps a hundred tiny dark pink flowers on it. After three weeks of almost unrelieved black and white, the color seems to burst out of the flowers and explode in his eyes. Such a dark, intense pink! Roger crouches to inspect them. The moss is very finely textured, and appears to be growing directly out of the rock, although no doubt there is some sand back in the crack. A seed or a scrap of moss must have been blown off the shield plateau and down the cliff, to take root here.

Roger stands, looks around again. Eileen has joined him, and she observes him sharply. He pulls his mask to the side. "Look at that," he says. "You can't get away from it any-where!"

She shakes her head. Pulls her mask down. "It's not the new landscape you hate so much," she says. "I saw the way you were looking at that plant. And it's just a plant, after all, doing its best to live. No, I think you've made a displacement. You use topography as a symbol. It's not the landscape, it's the people. It's the history we've made that you dislike. The terraforming is just part of it—the visible sign of a history of exploitation."

Roger considers it. "We're just another Terran colony, you mean. Colonialism—"

"Yes! That's what you hate, see? Not topography, but history. Because the terraforming, so far, is a waste. It's not being done for any good purpose."

Uneasily Roger shakes his head. He has not thought of it like that, and isn't sure he completely agrees: it's the land that has suffered the most, after all. Although—

Eileen continues: "There's some good in that, if you think about it. Because the landscape isn't going to change back, ever. But history—history must change, by definition."

And she takes the lead, leaving Roger to stare up after her.

The winds die in the middle of the night. The cessation of tent noise wakes Roger up. It is bitterly cold, even in his bag. It takes him a while to figure out what woke him; his oxygen is still hissing softly in his face. When he figures out what did it, he smiles. Checking his watch, he finds it is almost time for the mirror dawn. He sits up and turns on the stove for tea.

Eileen stirs in her sleeping bag, opens one eye. Roger likes watching her wake; even behind the mask, the shift from vulnerable girl to expedition leader is easy to see. It's like ontogeny recapitulating phylogeny: coming to consciousness in the morning recapitulates maturation in life. Now all he needs is the Greek terminology, and he will have a scientific truth. Eileen pulls off her oxygen mask and rolls onto one elbow.

"Want some tea?" he says.

"Yeah."

"It'll be a moment."

"Hold the stove steady—I've got to pee." She stands in the tent doorway, sticks a plastic urine scoop into the open fly of her pants, urinates out the door. "Wow! Sure is cold out. And clear! I can see stars."

"Great. The wind's died, too, see?"

Eileen crawls back into her bag. They brew their tea with great seriousness, as if mixing delicate elixirs. Roger watches her drink.

"Do you really not remember us from before?" he asks.

"Nooo . . ." Eileen says slowly. "We were in our twenties, right? No, the first years I really remember are from my fifties, when I was training up in the caldera. Wall climbs, kind of like this, actually." She sips. "But tell me about us."

Roger shrugs. "It doesn't matter."

"It must be odd. To remember when the rest don't."

"Yes, it is."

"I was probably awful at that age."

"No, no. You were fine."

She laughs. "I can't believe that. Unless I've gone downhill since then."

"Not at all! You sure couldn't have done all this back then."

"I believe that. Getting half an expedition strung out all over a cliff, people sick—"

"No, no. You're doing fine."

She shakes her head. "You can't pretend this climb has gone well. I remember that much."

"What hasn't gone well hasn't been your fault, as you must admit. In fact, given what has happened, we're doing very well, I think. And that's mostly your doing. Not easy with Frances and Stephan, and the storm, and Marie."

"Marie!"

They laugh. "And this storm," Roger says. "That night climb we did, getting Stephan down!" He sips his tea.

"That was a wild one," Eileen says firmly.

Roger nods. They have that. He gets up to pee himself, letting in a blast of intensely cold air. "My God that's cold! What's the temperature?"

"Sixty below, outside."

"Oh. No wonder. I guess that cloud cover was doing us *some* good." Outside it is still dark, and the ice-bearded cliff-face gleams whitely under the stars.

"I like the way you lead the expedition," Roger says into the tent as he zips up. "It's a very light touch, but you still have things under control."

Only slurping sounds from Eileen. Roger zips the tent door closed and hustles back into his bag.

"More tea?" she asks.

"Definitely."

"Here—roll back here, you'll warm up faster, and I could use the insulation myself." Roger nods, shivering, and rolls his bag into the back side of hers, so they are both on one elbow, spooned together.

They sip tea and talk. Roger warms up, stops shivering. Pleasure of empty bladder, of contact with her. They finish the tea and doze for a bit in the warmth. Keeping the oxygen masks off prevents them from falling into a deep sleep. "Mirrors'll be up soon." "Yeah." "Here—move over a bit." Roger remembers when they were lovers, so long ago. Previous lifetime. She was the city dweller then, he the canyon crawler. Now . . . now all the comfort, warmth and contact have given him an erection. He wonders if she can feel it through the two bags. Probably not. Hmmm. He remembers suddenly—the first time they made love was in a tent. He went to bed, and she had come right into his little cubicle of the communal tent and jumped him! Remembering it does nothing to make his erection go away. He wonders if he can get away with a similar sort of act here. They are definitely pressed together hard. All that climbing together: Eileen pairs the climbing teams, so she must have enjoyed it too. And climbing together has that sort of dance-like teamwork—boulder ballet; and the constant kinetic juxtaposition, the felt relationship of the rope, has a certain sensuousness to it. It is a physical partnership, without a doubt.

Of course all this can be true and climbing remain a profoundly non-sexual relationship—there are certainly other things to think about. But now . . .

Now she is dozing again. He thinks about her climbing, her leadership. The things she said to him back down in the first camps, when he was so depressed. A sort of teacher, really.

Thoughts of that lead him to memories of his past, of the failed work. For the first time in many days his memory presents him with the usual parade of the past, the theater of ghosts. How can he ever assume such a long and fruitless history? Is it even possible?

Mercifully the tea's warmth, and the mere fact of lying prone, have their way with him, and he dozes off himself.

The day dawns. Sky like a sheet of old paper, the sun a big bronze coin below them to the east. The sun! Wonderful to see sunlight, shadows. In the light the cliff face looks sloped back an extra few degrees, and it seems there is an end to it up there. Eileen and Roger are in the middle camp, and after ferrying a load to the high camp they follow the rope's zig-zag course up the narrow ledges. The fine, easy face, the sunlight, the dawn's talk, the plains of Tharsis *so* far below: all conspire to please Roger. He is climbing more strongly than ever, hopping up the ledges, enjoying the variety of forms exhibited by the rock. Such a beauty to rough, plated, angular, broken rock.

The face continues to lay back, and at the top of one ledge ramp they find themselves at the bottom of a giant amphitheater filled with snow. And the top of this white half-bowl is . . . sky. The top of the escarpment, apparently. Certainly nothing but sky above it. Dougal and Marie are about to start up it, and Roger joins them. Eileen stays behind to collect the others.

The technically difficult sections of the climb are done. The upper edge of the immense cliff has been rounded off by erosion, broken into alternating ridges and ravines. Here they stand at the bottom of a big bowl broken in half; at bottom the slope is about forty degrees, and it curves up to a final wall that is perhaps sixty degrees. But the bottom of the bowl is filled with deep drifts of light, dry, granular snow, sheeted with a hard layer of windslab. Crossing this stuff is difficult, and they trade the lead often. The leader crashes through the windslab and sinks to his or her knees, or even to the waist, and thereafter has to lift a foot over the windslab above, crash through again, and in that way struggle uphill through the snow. They secure the rope with deadmen—empty oxygen tanks in this case, buried deep in the snow. Roger takes his lead, and quickly begins to sweat under the glare of the sun. Each step is an effort, worse than the step before because of the increasing angle of the slope. After ten minutes he gives the lead back to Marie. Twenty minutes later it is his turn again—the other two can endure it no longer than he can. The steepness of the final wall is actually a relief, as there is less snow.

They stop to strap crampons on their boots. Starting again they fall into a slow, steady rhythm. Kick, step, kick, step; twenty of those, a stop to rest. Time goes away. They don't bother to speak when the lead changes hands: nothing to say. No one wants to break the pace. Kick, step, kick, step, kick, step. Glare of light breaking on snow. The taste of sweat.

When Roger's tenth turn in the lead comes, he sees that he is within striking distance of the top of the wall, and he resolves not to give up the lead again. The snow here is soft under windslab, and he must lean up, dig away a bit with his ice axe, swim up to the new foothold, dig away some more—on and on, gasping into the oxygen mask, sweating profusely in the suddenly overwarm clothing. . . . But he's getting closer. Dougal is behind him. He finds the pace again and sticks to it. Nothing but the pace. Twenty steps, rest. Again. Again. Again. Sweat trickles down his spine, even his feet might warm up. Sun glaring off the steep snow.

He stumbles onto flatness. It feels like some terrible error, like he might fall over the other side. But he is on the edge of a giant plateau, which swoops up in a broad conical shape, too big to be believed. He sees a flat boulder almost clear of snow and staggers over to it. Dougal is beside him, pulling oxygen mask to one side of face: "Looks like we've topped the wall!" Dougal says, looking surprised. Gasping, Roger laughs.

As with all cliff climbs, topping out is a strange experience. After a month of vertical reality, the huge flatness seems all wrong—especially this snowy flatness that extends like a broad fan to each side. The snow ends at the broken edge of the cliff behind them, extends high up the gentle slope of the conical immensity before them. It is easy to believe they stand on the flank of the biggest volcano in the solar system.

"I guess the hard part is over," Dougal says matter-of-factly.

"Just when I was getting in shape," says Roger, and they both laugh.

A snowy plateau, studded with black rocks, and some big mesas. To the east, empty air: far below, the forests of Tharsis. To the northwest, a hill sloping up forever.

Marie arrives and dances a little jig on the boulder. Dougal hikes back to the wall and drops into the amphitheater again, to carry up another load. Not much left to bring; they are almost out of food. Eileen arrives, and Roger shakes her hand. She drops her pack and gives him a hug. They pull some food from the packs and eat a cold lunch while watching Hans, Arthur, and Stephan start up the bottom of the bowl. Dougal is already almost down to them.

When they all reach the top, in a little string led by Dougal, the celebrating really begins. They drop their packs, they hug, they shout, Arthur whirls in circles to try to see it all at once, until he makes himself dizzy. Roger cannot remember feeling exactly like this before.

"Our cache is a few kilometers south of here," Eileen says after consulting her maps. "If we get there tonight we can break out the champagne."

They hike over the snow in a line, trading the lead to break a path. It is a pleasure to walk over flat ground, and spirits are so light that they make good time. Late in the day—a full day's sunshine, their first since before Base Camp—they reach their cache, a strange camp full of tarped down, snow-drifted piles, marked by a lava causeway that ends a kilometer or so above the escarpment.

Among the new equipment is a big mushroom tent. They inflate it, and climb in through the lock and up onto the tent floor for the night's party. Suddenly they are inside a giant transparent mushroom, bouncing over the soft clear raised floor like children on a feather bed; the luxury is excessive, ludicrous, inebriating. Champagne corks pop and fly into the transparent dome of the tent roof, and in the warm air they quickly get drunk, and tell each other how marvelous the climb was, how much they enjoyed it—the discomfort, exhaustion, cold, misery, danger, and fear already dissipating in their minds, already turning into something else.

The next day Marie is not at all enthusiastic about the remainder of their climb. "It's a walk up a bloody hill! And a long walk at that!"

"How else are you going to get down?" Eileen asks acerbically. "Jump?"

It's true; the arrangements they have made force them to climb the cone of the volcano. There is a railway that descends from the north rim of the caldera to Tharsis and civilization; it uses for a rampway one of the great lava spills that erase the escarpment to the north. But first they have to get to the railway, and climbing the cone is probably the fastest, and certainly the most interesting, way to do that.

"You could climb down the cliff alone," Eileen adds sarcastically. "First solo descent. . . ."

Marie, apparently feeling the effects of last night's champagne, merely snarls and stalks off to snap herself into one of the cart harnesses. Their new collection of equipment fits into a wheeled cart, which they must pull up the slope. For convenience they are already wearing the spacesuits that they will depend on higher up; during this ascent they will climb right out of Mars's new atmosphere. They look funny in their silvery-green suits and clear helmets, Roger thinks; it reminds him of his days as a canyon guide, when such suits were necessary all over Mars. The common band of the helmet radios makes this a more social event than the cliff climb, as does the fact that all seven of them are together, four hauling the cart, three walking freely ahead or behind. From climb to hike: the first day is a bit anticlimactic.

On the snowy southern flank of the volcano, signs of life appear everywhere. Goraks circle them by day, on the lookout for a bit of refuse; ball owls dip around the tent at dusk like bats. On the ground Roger sees marmots on the boulders and volcanic knobs, and in the system of ravines cut into the plateau they find twisted stands of Hokkaido pine, chir pine and noctis juniper. Arthur chases a pair of Dall sheep with their curved horns, and they see prints in the snow that look like bear tracks. "Yeti," Dougal says. One mirror dusk they catch sight of a pack of snow wolves, strung out over the slope to the west. Stephan spends his spare time at the edges of the new ravines, sketching and peering through binoculars. "Come on, Roger," he says. "Let me show you those otterines I saw yesterday."

"Bunch of mutants," Roger grumbles, mostly to give Stephan a hard time. But Eileen is watching him to see his response, and dubiously he nods. What can he say? He goes with Stephan to the ravine to look for wildlife. Eileen laughs at him, eyes only, affectionately.

Onward, up the great hill. It's a six-percent grade, very regular, and smooth except for the ravines and the occasional small crater or lava knob. Below them, where the plateau breaks to become the cliff, the shield is marked by some sizable mesas— features, Hans says, of the stress that broke off the shield. Above them, the conical shape of the huge volcano is clearly visible; the endless hill they climb slopes away to each side equally, and far away and above they see the broad, flat peak. They've got a long way to go. Wending between the ravines is easy, and the esthetic of the climb, its only point of technical interest, becomes how far they can hike every day. It's 250 kilometers from the escarpment up to the crater rim; they try for twenty-five a day, and sometimes make thirty. It feels odd to be so warm; after the intense cold of the cliff climb, the spacesuits and the mushroom tent create a distinct disconnection from the surroundings.

Hiking as a group is also odd. The common band is a continuous conversation, that one can switch on or off at will. Even when not in a mood to talk, Roger finds it entertaining to listen. Hans talks about the areology of the volcano, and he and Stephan discuss the genetic engineering that makes the wildlife around them possible. Arthur points out features that the others might take for granted. Marie complains of boredom. Eileen and Roger laugh and add a comment once in a while. Even Dougal clicks into the band around mid-afternoon, and displays a quick wit, spurring Arthur toward one amazing discovery after another. "Look at that, Arthur, it's a yeti."

"What! You're kidding! Where?"

"Over there, behind that rock."

Behind the rock is Stephan, taking a shit. "Don't come over here!"

"You liar," Arthur says.

"It must have slipped off. I think a Weddell fox was chasing it."

"You're kidding!"

"Yes."

Eileen: "Let's switch to a private band. I can't hear you over all the rest."

Roger: "Okay. Band 33."

". . . Any reason for that band in particular?"

"Ah—I think so." It *was* a long time ago, but this is the kind of weird fact his memory will pop up with. "It may be our private band from our first hike together."

She laughs. They spend the afternoon behind the others, talking.

One morning Roger wakes early, just after mirror dawn. The dull horizontal rays of the quartet of parhelia light their tent. Roger turns his head, looks past his pillow, through the tent's clear floor. Thin soil over rock, a couple of meters below. He sits up; the floor gives a little, like a gel bed. He walks over the soft plastic slowly so that he will not bounce any of the others, who are sleeping out where the cap of the roof meets the gills of the floor. The tent really does resemble a big clear mushroom; Roger descends clear steps in the side of the stalk to get to the lavatory, located down in what would be the mushroom's volvus. Emerging he finds a sleepy Eileen sponging down in the little bath next to the air compressor and regulator. "Good morning," she says. "Here, will you get my back?"

She hands him the sponge, turns around. Vigorously he rubs down the hard muscles of her back, feeling a thrill of sensual interest. That slope, where back becomes bottom: beautiful.

She looks over her shoulder. "I think I'm probably clean now."

"Ah." He grins. "Maybe so." He gives her the sponge. "I'm going for a walk before breakfast."

"Okay. Thanks."

Roger dresses, goes through the lock, walks over to the head of the meadow they are camped by: a surarctic meadow, covered with moss and lichen, and dotted with mutated edelweiss and saxifrage. A light frost coats everything in a sparkling blanket of white, and Roger feels his boots crunch as he walks.

Movement catches his eye and he stops to observe a white-furred mouse hare, dragging a loose root back to its hole. There is a flash and flutter, and a snow finch lands in the hole's entrance. The tiny hare looks up from its work, chatters at the finch, nudges past it with its load. The finch does its bird thing, head shifting instantaneously from one position to the next and then freezing in place. It follows the hare into the hole. Roger has heard of this, but he has never seen it. The hare scampers out, looking for more food. The finch appears, its head snaps from one position to the next. An instant swivel and it is staring at Roger. It flies over to the scampering hare, dive bombs it, flies off. The hare has disappeared down another hole.

Roger crosses the ice stream in the meadow, crunches up the bank. There beside a waist-high rock is an odd pure white mass, with a white sphere at the center of it. He leans over to inspect it. Slides a gloved finger over it. Some kind of ice, apparently. Unusual looking.

The sun rises and a flood of yellow light washes over the land. The yellowish white half-globe of ice at his feet looks slick. It quivers; Roger steps back. The ice is shaking free of the rock wall. The middle of the bulge cracks. A beak stabs out of the globe, breaks it open. Busy little head in there. Blue feathers, long crooked black beak, beady little black eyes. "An egg?" Roger says. But the pieces are definitely ice—he can make them melt between his gloved fingers, and feel their coldness. The bird (though its legs and breast seem to be furred, and its wings stubby, and its beak sort of fanged) staggers out of the white bubble, and shakes itself like a dog throwing off water, although it looks dry. Apparently the ice is some sort of insulation—a home for the night, or no—for the winter, no doubt. Yes. Formed of spittle or something, walling off the mouth of a shallow cave. Roger has never heard of such a thing, and he watches open-mouthed as the bird-thing takes a few running steps and glides away.

A new creature steps on the face of green Mars.

That afternoon they hike out of the realm even of the surarctic meadows. No more ground cover, no more flowers, no more small animals. Nothing now but cracks filled with struggling moss, and great mats of otoo lichen. Sometimes it is as if they walk on a thin carpet of yellow, green, red, black—splotches of color like that seen in the orbicular jasper, spread out as far as they can see in every direction, a carpet crunchy with frost in the mornings, a bit damp in the mid-day sun, a carpet crazed and parti-colored. "Amazing stuff," Hans mutters, poking at it with a finger. "Half our oxygen is being made by this wonderful symbiosis. . . ."

Late that afternoon, after they have stopped and set up the tent and tied it down to several rocks, Hans leaps through the lock waving his atmosphere kit and hopping up and down. "Listen," he says, "I just radioed the summit station for confirmation of this. There's a high pressure system over us right now. We're at 14,000 meters above the datum, but the barometric pressure is up to 350 millibars because there's a *big* cell of air moving over the flank of the volcano this week." The others stare. Hans says, "Do you see what I mean?"

"No," exclaim three voices at once.

"High-pressure zone," Roger says unhelpfully.

"Well," Hans says, standing at attention. "It's enough to breathe! Just enough, but enough, I say. And of course no one's ever done it before—done it *this high* before, I mean. Breathed free Martian air."

"You're kidding!"

"So we can establish the height record right here and now! I propose to do it, and I invite whoever wants to to join me."

"Now wait a minute," Eileen says.

But everyone wants to do it.

"Wait a minute," says Eileen. "I don't want everyone taking off their helmets and keeling over dead up here, for God's sake. They'll revoke my license. We have to do this in an orderly fashion. And *you*—" she points at Stephan. "You *can't* do this. I forbid it."

Stephan protests loudly and for a long time, but Eileen is adamant, and Hans agrees. "The shock could start your edema again, for sure. None of us should do it for long. But for a few minutes, it will go. Just breathe through the mesh face-masks, to warm the air."

"You can watch and save us if we keel over," Roger tells Stephan.

"Shit," Stephan says. "All right. Do it."

They gather just out from under the cap of the tent, where Stephan can, theoretically, drag them back through the lock if he has to. Hans checks his barometer one last time, nods at them. They stand in a rough circle, facing in. Everyone begins to unclip helmet latches.

Roger gets his unclipped first—the years as canyon guide have left their mark on him, in little ways like this—and he lifts the helmet up. As he places it on the ground the cold strikes his head and makes it throb. He sucks down a breath: dry ice. He refuses the urge to hyperventilate, fearful he will chill his lungs too fast and damage them. Regular breathing, he thinks, in and out. In and out. Though Dougal's mouth is covered by a mesh mask, Roger can still tell he is grinning widely. Funny how the upper face reveals that. Roger's eyes sting, his chest is frozen inside, he sucks down the frigid air and every sense quickens, breath by breath. The edges of pebbles a kilometer away are sharp and clear. Thousands of edges. "Like breathing nitrous oxide!" Arthur cries in a lilting high voice. He whoops like a little kid and the sound is odd, distant. Roger walks in a circle, on a quilt of rust lava and gaily covered patches of lichen. Intense awareness of the process of breathing seems to connect his consciousness to everything he can see; he feels like a strangely shaped lichen, struggling for air like all the rest. Jumble of rock, gleaming in the sunlight: "Let's build a cairn," he says to Dougal, and can hear his voice is wrong somehow. Slowly they step from rock to rock, picking them up and putting them in a pile. The interior of his chest is perfectly defined by each intoxicating breath. Others watching bright-eyed, sniffing, involved in their own perceptions. Roger sees his hands blur through space, sees the flesh of Dougal's face pulsing pinkly, like the flowers of moss campion. Each rock is a piece of Mars, he seems to float as he walks, the side of the volcano gets bigger, bigger, bigger; finally he is seeing it at true size. Stephan strides among them grinning through his helmet, holding up both hands. It's been ten minutes. The cairn is not yet done, but they can finish it tomorrow. "I'll make a messenger cannister for it tonight!" Dougal wheezes happily. "We can all sign it!" Stephan begins to round them all up. "Incredibly cold!" Roger says, still looking around as if he has never seen any of it before—any of anything.

Dougal and he are the last two into the lock; they shake hands. "Invigorating, eh?" Roger nods. "Very fine air."

But the air is just part of all the rest of it—part of the world, not of the planet. Right? "That's right," Roger says, staring through the tent wall down the endless slope of the mountain.

That night they celebrate with champagne again, and the party gets wild as they become sillier and sillier. Marie tries to climb the inner wall of the tent by grabbing the soft material in her hands, and falls to the floor repeatedly; Dougal juggles boots; Arthur challenges all comers to arm-wrestle, and wins so quickly they decide he is using "a trick," and disallow his victories; Roger tells government jokes ("How many ministers does it take to pour a cup of coffee?"), and institutes a long and vigorous game of spoons. He and Eileen play next to each other and in the dive for spoons they land on each other. Afterwards, sitting around the heater singing songs, she sits at his side and their legs and shoulders press together. Kid stuff, familiar and comfortable, even to those who can't remember their own childhood.

So that, that night, after everyone has gone out to the little sleeping nooks at the perimeter of the tent's circular floor, Roger's mind is full of Eileen. He remembers sponging her down that morning. Her playfulness this evening. Climbing in the storm. The long nights together in wall tents. And once again the distant past returns—his stupid, uncontrollable memory provides images from a time so far gone that it shouldn't matter any more . . . but it does. It was near the end of that trip, too. She snuck into his little cubicle and jumped him! Even though the thin panels they used to create sleeping rooms were actually much less private than what they have here; this tent is big, the air regulator is loud, the seven beds are well-spaced and divided from each other by ribbing—clear ribbing, it is true, but now the tent is dark. The cushioned floor under him (so comfortable that Marie calls it uncomfortable) gives as he moves, without even trembling a few feet away, and it never makes a sound. In short, he could crawl silently over to her bed, and join her as she once joined him, and it would be entirely discreet. Turnabout is fair play, isn't it? Even three hundred years later? There isn't much time left on this climb, and as they say, fortune favors the bold. . . .

He is about to move when suddenly Eileen is at his side, shaking his arm. In his ear she says, "I have an idea."

And afterwards, teasing: "Maybe I *do* remember you."

They trek higher still, into the zone of rock. No animals, plants, insects; no lichen; no snow. They are above it all, so high on the volcano's cone that it is getting difficult to see where their escarpment drops to the forests; two hundred kilometers away and fifteen kilometers below, the scarp's edge can only be distinguished because that's where the broad ring of snow ends. They wake up one morning and find a cloud layer a few k's downslope, obscuring the planet below. They stand on the side of an immense conical island in an even greater sea of cloud: the clouds a white wave-furrowed ocean, the volcano a great rust rock, the sky a low dark violet dome, all on a scale the mind can barely encompass. To the east, poking out of the cloud-sea, three broad peaks—an archipelago—the three Tharsis volcanoes in their well-spaced line, princes to the king Olympus. Those volcanoes, fifteen hundred kilometers away, give them a little understanding of the vastness visible. . . .

The rock up here is smoothly marbled, like a plain of petrified muscles. Individual pebbles and boulders take on an eerie presence, as if they are debris scattered by Olympian gods. Hans's progress is greatly slowed by his inspection of these rocks. One day, they find a mound that snakes up the mountain like an esker, or a Roman road; Hans explains it is a river of lava harder than the surrounding rock, which has eroded away to reveal it. They use it as an elevated road, and hike on it for all of one long day.

Roger picks up his pace, leaves the cart and the others be-

hind. In a suit and helmet, on the lifeless face of Mars:
centuries of memory flood him, he finds his breathing clotted
and uneven. This is his country, he thinks. This is the tran-
scendent landscape of his youth. It's still here. It can't be
destroyed. It will always be here. He finds that he has almost
forgotten, not what it looks like, but what it *feels* like to be
here in such wilderness. That thought is the thorn in the
exhilaration that mounts with every step. Stephan and Eileen,
the other two out of harness this day, are following him up.
Roger notices them and frowns. I don't want to talk about
it, he thinks. I want to be alone in it.

But Stephan hikes right by him, looking overwhelmed by
the desolate rock expanse, the world of rock and sky. Roger
can't help but grin.

And Eileen is content just to walk with him.

Next day, however, in the harnesses of the cart, Stephan plods
beside him and says, "Okay, Roger, I can see why you love
this. It is sublime, truly. And in just the way we want the
sublime—it's a pure landscape, a pure place. But . . ." He
plods on several more steps, and Roger and Eileen wait for
him to continue, pulling in step together. "But it seems to me
that you don't need the whole planet this way. This will always
be here. The atmosphere will never rise this high, so you'll
always have this. And the world down below, with all that life
growing everywhere—it's beautiful." The beautiful and the
sublime, Roger thinks. Another duality. "And maybe we need
the beautiful more than the sublime?"

They haul on. Eileen looks at the mute Roger. He cannot
think what to say. She smiles. "If Mars can change, so can
you."

"The intense concentration of self in the middle of such a
heartless immensity, my God! who can tell it?"

That night Roger seeks out Eileen, and makes love to her
with a peculiar urgency; and when they are done he finds
himself crying a bit, he doesn't know why; and she holds
his head against her breast, until he shifts, and turns, and
falls asleep.

• • •

And the following afternoon, after climbing all day up a hill that grows ever gentler, that always looks as if it will peak out just over the horizon above them, they reach flattened ground. An hour's hike, and they reach the caldera wall. They have climbed Olympus Mons.

They look down into the caldera. It is a gigantic brown plain, ringed by the round cliffs of the caldera wall. Smaller ringed cliffs inside the caldera drop to collapse craters, then terrace the round plain with round depressions, which overlap each other. The sky overhead is almost black; they can see stars, and Jupiter. Perhaps the high evening star is Earth. The thick blue rind of the atmosphere actually starts below them, so that they stand on a broad island in the middle of a round blue band, capped by a dome of black sky. Sky, caldera, ringed stone desolation. A million shades of brown, tan, red, rust, white. The planet Mars.

Along the rim a short distance stands the ruins of a Tibetan Buddhist lamasery. When Roger sees it his jaw drops. It is brown, and the main structure appears to have been a squarish boulder the size of a large house, carved and excavated until it is more air than stone. While it was occupied it must have been hermetically sealed, with airlocks in the doorways and windows fixed in place; now the windows are gone, and side buildings leaning against the main structure are broken-walled, roofless, open to the black sky. A chest-high wall of stone extends away from the outbuildings and along the rim; colored prayer wheels and prayer flags stick up from it on thin poles. Under the light touch of the stratosphere the wheels spin slowly, the flags flap limply.

"The caldera is as big as Luxembourg."
    "You're kidding!"
    "No."

Finally even Marie is impressed. She walks to the prayer wall, touches a prayer wheel with one hand; looks out at the caldera, and from time to time spins the wheel, absently.

"Invigorating view, eh?"

• • •

It will take a few days to hike around the caldera to the railway station, so they set up camp next to the abandoned lamasery, and the heap of brown stone is joined by a big mushroom of clear plastic, filled with colorful gear.

The climbers wander in the late afternoon, chatting quietly over rocks, or the view into the shadowed caldera. Several sections of the ringed inner cliffs look like good climbing.

The sun is about to descend behind the rim to the west, and great shafts of light spear the indigo sky below them, giving the mountaintop an eerie indirect illumination. The voices on the common band are rapt and quiet, fading away to silence.

Roger gives Eileen a squeeze of the hand, and wanders off by himself. The ground up here is black, the rock cracked in a million pieces, as if the gods have been sledge-hammering it for eons. Nothing but rock. He clicks off the common band. It is nearly sunset. Great lavender shafts of light spear the purple murk to the sides, and overhead, stars shine in the blackness. All the shadows stretch off to infinity. The bright bronze coin of the sun grows big and oblate, slows in its descent. Roger circles the lamasery. Its western walls catch the last of the sun and cast a warm orange glaze over the ground and the ruined outbuildings. Roger kicks around the low prayer wall, replaces a fallen stone. The prayer wheels still spin—some sort of light wood, he thinks, cylinders carved with big black eyes and cursive lettering, and white paint, red paint, yellow paint, all chipped away. Roger stares into a pair of stoic Asian eyes, gives the wheel a slow spin, feels a little bit of vertigo. World everywhere. Even here. The flattened sun lands on the rim, across the caldera to the west. A faint gust of wind lofts a long banner out, ripples it slowly in dark orange air—"All right!" Roger says aloud, and gives the wheel a final hard spin and steps away, circles dizzily, tries to take in everything at once: "All right! All right. I give in. I accept."

He wipes red dust from the glass of his faceplate; recalls the little bird-thing, pecking free of clouded ice. A new creature steps on the peak of green Mars.